I Am Ed

By R.A. Akerlund

For information, or to order additional copies, please contact:

Beacon Publishing Group
P.O. Box 41573 Charleston, S.C. 29423
800.817.8480| beaconpublishinggroup.com

Publisher's catalog available by request.

ISBN-13: 978-1-949472-41-7

ISBN-10: 1-949472-41-7

Published in 2021. New York, NY 10001.

Second Edition. Printed in the USA.

To my family....Fonsie, Hank, Wednesday, Angus, Sid and Andreas.

Table of Contents

Chapter 1:
Getting Out

Today was my sixteenth birthday, the seventh of August 1988, I'd had enough of waiting to grow up. I was tall enough to pass for eighteen and I already heard about a job in a supermarket stacking shelves. The plan was to get the most boring job I could get my hands on in order to motivate me to write hit songs. Living at home was no longer an option. Eating turds or rolling around in vomit must feel better than sitting around waiting to die alongside my brothers and my fragile mum.

A voice in my head kept telling me 'get out of this hellhole', and it was all I could think of. My brain was working overtime trying to figure out the great escape plan. I was ready to get away from all that I know, which was fuck all. I was attached to nothing, apart from my guitar, a gift from my dead father.

My mum and three younger brothers were like ghosts to me, we passed each other but rarely spoke, I didn't feel as if I belonged with them or to them, I guess you could say I was a loner or at least, I felt like one.

Our poor mum looked as if she was about to keel over, dragging her feet behind her and eyes dead like fathomless holes. One of my brothers, Steve, was already involved in circles you didn't want anyone you cared about to move in. It didn't take a brain surgeon to work out where this whole family was heading. I'd seen it around, too many times. You get the gist. I had to take drastic action even if it was selfish.

I jumped on bus 31 to Camden. I know.. only Camden, not very far from Kilburn but I felt as if I was on my way to somewhere far away, somewhere I could belong, surrounded by gig venues and punks, sharply dressed mods and smelly food stalls serving people from all over the world.

The supermarket on the high road was busy, before I entered I made sure my hair was neat and my shirt was tucked in properly. I took a deep breath and stepped inside the sharply lit store, I approached a till.

'Can I speak to the manager?' I asked the mousey girl; she was sweet looking. Her mouth was chewing a gum and she looked too young to have a job, which was encouraging.

'You're after Mr Brown? Over there.' She pointed to a tall, skinny, peak-faced man in a brown suit.

'Thanks.' I smiled at the girl and walked towards the man, who was busy helping an old lady getting some beans down from the top shelf and putting them into her trolley.

'Mr Brown?' I said sounding less confident than I had hoped.

'Who's asking?' He looked straight at me and I felt like the girl on the till: mousey and young, I mustered up courage.

'Ed, Ed Henderson, I'm after a job. I can do anything, I'm strong and reliable.' I had carefully researched first impressions after I read the relevant pamphlet at my school: 'How to Get a Job'. It seemed to have done the trick.

'Ok Ed Henderson…right. Come with me lad.' We walked into his smoky little office in the back and he chucked a form at me.

'First, you need to fill this in. Sit yourself down and take your time.' He pointed to a chair.

It was easy enough, I used my best handwriting and to be fair, it wasn't bad.

Mr Brown inspected my squiggles for half a second and then he looked at me, as if to work out if I was any good.

'When can you start?' he finally said.

I felt heat travelling from my neck towards my face. I hated when that happens. My not-so-cool interior exposed. At least it made Mr Browns face soften, he looked kinder.

'Eh… eh… any time,' I stuttered which didn't help with the tomato face situation.

'I need someone to stack shelves before the shop opens. Someone who is strong, not lazy. You will be paid weekly, and if I catch you slacking or stealing, you will be sacked on the spot and not paid for that day. Is that clear?' Mr Brown face looked scary again, his lips so thin that the skin above them crinkled like dried prunes.

'Yes, Mr Brown, that is clear, I will not let you down.' I said as if I meant it because I did.

'You can start tomorrow, five o'clock in the morning. Matt will be here to let you in and show you the ropes.'

'Thank you Mr Brown, thank you.'

As I walked out of the shop I broke into a triumphant smile. Perhaps I was becoming more of a man. This morning I could feel see beginning of a moustache appearing on my much too smooth face, a sign I was ready to take on the world.

I just a landed my first job. At last, the road to my new destiny was paved and I was on my way to freedom.

On the bus ride home I felt like whistling but I didn't, in case someone saw me. Walking up to our house, I decided it wasn't a good idea to share my news with the family just yet; it was all part of my plan, which had nothing to do with any of them. I needed to be clever about this, mainly because I didn't want to panic Mum, she was in such a bad way already. I could do it on the weekend when she was less stressed, moving out was going to have to wait anyways until I had some steady money coming in. Perhaps she would be pleased, I pondered, one less mouth to feed I guess. I'd visit her often, that's what I'll tell her.

Thinking about my plan made me feel good, I was someone, a young man with a destiny. I held my head high, my chest protruding though my grimy T-shirt with the deep breaths I was taking… I was happy; today I had moved one step closer towards my goal and it felt great.

As I got off the bus on West End Lane a pang of guilt struck me, my mum was always harping on about education but it just wasn't for me; I knew what I wanted to do with my life. There was only one plan and I was sticking to it, I was going to become a musician, a great one. I needed her to understand that. She knew that I loved playing my guitar but she always told me that music was a good hobby, but nothing to pin your hopes on. Better off with a proper job, like a postman or electrician, something reliable. She didn't understand the desperate urge that I had and I couldn't blame her for that, she didn't know how music made me feel, how I didn't have a choice in it. My head was buzzing, you see, I could feel it in my bones, that everything would work out. Now I had to convince my mum and the rest of the world, even if they didn't get it now, one day they would. I will show her, and everyone else, not today but soon.

As I walked into the house I knew something was terribly wrong, Steve, my little brother, was frantic, trying to dial 999.

'What are you doing?' I shouted.

'It's Mum, she's not breathing, she's gone all white, her body is cold and I can't feel the pulse.'

'Steve, calm down, are you stoned? Where is she?' I said.

'In the lounge, on the sofa, Ben's with her, I think she's dead Ed. Dead! Hello!' He shouted at the phone. 'Fuck! Answer! … Hello! Hello!…Yeah, it's my mum, she's cold… limp, we need help, she's on the sofa and I don't know what to do. What shall we do? Tell me what to do!' He paused, listening to a question. 'She doesn't seem to be…'

He gave the address, then put the phone down, his face pale as a sheet, his hands trembling, he didn't let go of the phone, his knuckles white as he squeezed it hard.

'She's in there.' he said without moving from the hall.

Fred, my youngest brother, was standing in the middle of the room, staring at me with his gaunt eyes, as if he was pleading to make it all ok. Then… everything slowed down, like it does in movies.

I was afraid. I didn't want to see her. My heart was racing fast. Steve had said the word dead. My chest was thumping and I felt like vomiting. Carefully I took another step forward, the messy room was shrinking around me, giving me no space to breathe. I had no air in my lungs, I was gasping and I felt dizzy and lightheaded. In front of me, sunken in on the brown sofa, with her hand hanging off the side was my small mother, crouching at the side of her, my brother Ben.

He looked up at me. He looked strangely calm so I sat down next to him. He whispered.

'She's gone all cold. I don't know what to do. I don't think there is anything I…'

My heart was beating fast and I could taste the sweat that was now trickling down my face. I have to keep it together. I am the eldest, I have to be... The panic felt as if it was about to explode, I took a breath, a deep one.

'Is there a pulse?' I managed to ask.

'I don't know, I can't find it.' Ben reached for mums' wrist.

I touched her knee. It was cold. I grabbed a grubby old blanket that our dead dog used to sit on it, I put it over her body. One of her eyes were half open, staring blankly towards the TV, which was blaring out the credits from *EastEnders*. I kicked the remote with my foot and the TV turned off. The room was still now, my other two brothers sat down next to me.

I could hear sirens getting louder, even though it felt like a second ago we spoke to the emergency services. There was a knock, no one moved, another knock, a little harder this time.

'Open the fucking door,' I shouted a little too loud as my brothers were right next to me, I couldn't take my eyes off Mum's body.

The house filled up with ambulance staff and chaos. Someone asked us who the eldest was, and I answered, 'Me. I'm Ed'

'How old are you?'

'Sixteen–I just turned sixteen.'

The slow-motion pace reversed and turned into a frantic fast-forward rush. They were prodding and touching her, machines were attached to her limp body, but it was no use. People were shouting above me but I was in a cocoon and it didn't seem real.

In the end they put her on the ambulance stretcher. They were starting to carry her out. Stop! I wanted to shout, don't take her! But nothing came out. I couldn't speak, I froze.

Mum was being carried out, her body leaving. The thought that she was never going to come back appeared and I screamed... 'Not again. Please. No. Not again.' This had happened to me, to us, before. The ambulance staff left after mumbling a few comforting words that I couldn't understand.

The living room was abruptly empty, medical debris scattered around the room. I sat down.

I could hear the ambulance drive off and the house was calm again, free of chaos, the four of us sat down on the floor in the hallway with our backs to the wall, heads buried in our hands. It was so silent, so fucking dead quiet, not even a breath. Fred had tears pouring down his face, although he didn't make a sound. The rest of us were static, staring into the floorboards.

We could hear a police car pulling up outside, the blue lights lighting up the house. Somehow, it felt right that something was happening, even if it was the pigs turning up.

They tried pressing the broken doorbell and then they knocked and we all stood up like robots. I was completely frozen, unable to move to get to the door handle.

'Anyone here? Open up. It's the police.' A firm, authoritative voice echoed through the door.

The knocking and voices got louder. I just had to make it to the door. My body felt disconnected from my brain. Walk, idiot! Get to the goddamn door.

I gripped the handle and opened the front door to a couple of policemen.

'Hi, my name is PC Plant. Who is the eldest out of you lot? You?'

'Yes, it's me,' I said, looking down at my feet.

'Can we come in?' The policemen looked at all of us sitting on the floor in the corridor.

'Sure' We walked through to our living room. The room had pizza boxes stacked in the corner, some empty beer cans and clothes thrown on the floor.

'Can we sit down?' The officer had taken off his hat.

'Sure.' I said, clearing the mess from the floor in front of them.

We all stood there, still, looking at the officers sitting on the sofa where our mother just laid dead.

'Boys, I'm sorry to hear that your mother passed away. We are very sorry for your loss.' The older out of the two paused dutifully. 'The doctors believe it was a heart attack. She is currently at St Mary's, being examined. After that she will be taken to the mortuary, and they will be awaiting instructions.

'How old are you… er…?'

'Ed, my name is Ed and I am eighteen years old,' I lied.

'Where is your dad?' The police officer took notes.

'Dead.' I was imagining the officer writing "Orphans" in capitals on his notepad.

'How old are your brothers?'

'Ben is fourteen, Steve is sixteen and Fred is thirteen.' I couldn't lie too much about Fred's age because he looked about eight years old right now. They scanned us up and down; a sorry sight, four teenage boys, limbs too long, spotty faces and greasy hair. We were tall but skinny, they probably wondered whether we were malnourished. We weren't, we just ate a lot of rubbish. Our weekly baths didn't do the trick anymore. We were scruffy and poor. Standard for the area we lived in. They'd seen it all before, judging by their unaffected expression on their faces.

'Do you have any other family that we can contact?' The policeman asked.

'Well, there's Auntie Linda. I can call her. And Mum has lots of friends. I guess I need to tell them,' I muttered under my breath.

'Do you want me to call your aunt? What's her number?' He looked straight at me, like he really meant what he said. Before I could answer his radio started making loud noises and he lost his concentration for a second. His face changed expression and he looked distracted and concerned. Something was up. He signalled to his colleague to take over.

'So, your aunt. Where is she?

'In Wembley, she's on her way here now,' I lied.

'Are you close?'

'Yeah, very,' said Ben.

I cleared my throat. 'She practically lives here.' I wanted them to leave so I could work out the best way to handle this.

'Can you cope with your brothers? As you are the only one of age I have to make sure that you can care for them.'

'I can care for them fine.' My voice sounded weak, barely a whisper.

PC Plant came over and whispered in his partner's ear. Their radio was going crazy; there was an emergency somewhere..

'Ok,' he said. He went quiet for a while as if to work out what he should do.

Ok what? I thought.

'Eh, well, that settles it. Ed, You are in charge for now. Let us know if you need any help. Here is the number for Social Services if you need it.' He handed me a leaflet and underlined a number twice that was already in bold letters at the top. 'You or your aunt, need to get in touch with the hospital right away about your mother's body.' The policemen stood up and put their hats on.

'We better be off. Boys, we are so sorry for your loss…' They looked genuine and I felt a pang of desperation. 'We'll be back to check on you later.'

I sincerely hoped they wouldn't.

After the officers left, the silence took over again. I decided that it was a good idea to give Fred a hug, he looked so upset and young. We weren't a family that showed affection as a rule. I squeezed his shoulder and patted his back, he fell into my arms and cried, I wanted to fix this for him so badly.

When dad died, mum had sorted things out. Now I was the head of the house and I didn't know what the hell to do. As I thought about that, it dawned on me that they were all staring at me.

'Fred, it's going to be all right, I promise, everything will be ok. Just give it some time. Trust me.' I was squeezing him. 'I just need to think. Work it all out. A plan…then it'll be fine.' I wasn't convinced about that.

I had no clue how to fix this, that was the thought that kept on spinning round my head, my life had taken a new turn. I know what I had to do, I have to be strong, I have to look after my brothers. For her…that's what she would want.

The kitchen was filthy and washing up was stacked around the sink. A pile of dirty clothes by the garden door gave off an unsavoury stench. This was a shit hole.

There was a time when things were better around here. After Dad died Mum just gave up and stopped caring. It was as if she was waiting for us to grow up so she could just curl up and die.

I had cooked, not even an egg. I found some beans in the cupboard and I gathered heating those up wouldn't be too hard. Adrenaline gave me an energy burst and I blurted out, a little too loudly: 'How about we clean up some of this mess?'

None of us knew how, but before long the four of us were making movements that suggested tidying.

We worked together in silence, grateful for something to do. I realised in that very moment that my

brothers were now my responsibility, we belonged together, and as I wasn't getting out of here anytime soon,
I needed a plan. We were the kind of family nobody
cared about, the dregs of society. We had to stick together; now more than ever.

Steve was a real handful. He did nothing anyone
told him to. He was fourteen going on forty-five.

'Steve, you got to go! Now.'

No reply.

'Get your butt out of bed. By the way, I found
your weed. If you don't get out of bed, I will throw it in
the bin.'

He decided to get up.

Mum was getting on his nerves, such a pain in the
backside. Always nagging him. Nag, nag, nag.

'You know nothing, Mum, you really don't.' he
muttered.

She handed him his school clothes and a piece of
toast and pushed him out the door.

He did what he liked and he liked being bad. He
already had the bad boy stamp so he might as well live
up to it. He shared a room with his two younger brothers..
The place was a dump, it stank, unrecognisable stains
and mess everywhere.

Him and his three brothers didn't say much to
each other, they all lived on top of each other and it was

intense, Ed drove them nuts with his constant doodling on his guitar.

'Shut the fuck up!' he felt like shouting but it was a waste of his voice. Ed locked himself into his cupboard of a room, and if you told him to stop he would play even louder, he did it for hours on end just to really piss everyone off.

His mum got on his nerves too, nagging away, never leaving him alone. He wasn't proud but on the odd occasion he had slapped her in the face. She just kept going on at him. Since his dad died, he listened to no one, he was his own boss.

He was going to end up on the dole or in prison. That's what everyone told him, and they were probably right and he didn't care much. This world has nothing to offer him and it suited him just fine. He liked to hang out with the kids from the estates, kids who had had a worse time than him, parents who were on drugs or proper drunks.

At least, they lived in a house - not in a block of flats. His mum was tired and constantly depressed. Since their dad died she had been like this but at least she wasn't a drug addict or an alcoholic, she was fine just weak. That made them a little better than the rest, he thought. He liked the scummy side of life; he liked peeled-off wallpaper and aggressive dogs. He liked to fit in with all the criminals and addicts. He felt he belonged there; it was his destiny after all. He already smoked fags and weed. Girls liked him too. His dad said it was best never to talk too much to girls, that way they would want you. He tried that, and it worked. They liked his skinny tall frame, his huge feet. His brothers use to call him banana man. It was stupid. His life was stupid. It was paved out, in the streets of Kilburn, at least that was sorted.

Chapter 2:
'£42.60'

In the cupboard there were some tins: spaghetti, beans, tomatoes, sweetcorn. There was bread, English breakfast tea. The fridge wasn't bad either: eggs, two pints of milk, sausages, cheese.

I knew Mum had a stash of money somewhere. After she cashed her benefits on a Tuesday she put the money in a tin to make it last the week. The tin was hidden somewhere impossible to find, as all four of us were light-fingered, well, all of us apart from Ben.

'Boys, we need to find the tin. Does anyone have a clue where she kept it?' I always made sure I didn't know–better that way.

Fred piped up: 'I think I know under the floorboards in her room. There's a loose board and I saw her crouching there the other day.'

Fred made his way into Mum's bedroom. There were some banging noises.

'Yass!' Fred looked pleased with himself; his spotty, freckled pixie face bore a smile. He handed me the tin; the Queen's face had worn off with the years, giving her a crooked smile that funnily enough suited her.

I shook it, there were coins in there, please God let there be some notes in there.

Slowly I opened the lid, we sat down around the dinner table and calculated that the tin housed the grand sum of £42.60.

'Right…You heard me lie to the police. I said I was eighteen. Do you know why I did that? I did that so we can stick together.' Ben, Fred and Steve nodded because they knew he was right.

I didn't even know if that is what we wanted. But at least this way, we had a choice. We had £42.60–that is not going to feed us for ever, but it is a start.

'Our mum died; we have no money. This is nothing. How are we going to survive on this amount of money?' Ben was the sensible one and he had a point.

He continued 'What do you think would happen if we told the police our real ages?' We were all scared. I was trying my hardest not to show it.

'Probably children's homes, like St Barnabas, or foster homes. We are too old to be adopted but too young to live on our own.'

I knew this, because it happened to a family on our street not that long ago, we all knew about it. They split the kids up all over the country and they never got to see each other.

I was surprised how protective I felt over my little brothers. Last week I couldn't care less about them and now I felt as if my life depended on it. I had to look after them. We had to stick together.

'We don't have to make up our minds now. Let's think for a while, make a plan.'

I wanted to ask about the afternoon. Had she been acting strange or did something happen. I decided against it. I couldn't think about it. Not yet.

We were hungry, dark circles under our eyes, shaken up like frightened animals. I decided that the safest thing to make was beans on toast; I knew how to use the toaster. I made all of us a piece of toast and we ate in silence. It was so quiet apart from the sound of the Jubilee Line, chugging away, comforting us like a constant beating heart in the distance.

I kept on trying to think of what to say but nothing felt right. I kept on catching my breath as if I was going to speak and then nothing came out. I wanted time to figure things out. I didn't have time. I had to grow up and quick.

Fred and Ben were looking for answers; they wanted to know that everything was going to be fine. Steve wanted to go out and drink with his friends, his leg was twitching and he was drumming on the table, usually I would have told him to stop or to get out but I didn't want him to go, not today.

I wanted solitude and my guitar, time to understand what had happened.

'I can't believe it. She was here yesterday. Sitting over there. She did say she was tired. She looked bad too,' Fred spoke softly.

'She always said that she was tired.' Ben was right, she'd looked exhausted recently, she said time and time again that she wasn't feeling good. I should have listened, we should have, tried to be nicer to her. I thought she was strong. I didn't know she couldn't take it.

The kitchen was still messy but at least you could see the table surface now.

'Those beans were cold,' Steve said, the first words he uttered since the ambulance came.

'Shut up.' I nearly smiled because he was right, they were fridge cold.

'The bread was burnt,' Fred said.

'All right. Leave me alone.' How the hell was I Going to do this?.

'I will make the toast in the future, I usually make my own,' Ben said.

'You do?' I never even knew we had a toaster, thought she grilled it.'

'Yeah, I like waking up early. Usually before mum.' A chill went down me when he mentioned her. I never knew Ben was an early riser. I didn't know any of the brothers that well. Our mother was gone and we were here together. Dead parents couldn't pay the bills so the stacking job in Camden was now even more important.

'I got a job today,' I said. 'In a supermarket in Camden.'

The boys look at me as if I was talking madness.

'You got a job? Why?' said Fred.

I said: 'Doesn't matter now. I wanna try and keep us together, for Mum's sake. So…I need information that might help me do that. For instance, what time does school start? You have to be on time, we can't raise suspicion, be on their radar. Don't tell school that Mum died, in fact, don't tell anyone. Yet.'

I was speaking too fast, rambling. I felt hyper. Saying out loud that Mum had died made me twitch a little. I continued to think out loud.

'They, the school, know that I am only sixteen, and if they ask, say that Auntie Linda is looking after us, living here with us. The police think I'm eighteen, hopefully they won't speak to school.'

Auntie Linda was our only living relative, Dad's sister. She survived on three Special Brew cans a day and had few teeth left. Hardly Mary Poppins, but she was our only hope. She lived in Wembley, not far. Perhaps calling her was a good idea after all.

Ben pointed out that Linda had moved house not long ago but that Mum had taken down her new number. As he said that the telephone rang. Ben answered. It was for me. 'Hi, yeah, ok. See you then. Bye.'

I scribbled down the address of the hospital. I felt nauseous thinking about not having a mother or father; it was much easier to think about how to survive, how to trick the system.

Next to the phone there was a piece of paper with Linda's number on it. Perhaps I will give her a call tomorrow. Or Ben could call her. They liked each other. All women, all old women liked Ben: he had a baby face, like Cliff Richard. I needed to get the boys to understand we had to work together otherwise we were screwed.

It was getting late, and I was exhausted. After another portion of beans on soggy toast, we sat in silence. The silence was uncomfortable and I was exhausted. 'We need to sleep,' I said.

My room was a tip and I sat down on my bed, my brain was racing, my body heavy and limp. Perhaps this was how my life was supposed to be, always a struggle, always pain. I felt hard done by and a little angry. I wiped my eyes because I knew there were tears there. I have to be strong. My dad's voice echoed in my head, 'Look after your mum son,' he had said. I had failed him.

I set my alarm for four o'clock. First day at my new work tomorrow. My eyes wouldn't shut, staring at the ceiling images of Mum lying on the stretcher wouldn't leave my head. Days, years, hours are just going to pass as they always have. My body will look the same, my dreary room, my brothers, the streets, and the people. Mum will still be dead, that's how it works.

My bed was a mess, the sheets use to be white but now they were yellow like urine and my pillow had no case on and gave off a mouldy whiff. This place was a tip. As my head hit the pillow I felt a tear trickle down my cheek. I wiped it away and hugged my stinky pillow hard until I fell asleep.

The alarm rang but I was already awake. The house was still like the night so I got dressed and sneaked downstairs, grabbed myself a stale piece of bread and headed out the door. As I stepped outside reality started to creep into my thoughts, it didn't feel right to leave. I decided to write a note for the boys, I went back into the house and wrote a message on an old envelope.

> *Ben Fred and Steve*
> *I'm going to work in the Supermarket*
> *Back at 10.*
> *Don't answer the phone or door to anyone*
> *Don't leave the house*
> *Ed*

Bus 31 was a smooth ride at 4.30 in the morning. It was only a few drunks scattered round the upper deck. The scenes from yesterday kept showing up in my mind and I wanted it to stop. I wondered how I was supposed to feel. How bad is it going to hurt? Is this enough pain? Should I be wailing on the floor or lying still in my bed staring at the ceiling. All I knew was that I wanted to play my guitar. Be alone. I wanted to hide or scream but all I could do was continue. For the boys' sake and our parents, I had to be strong clever and brave. I needed time to make sense of all the plans that were spinning around in my head. I was getting a headache, it felt like a giant hand pressing down on my brain.

This was the morning after we had been orphaned. It wasn't clear in my head, the reality of it, so I tried to brush the feeling off, pretend it wasn't true. I could pinch or punch myself all I like. This was now who I was and where I was. My mood car crashed and I had to shake my head violently to try and get rid of the panicky thoughts.

The sun was rising over the Swiss Cottage council estates. I was thankful for the quiet streets and the late summer's morning that gave me some space to think, muster up the strength I needed for my first day as a stacker of shelves. How everything had changed from yesterday and it felt unfair to the core.

I knocked at the delivery entrance and a black guy with an Afro, like Hendrix, answered the door. From the side of his mouth hung a cigarette without a filter. He was tall and skinny. With a raspy voice he said, 'All right mates? You must be Ed.'

I nodded; slightly taken aback by the coolest looking guy I had ever met.

The stock room was freezing, the radio was on, my heart was racing. There were pallets of stuff everywhere. Matt gave me a nudge and started to walk me through the mountains of groceries. He gave me some jobs involving heavy lifting. It was just what I needed.

I could do this all day and all night. I was a machine. After a while, people started to appear from the back. Mr Brown walked over to me. He looked like a mean, hungry bird, but when he spoke he looked nicer, 'Ed, I hear you've worked really hard. Keep up the good work. Same time tomorrow.' he said.

'Thank you, Mr Brown,' I muttered.

Four hours had gone by fast, it had felt more like fifteen minutes. £3.80 an hour was the agreed salary. I needed more hours. I had mouths to feed.

'Excuse me Mr Brown, if there are any more hours available, day or night, I'm your man. I really need the work and I will always work hard.'

'Ok' he replied and walked off. He must have sensed the desperation in my voice because just as I was about to step outside, he grabbed my arm.

'Wear a clean t-shirt tomorrow and you can stay on until one o'clock, stacking shelves while the store is open.'

The bus ride home felt different: a crowded bus but I still felt alone, hemming my thoughts in I was reminded of what was waiting at home.

Out of the corner of my eye I saw Matt, asleep, a few rows down. I walked over and sat down, don't really know why because usually I was shy.

'Hey' I said. He opened one eye and glanced over at me. Shit, he looked really tired and grumpy. I sat down.

'Hey Ed,' he said.

Small talk really wasn't my thing.

'Eh, so. Do you work there every day then?'

'Seven days a week. It sucks. I'm tired.' We both paused and drew breath as we were about to say something, but neither of us. I was relieved to see West End Lane approaching.

'This is my stop, see you tomorrow.'

'Tomorrow.' He said and casually waved goodbye.

I noticed his hands, covered in silver rings, I noticed his fingers too, the tops were covered in calluses, his nails lower than the flesh on his fingers, swollen tops bulging. I nearly said something but instead I stepped off the bus with a smirk on my face. Matt played the guitar, like me. He was probably amazing, better than me, that's for sure.

I got home at 10.10 a.m. and was met by silence.

'Hello!' I shouted.

The three of them, Steve, Ben and Fred, were sitting on the bottom of the stairs. They clearly had not been distracted and their faces were desperate and scared.

'Come here,' We hugged. I cried, we all cried. For our poor mum, for ourselves, for us who had no one, for everything that had happened so far in our short lives. Only we could change things. Somewhere in the hopeless moment I felt determined. There was strength brewing inside me I never knew I had. Being boys, we suddenly cleared our throats and wiped our eyes.

'Let's make lunch. Beans on toast? Warm this time.' Perhaps this had to happen to bring us together, that was fucked up. Just yesterday I felt like I didn't care about anyone, especially my annoying brothers. Now, I was worried sick about them. My voice was slightly high-pitched as I spoke.

'Ben, can you ring Linda? The number is by the phone. Can you see if she can come over later today?'

In the kitchen I heated some beans and toasted some now very stale bread.

'We need to get organised, if this is gonna work.'

Ben walked into the room. 'She's on her way.'.

'Ed, I have written a note for you, might be helpful. I kinda helped Mum with Fred's things anyway.' Ben handed me a bit of paper with some tidy writing on it.

I sat down; Ben had taken time to write a schedule that was incredibly precise.

'I would have included Steve but I have no idea what he gets up to. He's never at school.'

I knew that. Steve was a big problem. 'Don't worry about that. I'll handle Steve, if you can sort out Fred and yourself that would be ace.'

'No problem.'

I could rely on Ben. He was focused and judging by the note he just gave me more capable than I was at being organised.

'Good. We have enough food to last us a couple of weeks, my new job went well and they gave me eight hours per day, so that's great. We need to find out when school starts. We need to know who can do what.'

'No problem, I'll do that.' Said Ben whilst writing it down on a note pad. I was taken aback by his efficiency.

Concentrating on practicalities, I kept on nervously tidying the mess I had never noticed before. Life was a mess, and hoovering was not going to fix this but maybe it was a start.

Steve was on his way out the door. I stopped him.

'Where you going?' I said.

'I gotta get some fresh air. I need to get out here. I'm going crazy in here.'

I blocked him and stared right into his eye, 'I need you, otherwise I might as well call the social now and you could get yourself a cozy room in a teen hostel next to some psycho crack head. Try and stay out of trouble.'

'I'll be back in an hour. Promise.' Steve grabbed his coat and left.

I knew he was doing drugs and drinking alcohol, Steve didn't care about himself or anyone else. He was in with some dodgy people. The police had come around on many occasions to talk to Mum about him. Mum used to shout at him; he stressed her out on a daily basis.

Only last week I came home from school to find her trying to make him listen to her. She had found some weed in his dirty jeans pocket again. Steve didn't care much what she thought; he just snatched the weed off her and headed out the door. He didn't care about anyone, especially Mum. Things had got too out of hand for her to handle. The house, the money, the grief, the tiredness– it was too much for her.

I should have helped more; I should have been a better son. Steve's wasn't to blame, all of us were diffi- cult in our own way lack but his of empathy hadn't helped, but there was pressure from all angles and she was a very fragile woman. When our dad died, she had buckled; she couldn't cope without him. He held her up; without him it was too much of a struggle. They'd met when they were teenagers, grown up together. Even though it was tough, they belonged. Without him, she al- ways said, 'I might as well curl up and die.' She never spoke about it after he died, but we all knew she was bro- ken.

There were thoughts running through my brain I had never had before. I was a beginner at everything apart from playing the guitar. I wanted to do right by my dead mother; I wanted to be the person who saved the boys, but could I do it?

Exactly what was needed, I didn't actually know. I wanted to figure it out but all I could think about was the music. Chords. Notes. Noises I could make, melodies.

I headed up to my room in the hope of spending some time with my guitar. I needed music, as I got lost in the moment I noticed that Fred and Ben were standing in the door, listening to my playing. I ignored them and continued, letting myself go inside the notes coming from my rubbish amp. Melancholy sad notes ringing out in our scruffy little house.

The peaceful moment did not last long, as the doorbell rudely interrupted us.

It was mental Auntie Linda. She came crashing in, throwing her arms around us and sobbing.

I let her get on with it. It was strangely nice to see her, as she was the only living member of the older generation of Henderson's, our father's sister. She was also a living reminder why I *had* to succeed in my quest for change.

'I can't believe it; I just can't believe it! My poor boys. This can't be happening!' Linda was shaking and crying uncontrollably.

'It has,' I mumbled.

She carried on with her dramatic display and I couldn't help feeling grumpy. None of us had screamed or shouted. We were trying to keep it together.

In the end we all sat down in the living room.

I needed her on our side, it was a shame she was such a mess. She looked just liked dad and that was strangely comforting. It would have been helpful if she was a little more like him and less like a lunatic.

School was starting soon. Linda could help me with the boys. They knew our family well and I didn't want to raise suspicion. The fact that our school was rubbish could work to my advantage. No one would care too much about anything, I knew that.

Linda was surprisingly supportive and even offered to move in with us for a while. Perhaps she was drunk. I accepted before she could change her mind.

Ben and Fred were sitting close to her. Maybe I had misjudged how young these two were and how much they needed Mum. I was going with my instincts, and they were to protect.

Steve still wasn't home. Bollocks.

Steve was hanging out at the playground in the middle of the four tallest council blocks in Kilburn. He was sat on the swings, smoking a fag, swigging from a beer bottle. His mates weren't there for once, he was all on his own. Every time he thought of Mum on the sofa he took another swig and sucked on the fag a little harder. Now and again, he would hear someone shouting. Otherwise it was quiet, the sky spitting gentle drizzle on his blue Adidas hoodie.

It's all my fault, he thought over and over again. I pushed her over the edge. I should have been nicer. He kicked the sand and said 'Fuck' out loud. What just happened today was definite.

His youngest brother Fred was all right, but Ben and Ed were already blaming him, he was sure of that. He could see the hate in their eyes, and he didn't blame them. Fred was only thirteen and Mum's baby. He was quiet and looked exactly like their dead father. He was not a goody two shoes like Ben but he was sweet, likeable even. He would look out for him, take him under his wing, make sure he was at school. And Ed, he was all right. He knew it was his fault, killing her by acting like a complete idiot all the time. Fighting with her constantly, making her angry, not giving a shit.

Now they had to stick together. He was fifteen soon and capable of looking after himself, he thought. Ben and Fred were still young.

Ben, like a little professor and Fred, so young, a whippet, quiet, sensitive and frail.

A girl he knew walked up and sat down on the swing next to him.

'All right?'

He didn't answer.

'You Ok?' she said.

'Not really...Can you do one?' She didn't move. Steve looked straight at her in disgust. 'Please.'

The girl jumped off the swing. 'Fuck off...Who pissed on your cornflakes?' She disappeared towards one of the tower blocks.

He lit up the joint he had in his pocket and sucked on it, kept the smoke in for ages to get a good kick. He smoked it until it burnt his fingers. He didn't feel the buzz. All he could think of was his mum on the sofa. Ed was right: they had to stick together, he had to be better. Someone called for him from one of the windows; he liked that guy so he started to walk towards his flat. He always had booze and his parents were never home and if they were, they were so off their heads they couldn't speak anyway. It was rough, perfect. He sat down on the grubby sofa and was handed a vodka bottle.

'Someone said they saw an ambulance outside your house.'

'Yeah.'

'What happened?'

'My mum died.'

'Seriously?'

'Yeah.' He swigged the vodka, it burnt his stomach, slowed down his thoughts. The guy didn't say anything.

'I gotta go.' Steve stood up and got out. He started to walk towards Fairhurst Gardens. He was pretty loaded. 'Fuck!' he shouted out loud.

Chapter 3:
Funeral and the Beatles

The phone rang. It was the morgue. They wanted to know what we were going to do with Mum's body.
What was I supposed to say?

'Yeah, my aunt is sorting it. She's helping us. I will call you tomorrow.' I slammed the phone down a little too hard, relieved the phone call was over.

I walked into the living room. Linda was sitting on the floor with Fred. They were talking about school. Fred didn't like it much. He was telling her about how he loved playing the drum kit they had at school. He sounded a bit like I felt, like he knew it was his only hope of getting out. I didn't even know he played the drums.

'What's the point? I'm not clever enough to be anything anyhow.' He was drumming with his hands as he spoke.

'Everyone has to, you know, study. It's not so bad: just turn up, listen to the teacher. Wish I'd done more of that.'
I sat down next to them.

'Linda, we need a date, you know, for the funeral.'

She looked up at me. 'Ok Ed…I am on that. I called the vicar and he says next week Wednesday is clear. He liked your mum you know; he will say something nice about her.'

I didn't care what he would say. I needed her to be buried. I needed the phone calls to stop. 'Can you please call the morgue for me, I...'

'Darling boy...don't worry, I will call them. Where's the number love?' I handed her the piece of paper with great relief.

'You Ok?' I asked Fred.

'Yep, I just hate school, that's all.'

'Everyone hates school, but if you don't go, we will get in trouble: no more drums, no more us. You get it?'

'I know.'

'Let's hoover,' I said.

'That's worse than school.'

'I know, I have to stay busy. Get off your lazy ass, this place is a shit hole.'

Fred and I cleaned the house. Then we made dinner, frigging beans and out-of-date sausage served with Smash.

I had noticed Linda was writing things down on a piece of paper. When I came in one day after work, she asked me to come and sit in the kitchen with her. Her hands were shaking. On the upside, she wasn't that drunk.

'Ed, darling boy. There is a lot to sort out and I am really trying to get organised. Your Mum has made a real mess of things.'

I pulled my chair closer to hers and put my arm around her fragile shoulders. If I squeezed her harder she would probably break.

'Thank you auntie. I can cope but I don't know where to start. Explain to me how it all works. Bills, school stuff, you know. I don't want the Social to get involved, they will split us up. The police think I'm eighteen. It's fine for now, but if you can help me with the school, keep them off our back, that would be very helpful.'
I tried to look mature and calm.

'Ok darlin'. I don't want 'em to take the boys and split you up. I worry about Steve. That boy is trouble. The other two are all right.' She looked at me with empathetic eyes.

'And Ed love, I am very proud of you.'
It made me feel like crying, but I didn't.

She pushed some scrunched-up papers in front of me. I could see she was making an effort to look proper; she was one drink away from being drunk.

'The funeral is sorted out. I paid for it. For the electricity and gas, you pay with these slips at the post office counter. It's easier than you think. I will pay the rent until you are eighteen. Your dad had a bit of money– not much, but it will cover the rent for a while.'

Her eyes glazed over, as if she was about to start crying any second. I reached for her hand and held it. Her hands were shaking.

'I'll get you a drink, Auntie.' I said and she nodded.

Linda's face relaxed with every sip of the gin. I looked over the paperwork and I understood most of it. We were burying Mum and it was tough to think about. I didn't want to be reminded of anything. I wanted to lie in my bed and play the guitar, drink beer, eat shit food. There was no time for that now, I had to keep going. We had to give her a funeral. She liked the church. She cared about stuff like that, we would do it for her.

'I have invited some of your mum's friends to the funeral, and after we're going for a drink at the King's Head, where your Dad used to drink.' She looked straight at me to check if I was upset.

'I am so very sorry, Ed.' Her bony hand reached out to squeeze mine.

I cleared my throat, looked up at the ceiling to hold back tears.

'I wanna do it well, for Mum... and Dad. Not the funeral but everything, I wanna do right by them, they deserve that.' The tears started and I didn't know how to stop them, Linda stroked my head whilst I sobbed and it felt good.

This was clearly my time to grow up, take responsibility, whether I was ready or not was not up for discussion.

Linda and I spent the evening looking for appropriate clothing. We decided to look through the boxes in the cellar that stored Dad's old clothes. Reluctantly I walked down the cramped stairs. I hadn't thought about my father for a long time. I was little when he died, and Mum softened the blow, protected us and cocooned us with her gentle love. She was all right then. I let myself think about her for a moment and it hurt so bad.

'Come on, Ed. Let's get this done love.'

'Ok. Yes, alright then.' I snapped out of it and got on with the task in hand.

At the bottom of the stairs there was a Samsonite suitcase that had little stickers on it that spelled 'TED ENDERSON' in gold capital letters. The H must have fallen off.

'This is the one. I know he had lots of nice suits. He bought some for the sales job at that hoover company.'

Linda laid it down and started to open it. I just froze. My dad had worn those suits.

I started to think about how tall he was. I was taller. He was wider, I think. She pulled out a dark blue suit jacket and I tried it on dutifully. It was far too big. I remember my Dad wearing it, it was so dated too, large lapels, too big for my little head, I felt ridiculous.

'My days! Ed! You look just like him.' She was now bordering on hysteria, talking fast and pulling out items from the suitcase. 'Right, just grab a few and we will try things on upstairs. I can't be down here, it smells.'

As Linda grabbed some more suits out of the suitcase, something metallic and heavy fell on the floor. A watch; I remembered that watch. I suddenly recalled my dad's hands and wrists. I looked at mine. They were exactly the same; I had never thought about that before. I put the watch on.. I'll take the watch, but what I really need is you, here.

Between the old suitcases and school uniforms we threw together suitable clothes for our mother's funeral. We looked a right mess.

'That one's perfect!' Ben had just walked in with me trying on a black suit, a few sizes smaller than the others.

'That's your Granddad's.' Linda was brushing dust off the shoulders.

'This one will do.' I Said, relieved it was over.

'Don't worry about me, I'm sorted,' said Ben.

'How?'

'I've got a suit. I bought it in a second-hand shop for a couple of quid.'

'Really? Ok. Fred, come here. This one?'

We managed to put together outfits for Steve and Fred. Steve walked in. His clothes were stained and his trainers had gaping holes in the front and he wore no socks. He stank of BO, booze and fags. We were all relieved he was home. Now we needed to keep him in, like you do with stray cats.

'All right? You look rough. Have a bath will you? Linda is making eggs and chips. Sort yourself out, then we will eat.' I avoided his eyes and continued getting about my business.

'Ok. I feel like shit actually' he said eventually. 'I didn't recognise the room for some reason. What did you do to it?' he slurred.

'You look like shit,' I said with a smirk on my face, now looking straight at him. 'I just wanna get the funeral out of the way. And Steve, let's all try looking half decent. For her. She would have liked that.'

'Yeah, she would. She always made me brush my hair. It's strange, since she died I do it. Not today, but usually. I mean, I want to do it… I'm gonna get cleaned up, I really feel bad.' He wobbled over to the sofa and parked himself on the couch.

'Can you help me pick a song? You know, for the funeral? Linda suggested a few that she knew Mum liked.'

'Yes, I'd like to.'

We started to put on songs from our parents' tiny record collection. Simon and Garfunkel, The Beatles, Dylan, Tom Jones. Elvis and Van Morrison. Linda kept on signing along.

Ben and Fred surfaced and we all sat down on the floor, looking through the records, laughing at the covers. There were lots of memories in that collection. Songs bringing our parents back for a brief moment. It was comforting to listen, even Cliff Richard sounded good. We didn't have a choice; everything was harder than we thought.

I woke up with the sun. Staring at my ceiling and feeling numb I decided to just lie there. I felt hollow, like a dead tree trunk. Staying busy was the only thing that helped me. My guitar was my lifeline. I want this hollow crap feeling to go.

The punch was going to get me somehow, the thing was, there was nowhere to hide. Today I was putting my young mother—only thirty-eight she was—in the ground with the maggots and worms to chew on her tired body. I had no idea what to expect today or what it would feel like. I didn't care much either. Today was for her, showing our respect, saying thanks for giving us life.

Steve had sorted himself out, got a good night's sleep and some food in his concave body. We sat down and talked about the song that Mum might have liked the best. It was strange to speak about her as a person who used to like things but somehow, as we spoke about her, we remembered her, what she was like when we were little boys, how she used to be carefree and sweet. How she kept her long brown hair in a tight bun, her face soft and her cheeks pink and flushed. We remembered her long red kaftan with sunflowers on it, how it touched the grass as she ran on Hampstead Heath with no shoes on. Those were the memories I wanted, not the hunched-over grey scarecrow she'd turned into after Dad died.

We remembered her and Dad drinking red wine and listening to The Beatles, singing at the top of their voices with the four of us telling them to shut up. Mum and Dad falling over laughing, tickling us and singing, 'You want me to!', 'Let it be, Let it beee! Well, I' m not going to!' and the tickling went on and on, we were happy. We decided that 'Let It Be' would be the song we played in church today.

Linda was on form. Each one of us had a tidy pile of clothes to wear and she was already dressed in a black dress from Marks and Spencer's. She even cleaned our shoes for us. Fred was quiet as a mouse, his little face serious and desperate. Ben managed to look super hand-some and stern. Even Steve looked half decent. Me? I don't know. It didn't feel like reality. But it was, I knew that.

Auntie Linda had sorted the funeral, as promised. I found out that the whole thing cost £300. The cheapest funeral you could have. The church had agreed to do it for free and the rest was spent on the funeral director, simple coffin, transport and a wreath that said Sue in a heart shape. She was going to rest next to Dad, Linda told me everything but I barely listened, I wanted it to be over and done with.

As we walked down the road I had butterflies in my stomach and again that now familiar feeling: numbness.

Outside the church there was more people than I had anticipated, I vaguely recognised their faces. They all looked at us with pity, shook our hands and mumbled faint "So sorry's".

That word again, 'sorry'. The police, Aunt Linda and now the fucking funeral-goers. I wanted to shout, 'For what exactly? Sorry that we were born to two weak people who had four kids then crumbled under the pressure of life and died, leaving us alone, poor and orphaned?' Yeah, I would be 'so sorry' for anyone in that situation but life has to go on. At least I felt something now, I felt pissed off. I wanted to hit someone, hard on the nose, my fists were clenched as I walked into the church.

Grateful to make it through the little crowd, we huddled together on a bench. Adrenaline pumping through my veins, I was so close to panic, as close you can get before you lose control. I had to calm down, I slowed my breathing down. I looked over to my little brothers, they were relying on me to hold it together, so I tried with all my might.

The priest, whom I recognised from Dad's funeral, spoke; I can't remember what he said. Something about being taken too early, bla bla bla. Something about her boys and then he mentioned God.

It went on for a while and then Linda stood up and said a few words that no one could hear as she was crying so hard. Then, out of the speakers, the music started playing. I closed my eyes. The intro chords of 'Let It Be' entered my ears and I felt something, euphoria maybe.

It was so soothing and exactly what I needed. The notes echoed in the church hall; the stained-glass windows let in some sunlight through the Virgin Mary's halo. I thought about Mum, and tears were rolling down my cheeks, I tasted the salt. As the signing begun I could hear Steve's voice clearly. He sounded good, raspy yet tuneful, he sounded better than the Beatles. I lost myself to the words of the song, the tears now making a small puddle on the wooden seat and for the first time I didn't care. The music soothed me but the devastation of the situation hit me like a lightning bolt; there was no way to hide. Finally, I felt it, I wanted it to hurt and it did. It was nearly unbearable, a sharp pain cutting me up from the inside.

'There will be no sorrow, let it be.' Steve's voice cut through the pain and he took my hand in his.

After the service we all walked together to the pub. Linda's face was bright red and her mascara had run down her cheek. Ben was staying close to her and Fred and I walked together, even Steve felt calm and present. Our oversized suits looked cheap and tatty, it sure was a sorry sight.

We ate some grey sausage and mash and drank some beers with the mourners. Linda was knocking the gins back. After lunch, she came over and sat with us, drunker than usual. She took me to one side.

'Ed, darling boy, I just can't do this much longer. I thought I could, for Sue and for your dad, but I am too old. I want to go home.' Her dress was askew and one earring was missing. Her words were slurred. I wanted to get away from her so bad but she was leaning on me.

I assured her that there was no need to be upset. I was ready, I could handle it.

As I spoke I glanced down at my father's watch. Linda's state was worsening; her smell, a mix of sweat and piss, was getting too unbearable to be around. We needed to get on with our future. Auntie Linda was not someone we could rely on. I had to accept that. The boys were not going to agree with me on this, but we had no choice. She was in no state to look after herself, let alone us, she had to go.

We didn't stay long. The funeral-goers were getting on my nerves. All the people in that pub were broken, on borrowed time. I wanted to get out of there. As we left the pub I took a deep breath. The suffocation eased. Again, didn't feel real. But it was. There was only so long I could muster hanging out with a bunch of dramatic drunks in a shitty pub in Kilburn. Linda stayed on, by the time we left she was pretty legless.

Back at the house the mood was bleak.

'Guys, I'm gonna play my guitar. You wanna come up to my room and hang out for a while?' Without answering they followed me up to my little room and sat down on my mattress. I started to play the beginning of 'Let It Be'. When I looked up I noticed that all my brothers were nodding, swaying in time to the music instead of telling me to stop. Without me asking, Steve started to sing. The sound that came out of his mouth was hypnotic, he sounded so good.

It drew me in, my fingers were dancing over the strings in time with the sound of his tone. If only Mum could have been here to hear this. This is what she had needed, some hope for our future, see that were good at something.

Fred and Ben nor I knew Steve had this singing voice. I don't actually think he did until that moment. I even harmonised on the chorus and he kept in tune. The blend was perfect; the way siblings voices do. Fred was tapping the time on time.

A still moment for our mum, the four of us, united, actually liking being with each other. Sticking together was what we needed to do.

'Didn't know you could sing,' Fred said

'I can't really, but I quite like it. It feels… good,' said Steve.

Ben looked amazed. 'No, you can *really* sing. It sounds amazing. I mean, with Ed's playing as well, it's really good. I mean it. It's great.'

I was lost in picking the strings, still stuck in the moment of the perfect match to my playing, Steve's voice. He was only fourteen, far too young to be in a band. Like myself, he was tall and looked older than his years. Looking round my tiny room, I saw the four of us together and strangely I felt more that I belonged, more now than ever before. I had all these big plans to flee the house to find members for my band and all the while I had the best singer right in front of me, sleeping in the room next-door. My brother, the useless layabout, future-mapped-out-as-a-drunkard Steve Henderson.

It felt like the perfect time to drop the bomb.

'Guys, Aunt Linda is going back home tomorrow. She wants to live in her house. We'll be fine, right?'

Steve was probably relieved. I just wanted to get on and grow up. Make a change. Make music. I avoided to look at the other two.

The end of the longest ever summer was at our doorstep. School was starting for the others, and I was working, and now looking after my three brothers. Even though I was determined to a make this work I had a niggling feeling it might be harder than I thought. I suggested food but no one was hungry. I put on the last Ozzy record.

Ben said that he wanted to learn to play guitar. I suggested the bass.

It was time for bed, grateful that this day was coming to an end. I hit the pillow after playing guitar four hours straight.

Goodbye, Mum, I love you, I will always miss you.

Steve couldn't believe how a human could actually reek that badly. He wished Linda would piss off. Fred and Ben were so into her being there, but he was over it. Another car crash in their house was the last thing they needed right now.

The funeral had been all right, better than he had anticipated.

Something amazing had happened. He had felt something in the church, like a calling, an awakening even; perhaps it had something to do with God. Perhaps God or Mum was trying to tell him something. That he wasn't useless, that he was good at something. It was the music, he felt it move inside him. It was as if his cold heart had been moved by the notes. They had opened up his mouth and this voice came out, a voice that sounded good. He liked to sing along to pop songs, he had always liked a good tune. He never just sang, though, singing was for girls. It was odd, like he didn't have to even try;

he just knew what to do, like someone greater was doing it for him. Perhaps his dead parents had tried to save him from his future. He didn't care about the fact he was a waster. He always knew what would happen to him in life and he had accepted that. He already had unprotected sex and done lots of drugs with girls from the estate. It was OK. He would shag anything he could get his grubby hands on.

This music thing was strange. And Ed liked it, he could tell. Ed always acted as if he hated him, but since he had heard his voice he looked at him with a bit more respect. Being at home seemed better now than before mum had died. When he closed his eyes and listened to music he felt calmer. This urge to sing would start to linger. Then he would open his mouth and the noise that came out was sweet. Sometimes the sound would be hard, raspy, whatever his mood was. Even though he didn't know what he felt the voice would express it. It was innate, straight from his soul. Guilt and fear would vanish and leave him feeling good for the first time in years, in fact, ever. It dawned in him that this might be his calling, he never thought he had one. He'd always been told that everyone had a calling, not everyone finds it. Maybe he had. He knew he was good and it had changed everything. Was this what hope felt like, he wondered.

Chapter 4:
Benson & Hedges

The next day I had to get up and go to work, leaving the boys to fend for themselves.

Linda was still there, snoring on the sofa like a little piglet. I kept on thinking about the day before. Mum's coffin, the people, the priest and that feeling of despair, the lump in my throat. Then, there were the boys, my innate feeling to protect them and poor Aunt Linda, who already had one foot in the grave. I put my practical brain in gear, thinking too much wasn't good, action was what was needed.

I made a mental list of things that needed to be in order for us to stay together. I spent my working day and the ride home perfecting it.

When I got back Aunt Linda was still stinking the place out, still fast asleep. I called the boys into the kitchen.

Hardly the summit of the housewives' society but we worked out a plan.

1. Getting everyone up and out in the morning. Fred. (Fred had always been the first one to wake up so he was the most suited for the job. Some mornings he

didn't manage to get Steve up, though; he probably managed three mornings out of four.)

2. School scheduling, keeping up appearances, making sure we're not getting found out at school. Keeping the Social away. Ben. (He was kind and liked to be good so he was perfect for the job. He also knew how to use a hair- and toothbrush.)
3. Food on the table and roof over our heads. Ed.
4. Steve has no job. (Apart from being Steve.)

Steve was a mess, he did look better today, He just wasn't up for any responsibilities but at least he wanted to be with us, I could tell something had changed.

After our meeting we decided we should probably wake Linda up. Ben nudged her gently and she slowly came back to life. The state of her made me think of sewers, rats and stinky sewers. Ben seemed not to mind so much, which was odd, as he was the cleanest out of all of us. He even made her a cup of tea. There was no need for her to get dressed as she was still wearing her funeral outfit–didn't look so good now, though. I offered to see her to the bus. She looked relieved when I suggested it. Fred and Ben had their brave faces on and I couldn't help to think it was sad this was our only living relative that we knew of. Steve didn't handle the situation as gently: 'Auntie, you really stink.' I kicked him.

'Sorry, Steve.' she replied sheepishly.

Linda was a nice woman, just not very functional, that was all.

We gathered her things for her and left for the bus stop. She wasn't able to speak much but she did say, 'I am just on the other side of the phone, Ed. Remember that love.'

'I know, Auntie, I know. Let's get you on your way.'

Let us get on with our lives; we can't rely on anyone, especially not you, I thought. I slowly walked back home after the bus drove off. I took a deep breath, the list and the boys and I will be just fine. You'll see auntie Linda. We will do great.

It was pretty clear from our young years that none of us was going to be a professor, but Ben was doing his homework and was showing signs of not becoming a waster. He seemed more proper than the rest of us. Fred was still so young and relying on Ben to talk for him.

Ben was practising the bass now. I discovered Fred was a decent drummer; he'd been playing for a while at school. He seemed to like it a lot and luckily his sense of rhythm was all right.

'I bought a kit and a shitty old bass guitar from *Loot*. £20, for both.' I announced one day after work.

We put all our instruments in the living room, together with a mike, amplified by my old guitar amp (I had bought myself a new one.) We threw out the green sofa had Mum died on, it just wasn't possible to sit on, it had to go. A constant reminder of that dreadful day.

We had a full band set up in our own living room. Noisy, not the best for neighbourly peace, I admit, but it gave the room new life, I loved it.

The Supermarket was still happy with my efforts so money kept coming in and slowly I started to get to know some of the other workers. The mousey girl at the till had a pretty name–Veronica–and Matt and I were getting along well. We were both heavily into music and every morning we played the latest albums on the tape deck before Mr Brown turned up. Blaring out on the shop floor were our heroes, making us work faster, nodding to each other when a particularly brilliant tune or solo came on. We were in our own little shit kingdom until 8.30, when the other employees started to arrive.

I desperately needed the money: feeding the boys was more expensive than I thought. I had started to take things out of the bins that were out of date but looked fine. It was amazing how much food was left over. I made it my business to manage the leftovers. We ate some fine foods from there, stuff we had never tried before.

Veronica had started to put lipstick on recently and from what I had gathered girls only did this when they liked someone. Suddenly she seemed less mousey, more like one of the dancers from *Top of the Pops*. When I looked over at her, she smiled and sometimes blushed.

She had large grey eyes, a wide smile and a thin long nose. She was skinny and short, but she looked sophisticated, sort of. Her grey coat looked more attractive against her red lips and pink cheeks. In fact, she looked pretty. Really pretty.

I spent time thinking about Veronica and her smile while I was stacking shelves. 'I felt a strange sensation in my belly. I dropped a tin of tomatoes on my foot. Damn it! To stop myself thinking about her I listed the products location in my head.

Aisle 5. Baked beans, tinned tomatoes, peas, pasta shapes in tomato sauce, kidney beans, tuna in brine, and tuna in sunflower oil.

Aisle 6. Bread, cakes, baking ingredients, cookies and jams.

Aisle 7. Pasta, rice, eggs and spices.
And so the list went on. Sometimes it kept me awake at night, occupying my head monotonously and then Veronica would appear and all I could thing about was her.

I was good at my job. It was possibly the dullest job in the world but that didn't bother me. I was efficient and I was effective, there was no one who needed the job more than I did.

Matt asked me if I wanted to hang out after work one day. He suggested he would wait at the record shop on Parkway, I accepted.

It occurred to me that perhaps we were becoming good friends. I had never had a proper friend before, at least not one that I liked this much.

Mornings at work went faster after the store opened, especially as I was keeping myself visible for Veronica. Around eleven o'clock she was due for her coffee break. I knew this after carefully studying her routine. I had held off my own break so that we could meet in the staff room accidentally.

She was sitting in the smoking room. I wasn't a smoker but now that I knew she did, I had to give it a go and start as soon as possible.

'Hey, didn't know you smoked!' I tried not to cough.

'Yeah, I smoke, since I was thirteen, love it. You want one?'

'Nah, too early in the day for me. I like being around fags, though, they smell good.' I was nearly vomiting by now.

'Do you like it here? Sucks, right?' She looked straight at me.

'Kinda sucks, but it beats going to school, that's for sure. I'm gonna meet up with Matt after work. You wanna meet up sometime?'

I was scratching my head, left hand in back pocket, as I spoke to her. She made me so friggin' self-conscious. Nervous ticks I never knew I had jumping out of me. I needed to pull myself together to do this. Not so easy when my whole body was jittering with nerves.

'I work until six, but yeah! Sounds cool. Where?'

Shit, I really hadn't thought this through.

'Where? Er, Good Mixer?' It was a pub near the record shop that I had seen some youngish people hanging around outside. 'Outside it at 6:15?'

She smirked and I could see her cheeks getting flushed.

Casually I wandered out. I didn't want to embarrass her but I needed some giant breaths before I could continue through to the aisles. I made it to the loo and vomited a little.

As arranged, I met up with Matt at Rough Trade. We were looking through the new releases and asking the shopkeeper to put some obscure records on. Afterwards we went down to the lock with some beers that Matt had nicked from work.

He was wearing his denim waistcoat with some amazing patches on it, black drainpipes and vans. He was a beanpole, taller than I, and his hair made him even taller. His hands were typical guitar-nerd. Calluses on his left hand and nails slightly too long for a man on his right hand. I wondered what his style was like.

He looked like a young Hendrix, so I imagined he was an amazing guitarist.

'How old are you?' Matt asked.

'Sixteen, but I'm pretending I'm eighteen so the social won't take my brothers away. My parents both died.'

Shit…Why was I telling him?

'Ok, I see, so you're eighteen, cool,' Matt smiled. I noticed he didn't want to go into it further. I was relieved.

'Yeah, I feel old, though.' Swiftly I changed the conversation to something lighter. 'I asked Veronica to meet us at the Good Mixer at sixish.'

'You did, why? You like her or something?'

'Dunno, I like girls, and…she's alright, I guess.' I swigged my beer and felt manly.

'We should play guitar sometime.' Said Matt ignoring my girl comment.

Yes, we should, I thought. 'I have a set-up at my flat in the front room. Come round to mine one afternoon and we can jam if you want?' Another swig.

'Will do, you know Ed, I think I will leave you and young Veronica to your little date this evening, should be heading back to my house anyhow, my nan has cooked for me.' I could tell he was amused and didn't know whether he made the grandma thing up as he was smiling when he said it.

We sat there for a while, looking at people walking past, making comments on passers-by and discussing Black Sabbath and why Status Quo were in fact cool. Jimmy Hendrix is the guitar God but Yngwie Malmsteen lacked soul; he knew how to play, though, we agreed on that. We liked Queen, the melodies, but we hated pop music and were into the new crunchy sounds the Americans were making. We agreed on nearly everything, apart from girls and guitars. I quite liked them together; Matt thought they made cooler drummers.

We ducked when punks walked past, as they probably wouldn't like our look.

We laughed at their hairstyles, making sure they didn't notice. Punk music was cool though; piercings and Mohawks just weren't my thing.

They looked like they wanted to fight, but they were usually alright. I didn't like violence much. A self-confessed coward, I never felt the need to lash out.

Life was working out a lot better that I had imagined a few months back. The beers were going down nicely and Matt and I were friends. I felt warm and confident.

'You wanna smoke?' Matt offered me a Benson & Hedges.

'Hook me up.' I laughed nervously thinking about the vomit earlier.

I needed to do this so I could hang out in the smoke room and spy on Veronica, I took a drag on the cigarette and through sheer determination I managed not to cough. It tasted like shit but the image of myself with a fag in my mouth made me feel amazing and cool. After the first cigarette, or maybe the second, I was hooked.

Walking down Camden High Road, I was thankful I had all those beers, they gave me the confidence I needed.

Turning into Inverness Street, I could see her sitting on the pavement. Without her cashier uniform she looked completely different. She wore tight spandex leggings with an oversized Twisted Sister t-shirt on the top, black Dr Martens on her feet and lots of eye make-up. Veronica was the most beautiful girl I had ever seen; I was getting closer to her. Shit, get it together, this is it.

'Hi.' I was drunker than I thought. Hopefully she wouldn't notice.

'Hey Ed, so glad to be out of that mood murdering place.' I couldn't believe how pretty she was. My nerves were jittering and I used all my focus to keep it together.

'Yeah, it sucks, working is shit. You want a beer?' I wanted to agree with anything she said. Wherever she leads me I will go, I thought in my mushy head.

'I do, yes please.' She smiled the naughtiest smile I had ever seen. I handed her the beer and my heart too.

We started to walk towards the canal. The night was still and light and the two of us chatted about work, music and cigarettes. I had two cigarettes left. She smoked Marlboro lights; I decided I was a Benson & Hedges kind of man.

We parked ourselves on a green bench by the stinky water and sat quietly for a little while, watching rubbish and dead ducks floating by.

'It really is a shit hole, this canal.' She said.

I leaned over, reached for her hand and gently squeezed it, she squeezed it back. I wanted to kiss her so bad and I thought to myself, this is the right time.

I turned my face towards her, looked straight into her eyes and leaned in, she did too. Our lips met. Hers were soft like marshmallows; she tasted like strawberries and cigarettes. I lost myself in the moment, her breath gently caressed me and the surroundings, everything stood still for a while and there was a tickle in my stomach. This was another first, not the kissing but I think these feelings were perhaps what all the songs I liked were all about. Being in love.

We sat on the bench for hours until I realised I had to go back home. My neck was aching from hunching over, my lips dry from kissing.

This was also the first time I hadn't gone home straight from work. I relaxed and for a minute I remembered what it was like before Mum had died: only myself to worry about.

Veronica lived with her family in Kentish Town, so we started to walk towards her house.

The lipstick had worn off and somehow I liked her better without it. I wanted to do things the right way.

'You wanna come back to mine after work one day?'

'Tomorrow?' she answered a bit too fast but it was exactly what I wanted her to say.

'Tomorrow would be perfect.'

She wouldn't let me walk her to her door so we parted ways in Chalk Farm. Her eyes were all glittery as she looked over her shoulder twice after we parted. Bus 31 felt like a limousine and I was smiling from ear to ear.

It was ten o'clock by the time I got home. The boys were practising their instruments. As I walked into the living room they all stopped playing.

'Where you been?' I noted that Fred looked scared.

'We thought you'd done one.' He muttered

'Done one?' I didn't understand what he meant.

'You know, done a runner.'

'Don't be stupid. Just hooked up with a mate from work. Next time, I'll warn you. Promise.' I grabbed my guitar and sat down on a chair. 'Now then my brethren, let's play a tune.' My mood was too good to be ruined.

The room was strangely cosy, takeaway boxes and empty cans aside. We had started a hoover schedule and were somehow keeping to it. Well, everyone apart from Steve.

We stayed up, playing quietly on our instruments. Amps were off and we were working out song structures. Fred and Ben's playing was coming along and Steve's voice was possibly the best voice I had ever heard. It was raw, rough but easy on the ear. We had some more beers and suddenly I just blurted out something I'd wanted to say for a while.

'Perhaps we should sort Mum's room out. The three of you are really crammed in the big room, I guess, we need to do it at some point.'

There was that dreary silence again. We had been happily plodding along, and as soon as I mentioned her name we all clammed up.

'I mean, I could move in there, Steve could have my room, and the two of you could share the big room. What do you think? It makes sense.'

Still silence.

I started to play my guitar again, thinking that the boys needed to digest the thought of someone in Mum's room, even if it was me. I stopped playing again. I wanted to press this.

'I mean, perhaps we should ask Linda to come over and help us sort her things out. I need her to help me with some other things too. Could you call her for me, Ben?.'

I reached for my jacket and took out my newly bought packet of Benson & Hedges.

I had the attention of my brothers. They stared at me as I lit one up. I took a deep drag and slowly let the smoke out.

'I mean, we need to do it. Steve, what do you say?' No one seem to care about what I said but they all just stared at my face.

'Can I have one?' Steve piped up.

'Course,' said I.

It was odd, even though I was bringing up the taboo subject of Mum's bedroom; I felt so much closer to my brothers. They were looking to me for guidance, which was weird to think about, especially since I was just a big kid who loved to play the guitar. I liked it; I liked being responsible for them. It was important. I had never been important before.

We stayed up for another two hours playing and for the first time it clicked, I got a taste of what it could feel like to be in a real band. It was better than I had imagined. We blended together; the sound was interesting, edgy even. Perhaps us being in a band was what we needed to stick together. We never spoke about it. There was something here, growing. Like the beginning of a fire or even an explosion, I could feel it. I wanted to smoke more fags. I needed to get used to it, for her…Veronica.

Waking up at four o'clock after two hours' sleep wasn't an easy task, but Mr Brown had been known to sack people who were late. With that in mind, I crawled out of bed into my clothes and on to bus 31 to Camden. Even though I was knackered and my head was a little sore from the beers, I was in a fine mood this morning, smiling to myself as Veronica was dancing around inside my head. The early morning went in slow motion, Matt was in a grump and I was just waiting. Waiting for her to turn up.

When she finally arrived I felt exhausted. She came straight over and touched my hand. I squeezed it back and didn't let go.

'Hi.'

'Hi yourself. Are you ok? You look knackered.' She looked me straight in the eye and I glanced down at the floor.

'I'm tired, didn't get much sleep last night, that's all.'

It dawned on me that I was tired too. I'd worked four months straight, every day for eight hours, apart from the day of Mum's funeral. I needed a break.

'Well, you should rest, then.' She smiled.

'I might ask Mr Brown for a day off.'

'Sunday–ask for Sunday. That's when I'm off.'

It would also free up time for practice with the boys. Money was needed but we could make it on a six-day week salary. With the amount of out of date food I was getting from the bins I hardly had to buy anything. Something had to give.

'Good idea.' Any ideas from Veronica were good, I thought.

It was getting to the end of my working day and I was hovering around the smoke room to get to talk to her.

Just as my break was about to end, she turned up, her large grey melancholy eyes looking straight at me.

'Hey, I'm off soon. Gotta get back home to see my brothers. They were a bit freaked out yesterday.'

'Your brothers were freaked? Why?'

'I'm kinda looking after them. You see, our mum died.'

Thank God for the floor. Useful to stare at while feeling awkward.

'Oh, I'm sorry.' She fidgeted and her eyes widened in empathy.

'If you wanna come by after work, here's my address.' I handed her a scrunched-up paper.

'Yeah, I would really like to do that.'

I think it was happening, Veronica and I were on.

Chapter 5:
Veronica and Ed

I got home at 1.30 p.m. to an empty house. The familiar smell of old socks, damp and sweat welcomed me home. I wanted to rest but, a girl I really liked was coming over to our shithole of a house. I started to tidy up as I walked through the house, it was worse than I thought, in fact it was so bad I might as well give up so, I sat down on my bed instead, guitar on my knee, started to strum a little tune that I had thought up while thinking about her…Veronica. The tune was far too cheery for my taste but it was a good melody. I dozed a little, my body was aching, I needed a rest, I let myself go into dreamland with a half-smile on my face.

The next thing I knew Ben and Fred were standing above me, laughing. 'You were sleeping holding on to your guitar like it was a person.' I let go and grabbed my pillow instead and whacked them over their heads. They were both in hysterics. I remembered my dream. She was in it. Naked. If she really looked anything like that, I don't know whether I could handle it.

'Man, that was the best nap ever. Shit! What time is it?' It was dark outside.

'Five.' Ben always knew the time.

She wouldn't be here for a couple of hours. The house was a dump, my bed was a mess.

Ashtrays, cups, crisp packets and crap was lying around. I shouted a little too loudly. 'Guys, Let's clean this place, it's a dump.' No reaction. I tried a more pleading voice.

'Come on guys, help me.'

No reaction, nothing.

So, I sat down, decided there was nothing more I could do. This was me, us. Take it or leave it.

Steve came home, off his head. Again. I knew nothing I could do or say would change his ways. Thankfully he was a nice drunk, not aggressive, sweet and gormless, like a little creature. He wasn't that happy before Mum died and now he was drinking with a reason, trying to forget. A bottle of vodka in his jacket pocket at all times. He was pissed most days. He thought I didn't notice, that's how drunk he was.

'Let's play that song we played last night. It's been going round my head all day. It's really catchy,' he said, slurring his words.

The doorbell rang, it made everyone jump. Everyone froze, all for different reasons. Ben said, 'Who's that? Shh…Don't answer it.' Steve sat down on the floor making a hush sign with his finger over his mouth. I smiled.

'It's my friend. From work.' I jumped up.

I opened the door to Veronica, it was surreal seeing her on my doorstep, wearing a Motorhead t-shirt, red tights and white converse. The brothers looked confused, I felt proud and weirdly confident.

I introduced her to the boys, they just stared at her like she was some sort of strange alien or something. She didn't look like any other girl they'd ever met before. She wasn't from round here, that was apparent.

We haven't had any visitors, apart from Linda, since Mum died. As a rule, the boys never brought back friends, none of us did. We didn't want people to talk about us, draw attention to ourselves. Seeing a female in our living room was not something we were used to. I think we all fell in love that instant. Our jaws were stuck in an open position and for an moment there was silence.

'Who wants pancakes?' Veronica held up a plastic bag.

'Pancakes? You're mad. But yeah.' said Steve, sounding slightly more sober.

'I'm great at making them, my mum and I make them every week since I was a kid. I brought all the ingredients.'

We all followed her into the kitchen, watching her cracking eggs and whisking the mixture like a pro.

'Voilà, un crêpe pour toi.'

French for pancake, apparently, and she served up a perfect one.

'I'll make the table.' Ben said.

'The table?' I repeated.

We never lay the table.

'Do you have any jam?'

'Think so,' Thank god for Ben.

We had five pancakes each, sat around the table and talked rubbish. It had been a long time ago since I'd felt like this. For a moment, it felt all proper, like a happy normal family.

She also brought a pack of cigarettes and some lagers that she had managed to sneak out of the shop. Fred was getting good at smoking but Ben kept himself from the influence of peer pressure. I like that about him: he was strong, from the core. Fred was coughing like an old man. I remember thinking 'He'll get used to it.'

Even though I didn't know Veronica well, I felt as if we'd been friends for a long time. We moved into the living room, now music room and picked up our instruments.

She listened to us play until midnight.

'You guys sound amazing. I'm not just saying that it's really good. I never heard anything like it. A mix of heavy metal and punk with a bit of folky melody thrown into it.'

I knew what she meant; it was an original sound. The songs were shaping and I could see the brothers, especially Steve, were getting excited.

Music could do that. That's why I love it so much. It makes people feel things they should and forget about trouble.

Veronica was our first ever audience, I couldn't stop staring at her and she kept catching me and we locked hungry eyes. I had especially noticed how she threw her head back when she laughed.. Her dark brown hair nearly touched her bottom, her grey eyes sometimes lost their focus and wandered off into the distance, making her look melancholy and a little sad even, I wonder if she was and I hoped not. I wanted to make her happy.

My stomach would turn a little when I caught her eyes. My hand searched for hers if I sat down close to her, making sure the boys wouldn't notice; my foot touched hers and it felt like electricity, every time we made contact my whole body tingled. What the fuck was happening? Whatever it was, I was hooked.

Veronica stayed until midnight then she had to leave. We spent half hour kissing in the hall and my whole body trembled with desire.

'You want to be my girlfriend?' I whispered in her ear. She blushed.

'Yes,' she replied.

I couldn't believe that she liked me. But she did, that much I knew, I could feel it. I had a girlfriend, a pretty one that made pancakes and had soft, cushion-like lips. I walked her to bus and off she went in the night. This had been the best night of my life. So far.

.

Ed had some bird around. Steve felt weird about it. I mean, she was nice enough but who the hell would be all cheers and laughter just after they've buried their mother. It wasn't right. He thought *he* was a fucked up and all, but this? All three of them were looking at her like she was the mother fucking Madonna. She wasn't. She was just a girl Ed wanted to fuck.

He knew about that–he had slept with lots of girls. Since he had started selling weed all the girls loved him. He liked no one, he wasn't that stupid. All they wanted was a piece of him. He couldn't even remember their faces. Last night he had some speed, didn't like it much so he had made a mental note he liked to be mellow not mental. Weed. Oh yes, how he loved that weed.

The thing is, it was his birthday today. Some fucking birthday this was. No one remembered and why should they?

I had to get Aunt Linda round the next day to help us sorting Mum's room; going in there would be too much especially if her things were still in there. We had kept the room a no-go area.

Another problem was the post that kept coming, there were piles of it stacking up in the hall. All this was easier to think about when I felt happy. Nearly skipping down the road, feet light as feathers, I entered the house,

I heard Steve, strumming the guitar and singing along with his voice of angels. He was writing words down on a piece of paper. He sounded sad, I sat down next to him. His voice pierced through the melancholy notes, making me shiver. He sounded so heartfelt and low I couldn't help suspecting something was up. I sat outside and listened for a while before I walked in.

'You good?'

'Yeah, I really like this song. It's a strange one, but it's really catchy. You know Ed, I wasn't going to say anything but… it's my birthday today. I'm officially fifteen.' I felt as if I someone punched me in the stomach, I deserved someone to I've been so wrapped up in my own world, I completely forgot. I knew his birthday was around now so I should have asked, should have made sure I knew. How could I have missed it? I've been too busy thinking about Veronica, work and the music consumed me, feeling happy about us playing together. I looked down at the paper and I read the words.

Why did you have to go?

'Steve, you should have said. You really should have reminded me. I have a day off on Sunday. Let's do something. What do you wanna do? Anything. Whatever you want.'

He paused. 'It's ok Ed. Relax. I get it, it's hard for you to remember these things. I mean, you're not my mum. You know…I really wanted a bike. Mum always said she was gonna get me a bike when I turned fifteen.,

… we can't afford a bike. It's all good. Mum couldn't afford one either and it doesn't matter anymore.' Steve continued playing, hunched over the guitar, strumming slowly. I'm such an idiot. I lit a fag and offered him one, he stopped playing and accepted the cigarette.

'The pancakes were nice. Veronica seemed alright.' He said.

'Yeah, we had a nice night. Give me my guitar.'

I started strumming. 'Happy Birthday to you, Happy Birthday to you… Where am I gonna get a bleeding bike from?' I made him smile. I put my arms around him and our foreheads met. We had a moment and for a second I thought everything was going to be fine.

The next day came along in what seemed like two seconds, the alarm clock went off, and my eyes ached when I tried to open them. At least it was Saturday.

Before I left the house I jotted Linda's number down on my hand. I needed help and I needed it now.

Throughout the morning I had this uncomfortable feeling in my belly. I could see Steve felt sad, he wanted to be brave, but at the same time it had truly sunk in that we were on our own. Orphans. From now on I will have to make sure to remember all their birthdays. If we were going to make it we had to stay away from dark thoughts that reminded us of her.

Break time was spent in the smoke room and as expected; Veronica turned up.

'Morning. How you going there? You look… exhausted, you tired?' She didn't look that great either, dark circles under her eyes and pale skin.

'Eh, yeah, I realised after I walked you to the bus that it was Steve's birthday and none of us remembered.'

'What? Why didn't he say anything?' She paused. 'It was late last night, later than I thought. My dad was really angry when I got back.'

'Really? Didn't know you had a curfew. Being parentless and all that.' I knew that Veronica was seventeen. She never mentioned her family, probably because it felt odd as I didn't have parents.

'He gets stressed when I'm late, that's all, worried Dad syndrome, he is French you know.' She looked down on her hands as she spoke.

My mind had already wandered back to Steve and my own problems.

'He wanted a bike. Mum…had promised him a bike,' I said.

Veronica sat down and reached for my hands, they were soft and calm. Just touching her made me think of all the things I wanted to do to her, with her, it was impossible to focus on anything else. Our lust filled eyes locked in and it was so intense it fried my brain. After some careful plotting, we, or actually *she* came up with the idea of stealing a bike. It had to be late at night, she said, and it had to be far away from the north-west of London. She hatched the plan meticulously, I couldn't let her down by telling her I wasn't that into stealing, in fact I hated it.

She decided that we would spend tonight searching for bikes across the river. I agreed even though I was riddled with nerves.

After work, I went to find a pay phone, ours was cut off, and dialled Linda's number. After twenty rings she finally picked up. Her voice was sleepy and croaky, she listened and agreed to come over the following Sunday afternoon. Our aunt was in a bad way but I needed her to be there.

I rushed home to get the boys sorted before we I went out. I'd bought a cake from the shop; it had Superman on it. I thought it might make Steve laugh, as he used to love Superman. As expected, he wasn't in; Ben and Fred said he'd been gone all day. I told them about missing Steve's birthday and I could see they felt bad too.

We decided to go and look for him. It didn't take us long to find him. Some of the boys at school hung out at a block of flats off West End Lane, so we decided to head there first. Steve was standing in the playground, smoking weed with his mates.

'Come on young man, let's go home and play music.' I literally pulled him along. His eyes were glazed over and I could smell him. He was in no hurry to leave.

We managed to lure him home with the promise of band practice and cold beer, and even though he protested I think he liked that we looked out for him. On the way up to the house Ben spotted a man in a grey suit standing outside, clipboard in hand. We waited around the corner until he was gone. There was an envelope on the floor by the letterbox. Delivered by hand, it said on it in bold black capital letters. It looked important, so I decided I'd better open it even though my plan had been to open scary-looking mail with Linda the next day.

The letter was from the council, apparently we owed three months' rent. I knew this was bad news.

Linda had obviously not kept her promise. I went to the phone, forgetting it was out of service. I didn't want to worry the boys so I grabbed my coat, said we needed milk, I practically ran to the phone booth. How could I have been so stupid, putting my trust in an old pisshead? Anyone could see she wasn't fit to look after herself, let alone a promise to four teenage boys.

Again, it took plenty of rings for her to get to the phone. I had to try and stay calm.

'Linda hey, Ed here. The council just dropped by a letter. We owe rent. I thought you said you sorted it.'

She sounded confused and her voice was so slurred. I could barely make out the words. I am such an idiot. She was off her head. From now on, I'd trust no one.

'What was that all about?' Ben was the only one who had clocked that there was a problem.

'Nothing, don't worry. Let's play. Get your bass out. Is it tuned?'

We all sat down and practised our song, the first one that we actually finished. Steve had even written the words. We ate the Superman cake and played music for hours.

Veronica knocked on the door at 6:15. She brought a card and some beers for Steve. Her energy and the smell of her sweet perfume made all of us act nicer. Like fresh air she was and all four of us were following her every move, like dedicated fans.

After a while she and I decided to get out of the house. We had a mission after all, besides, I wanted Veronica all to myself. I grabbed her hand.

'Let's go!'

We jumped on the tube and got off at Blackfriars, lurched around for a couple of hours like tourists, holding hands and chatting about nothing.

We stopped in doorways, snogging and my body was burning up, I wanted more, I wanted all of her. I knew she was going to let me, I could tell, and I couldn't wait. Her body was warm, her breasts, soft and her knickers hot when I touched her down below.

After the pubs closed we scoured around the area to find a bike. Veronica seemed to know what she was doing and I followed her lead.

We found the perfect bike at the end of a garden: no lock and a good size for a young lad. It was freezing, but with the help of incentive and adventure we got the bike back to north-west London. It took ages, as we kept on finding parks and alleyways to sneak in to. It was cold but I was a little tipsy on beer and love I couldn't care less.

When we got back home, the house was quiet, so we crept in like a couple of burglars. It was in the early hours of the morning and we were freezing and giddy. We left the bike in the hall and Veronica had brought a red ribbon that she tied around the saddle. It was a good bike; Steve would love it.

We stumbled up the stairs and fell onto my bed. We both knew what was going to happen and we wanted it to. We undressed in a hurry; I was scared to let go of her eyes. It was over pretty quickly but it was perfect.

At five in the morning she leapt out of bed and ran out of the house.

'Bollocks! It's five o'clock in the morning!'

She ran out the door but she left her panties behind…I was no longer a virgin.

Chapter 6:
Never Trust a Drunk.

It was my first lie-in for what seemed like a lifetime, I opened my eyes at exactly ten o'clock. The house was still quiet and I sneaked downstairs. The bike was still there where we left it.

I wondered if Steve would like the bike. It had yellow writing on it, Spelling out the word 'STYLER.' Apart from that it was matte black. It looked even better in the morning light. I sat on the stairs and admired it, thinking about Veronica and last night.

I should have left the boys to sleep in as it was Sunday, but the combination of having a day off plus the excitement about the previous night's events made my adrenaline pump. I ran up the stairs and shouted on the top of my voice: 'Good fuckin' morning! You lazy little bastards.'

Steve was impossible to get out of bed but in the end they all started to make movements. Ben and Fred saw the bike first. Steve had to practically walk into it before he noticed.

'Bloody hell! What's this? Where did you get this from?' Through his half-opened eyes he was clocking what was going on. I could tell he was excited but there was a slight serious mood hovering in the air. Not what I expected. I started to talk too fast.

'Veronica, she helped me. Some mate of hers sold it to me real cheap,' I said. I couldn't tell the truth. And it also made Veronica look good. I wanted them to really like her. It was working. So far, so good.

'It's great, in fact, it's amazing. I love it. Is there a lock? I mean, people nick bikes round here all the time.'

'Nah, we should probably get one before you leave it out of your sight.' I saw a pang of sadness in his eyes, then I got it, the bike reminded him of Mum, their conversations about his birthday, him nagging her for a bike. I knew he was happy but this was hard, everything to do with mum was painful and I know we all missed her terribly, we were all mourning her in our own way, being as brave as we possibly could. I went into my usual hyper mode and it seemed to work.

We took the bike out to a little park in Kilburn and messed around with it. Fred was useless on the bike and Ben kept falling over. I was in stitches watching them, they looked happy and for a minute we were a normal family. Steve had good balance, he always found everything so easy. I'd always found it irritating but now I was grateful. He was smiling from ear to ear. I think it did the trick on the end.

I suddenly remembered Linda was coming over today.

'You guys stay here, don't leave the bike, I have to go home. Aunt Linda is coming. I need to talk to her.'

Five minutes after I got back home the doorbell rang, Linda, looking like a car crash had arrived on our doorstep. I actually think more teeth had fallen out since the funeral. It was a miracle she made it here. We sat down in the kitchen. I opened the garden door as the sour stench coming from her was even worse than last time. After a few pleasantries I cut to the chase.

'Auntie, what's going on? I had this letter. You said you were going to sort out the rent. Some man came by yesterday.' I placed the letter in front of her. 'We might lose the house, that can't happen.' I tried not to sound pissed off, but I was.

'Edward, darling boy, I let you down, I'm not in a good way. I'm sorry, I really am. Since the funeral I have just been falling apart. Worrying myself sick. I can't sleep or eat; I can barely walk.' She let out some sobs followed by a violent coughing fit. 'I can't stop thinking about your parents, this tragic family, you boys.' Tears were rolling down her tired face.

'Linda, it's fine. I promise, we can cope. You have to show me, you know, how to pay the rent and the bills. I can do it myself. You said there were some money, you know, from our dad?'

I got her a cup of tea and some tissues. I needed to know where that money was and how to pay stuff. We needed a roof over our heads. I had to act quickly.

In the end, after two glasses of gin, I got it out of her. She told me Dad had left some money that came from their mother; it was more than I thought. Eight Grand. I couldn't help thinking it was mean of her not to have told Mum, it could have saved her life. But there was no time to dwell on the past, forward was the only way. She had the cash in a saver's account, and apart from Mum's funeral costs, she hadn't spent any of it.

'You know, I have a job now. I'm never late for it and get paid weekly. Steve is doing better too. He is coming home after school so you don't have to worry about us.'

All I could think about was that I needed to get my hands on that money. After all, it was ours. Auntie Linda was a ticking time bomb and when she went, so would the money that could save us.

She rambled on how she had promised Dad not to give it to us before we were eighteen. She also understood that things were different from when he had died and that she knew that we really needed the money. In the middle of our conversation the boys arrived back. We played her a couple of songs that we had been working on. Her feet were tapping along to the beat.

She cared for us, I could tell and that counted for something. She closed her eyes and swayed from side to side erratically. Looking at her, it was obvious that she was a proper drunk, her movements shaky like leaves and her body frail like a dry dead stick. She was close to the end. Whatever time she had left was borrowed; Linda was broken beyond repair. This made me anxious. We needed to get our hands on that cash and quick, it was ours after all.

Before she got too drunk I asked Linda if she would help me open up some of the mail. Even though I had now worked out that perhaps Linda was not someone I could rely on, at least helping would make her feel important, and she was organised when she had her head on.

There were a few letters from school, one from Steve's teacher that required a meeting. It was set for Monday afternoon. I pleaded for her to stay the night and go the next day. She could wait for me to come back after work and we could pay the rent and some other things that I needed help with. She was in such a good mood after our playing (and probably a few swigs of gin) that she agreed to help me out.

Next on the agenda was Mum's bedroom. I explained to Linda that we needed the room.. I was worried about seeing and touching her things. It was not going to be easy. The brothers seemed calm this evening, so I figured tonight was as good of a night as any.

Steve cycled to the fish and chip shop and we all sat around and ate in silence. The ticking of our kitchen clock and the odd cough from Linda were the only sounds. I cleared my throat and mustered up the courage to speak.

'We need more room and we need to sort out Mum's things.' The boys kept eating, no one protested so I continued to pursue my mission. 'I mean, it seems stupid for it to be empty. She would have wanted us to use it, and Steve could use his own space. Linda, will you help?'

She looked unsure but she agreed. We had some black bin liners and I had taken some boxes from work. Mum didn't have a lot but there were some things. I decided that we needed music. We put Bob Dylan on the record player and we all entered the room together. Nerves were hanging in the air. Fred banged his head on the door and Ben sat down on the unmade bed. I guess it was unknown territory, going into your dead mother's bedroom.

I scanned the boys, trying to work out how they felt. They looked calm. We took everything out of her closet. Her smell was suddenly everywhere but it didn't matter, it felt nice. We started to open her drawers. We found photos underneath the bed, us as babies, Mum and Dad looking young, alive and carefree.

We found her jewellery box with some necklaces and a couple of rings. Dad's wedding ring was there as well. The strange thing was, I had been dreading this day, but instead it felt safe and soothing, like I was close to her. I remembered her when she was happy before she started to fall apart. It made me even more determined to succeed for her, for her dreams that I know she had when we were little, I remembered her being full of life and proud of her family. Sometimes I wondered what happened to her, what made her so sad. I know when Dad died things changed, but somehow I knew there was more to it than that. Steve took a sweater of Mum's and put it on; it fitted him. I could see he liked it. He looked good in it.

'I really like this.' Steve sat down, singing along to 'Maggie's Farm'. He knew every word. It surprised me but that was how Steve was. Never predictable, I give him that.

Linda boxed the nice things and wrote neatly what was in it. Looking at her, I wondered how she ended up in this state. There were signs of a proper person in there, a person who could write, look clean and think. What was wrong with our family...why was everyone so messed up?

We stored everything carefully in the top cupboards. Some of the trinkets we decided to give to the charity shop but most of the things we saved. Sleeping in her room would be weird but somehow it didn't bother me as much as I thought it would. Being this close to Mum was a good thing, reminding me I had to make a change for her and for us. The determination I had inside was there before she died. Now, I felt even more determined to succeed.

Linda kept on going out to the hallway. I gathered she had a bottle of gin in her jacket pocket, as she looked more and more purple as the night progressed. She cracked some jokes and waved her hands as she spoke. Her mood had improved but we all knew she was soon going to be too drunk to speak. I guess she wasn't here to clean herself up. I did need her to be functional in the morning, we found her an outfit from Mum's things that she could wear. I had to get her into a bed to stop her drinking.

We decided that Linda would sleep in my bed and I would spend the night in my new bedroom. I walked Linda to my bedroom. She was so drunk her legs were giving way, I carried her to the bed, she was light as a feather. I tucked her in and carefully took her shoes off.

I braced myself and went into my new bedroom. Mum's bedroom. I grabbed a beer from downstairs and found some new sheets from the cupboard. After the boys and Linda were in their beds I went upstairs. I was about to change the linen. I sniffed the pillow like a dog; it still had her smell. I couldn't bring myself to pull them off. I didn't want to. I wasn't ready.

I battled with the feelings that were spinning around in my head. I decided I didn't want to change the sheets so I wouldn't. Not tonight, maybe not ever. The bed was comfortable. I closed my eyes and wandered off into the strangest of dreams, I walked into the kitchen where Mum was standing preparing dinner. In the dream I knew she was dead, so I was surprised and happy to see her. I walked up to her and hugged her hard and she told me to stop being so silly, it was only a joke, she never died. Everything was fine. She'd pretended to die so that we would shape up. All was well. No need to worry. We hugged and I felt so happy.

The alarm clock rudely awoke me at 4 a.m. as per usual. I leapt out of bed and quickly pulled off Mum's sheets so that the boys didn't see that I had slept in them. I went off to work on my usual ride, Bus 31.

The working morning went by like a speeding train and I was eagerly awaiting Veronica's arrival when the store opened. She didn't turn up. It occurred to me that I didn't have her phone number or address. My head was spinning with different reasons why she wasn't here, mainly ones that had to do with her and me. It didn't make any sense. We had had such a great night. We had connected, properly–she must have felt it too. It wasn't the sex thing. It was more than that, it was the real deal.

After work, I rushed back home as I was worried that Linda might have changed her mind and left the house. I needed to make sure she was in an acceptable state to handle Steve's school meeting. I arrived back home at 1.35. The meeting was at 2 p.m. Walking in the door, I spotted Linda crouching over the kitchen table. She looked like death itself; there was no way she was going to be able to attend a school meeting. She stank of booze and she was slurring her words.

'Ed, hesh…looo, boy. Your home…schh…already. Good boy.'

I went over to her and stroked her cheek, which felt like sandpaper, I felt like slapping her.

'Oh, Auntie Linda, you don't look so good. Let's get you back in bed for a little rest.'

How was I to get her to the bank? I needed to sort the rent situation. I had to get her there. It wasn't the first time a parent hadn't turned up for a school meeting in our area. I could get around that but the rent was a different matter. That letter yesterday didn't feel patient, not one bit. The money from Dad was ours after all.

I let her sleep for one hour, then woke her up with a strong cup of coffee. I took her to the bathroom, cleaned her face with a flannel, gave her a toothbrush for her teeth, applied the toothpaste for her and brushed her hair gently. As I cleaned her face she looked up at me like a little girl and said, 'Sorry, so sorry, Ed. You're a good boy.' Her words clearer now.

'That's Ok, Auntie. Let's get you sorted. Put this on.' I gave her mum's clothes that we had chosen the day before.

It was getting late for bank opening hours, the two of us walked towards the High Road. We didn't say much but there was a mutual respect and determination the air. I had the letter about the rent in my pocket and my birth certificate, which I had fished out of Mum's stuff the night before.

The last thing I needed was to worry about our house being taken away. Linda thankfully took charge at the bank, handing over her red saver's account book. The cashier updated it and there was nearly £9,000 in the account.

'I would like to open an account, in my nephew's name, a saver's account. His name is Ed Henderson, born on the 7th August 1972.' I was surprised she knew my birthday, a sign that there was a normal, well person inside her dishevelled shell.

The woman behind the counter was sweet and helped us with the formalities, I handed her my birth certificate. She also helped me pay the rent we owed.

'Can you transfer the rest of this money into his account, please?'

'Aren't you a lucky boy.' Said the cashier.
I nodded but wondered what she would think if she knew the truth. Linda pushed the savers account book towards the cashier. It was a huge amount of money and it was going to save our asses. Linda wanted to go home so I walked her to the bus station and waited for her bus to arrive, she was pleased to be leaving me. She was holding on to my arm and I hoped she wouldn't fall over once I let go.

'Ed, I have a letter here that your dad gave to me about the money. Doesn't matter much now, I had to go against his wishes. You have to promise me to share the money equally with your brothers. I have to trust you, and I do. You are doing a fine job with the boys.' She handed me a once white envelope.

This could be our last goodbye, I thought as I hugged her frail body carefully. She just wasn't able to cope with life, our situation. Her body looked fragile and whatever was left of the old Linda that used to come around and play with us was definitely long gone. I had to look ahead. The future was all I had.

'I promise.' I said and I meant it.

On the way home I thought about Veronica. Where was she?

I went home and waited for the guys, still holding the letter from our Dad.

The door went just after three, Steve handed over another letter from school. He gave it to me with a smirk on his face and I wanted to punch him so bad. All I had asked of Steve was to stay out of trouble, nothing else; he couldn't even do that. Ben told me his teacher had been asking about mum. I zoned out while I pretended to listen to their school problems. Right now I a bit of silence to work out what to do.

With the rent and our immediate future sorted, I suggested we go to Wendy's for dinner. We were all starving and had two cheeseburgers each. Afterwards, we all went back home and practised our instruments into the small hours, I didn't mention the letter or the money, I was worried it would cause fights.

Our neighbours had started to complain about the noise coming from our house. It was another big problem. Another worry one was the time of year: only one week away from Christmas. It was going to be a tough, I pushed it to the back of my mind.

The only effortless part of our lives was the music, playing together. We were starting to sound so good.. Sometimes I wondered how the last four months had happened. In fact, we were in a strangely harmonious place. I wrote a song about it and I knew it was a good one, the best one yet. I couldn't wait to play it to the boys. I was excited to hear Steve sing it.

When everyone had gone to bed I went into my newly acquired bedroom with new clean sheets on. I got the letter out from my coat pocket. It said 'Linda' on it. Slowly I pulled the note out and apprehensively rested my eyes on the paper.

Linda,

I asked you to open this letter in case I went and died on you all. If you are reading this, it means that I am gone. Hopefully, I wasn't too young when it happened.

The money we had from Mum and Dad is for the boys. Sue can manage until the boys are eighteen. I want them to have the money when they are young adults, something to start life with.

I also want you to tell them that I am proud of them, I never thought I'd have four boys. Didn't think I had it in me.

With my dodgy heart and the bad Henderson luck I just know I won't make it to an old age.

Please look out for my family. It's important to me that they will have a good life. Sue is a weak woman, make sure she eats well.

You are a good little sister, I love you. I thank you from the grave.

Much love,
Your big brother Ted

The letter made me feel weird, I wished I had never read it and that we didn't need to use the money. I understood why Linda had been reluctant to hand it over, his wish was sacred but I had no choice.

I promised myself that the money was to be used for the rent and emergencies only, I would keep it quiet for now, it was for the best. When the boys were old enough we would split what was left. It was that little bit of luck that we needed.

Thank you, Dad. You saved our bacon.

School was getting unbearable for Steve, all he wanted to do was smoke weed, drink and sing. Rehearsing with the band was great. Ed got him this great bike for his birthday and he had started to sell some weed for his friend's dad, the cash was good. The bike made it easier for him to get around. He bought himself a backpack so he could whizz around the area.

Fred had looked so thin recently so he made sure he had money for lunch at school. Last week he had made £40 from his dealings. A decent amount of cash. If Ed knew he would kill him, but Ed wasn't his keeper. Besides, he was careful not to get caught, used a false name, Rob, and never let on where he lived or his age. After this school year he could leave. He kept showing up at school now and again for the boys' sake. Now with the band it was even more important that they didn't get found out, he liked this new thing they had going on with a band.

Ed's new girlfriend was better class than any of the girls he got off with and she was a nice bird too, so home life was better.

Every time he went straight home after school he found Ben sitting in the kitchen reading, doing home-work. He was from a different planet from the others. At least Fred was more like him. Steve had become curious and slightly guilty that he liked the family more now, without their mother in it. They had all lived under the same roof but there had been no connection, until now.

This whole band thing had made him care, it was the music, it moved him, made him a better person. He actually now gave a fuck whether Ed knew he sold weed. He had promised him to stay out of trouble and dealing was trouble. He felt guilty, especially after the whole birthday thing. A few months ago Ed would not have cared when his birthday was; now he was acting like Ted, their father, not Ed the loner brother who never bothered to say hi. Not that he ever did either. Steve used to be happy keeping himself to himself. Not now, though: now he cared. Who would have thought that music could change your life? Family was important but music could make you a better person. He knew that now. Walking home from school, he remembered he had to go get some more skunk from the flats. He changed direction, dragging his lazy ass to make more secret money. If only Ed knew…He would kill him and that didn't matter *as* much. He was his own boss.

Chapter 7:
The Band Is Born

Veronica was still a no-show at work. She had completely vanished. I had to pluck up the courage to ask Mr Brown where she was. I walked confidently towards his office.

'Mr Brown, sorry to disturb you, but do you know where Veronica is hiding? She's been off for days now.'

'Yes, she's ill. Some sort of broken bones accident,' he said.

'Oh, that sounds bad. Perhaps I could have her number to check how she is. Or address?' I tried to look casual. She was absolutely fine when she left me the other night; I had to find out where she was..

'Can't do that, I'm afraid. She's coming back next week, that's what she said.'

Mr Brown walked off whilst I was still trying to think of what to say.

I didn't even know my so-called girlfriend's surname so I had no means of getting a hold of her. It was annoying as hell. I guess I would have to wait.

It was a Friday and I'd invited Matt around for a drink and a jam, I'd warned the boys, told them all about him and how extremely cool I thought he was.

I'd made sure we had plenty of lager and smokes in the house. Even though I felt a bit tense about bringing him into our bubble, somehow I knew it was the right thing to do. He arrived on time, carrying his guitar case; he played a Les Paul, it was black, matt black with chrome knobs, AC/DC stickers on the back and a zebra shoulder strap.. I knew, because he told me, that he had saved up for a year to buy it, now I understood why, it was incredible.

Matt didn't say much about himself, he told me he lived in Golders Green with his maternal grand-mother, his mum and dad had gone back to Trinidad when he was a little boy. His nan was a nurse, she fed him jerk chicken and made him breakfast no matter what time of day it was. After we'd admired his guitar we opened a beer and attempted small talk.

I tried to sound casual,

'Do you know anything about what happened to Veronica? Apparently she's had some sort of accident.' Matt sometimes had more information than he let on.

'No, not really, I know her old man looks kinda scary, saw him pick her up once, seemed the grumpy type. Huge French guy.'

Matt was taking his guitar out of its black case, which was covered in gig stickers. He plugged it into the amp and started to tune it. As he strummed the guitar gently, his foot was tapping the tempo. I stopped talking and sat down next to him and plugged myself into Ben's amp. We started playing; we locked in with each other instantly.

As I suspected, Matt had incredible feel...he was a natural. His long slim fingers were dancing over the metal strings. I was steadily playing riffs and together it was perfect, absolute perfection, it reminded me why I wanted to be alive: nothing else mattered in the world when I connected with music like this. This was what I lived for, moments like this one.

Hours went by, we only paused when the boys came home from school. I could tell they were impressed by Matt and his playing. He was a little older, confident in his own skin–just his appearance and the guitar were enough to earn any teenage boy's respect–and his playing was mind-blowing. He played like the guitar was part of his body. Because music was our lives now, Matt fitted right in, like a missing link.

I thought about Veronica. Where is she? The information I had got out of Matt didn't help; it was worse. Her dad was probably an aggressive guy. She had left my house at five, probably bad news, she was definitely panicking. I had to find her. I had this niggling feeling things were not right and maybe it was all my fault.

I asked the brothers to join in. They started to sort out their instruments.

Fred sat down behind the kit and started to play along; it was amazing how his style had developed so much in the last months. It was simple and steady. He played a small jazz kit and the noise that came out was crunchy and round. No frills, just straight beats. I could tell that Matt liked it.

Matt asked us about our songs we had been working on and if we could play him something. We decided on the song I had written, the one that was nearly done.

Matt lit up a fag and grabbed a drink, then sat back, relaxed as if he was ready to listen. We started playing. I kept looking over; his foot was tapping, and his eyes closed. He grabbed his guitar and started to play along. The room shrank, the air vacuumed us in, we morphed together–it was like magic. The first time it had really happened and we were all hooked.

The doorbell rang; it was the neighbour screaming through the letterbox.

'Boys, for fuck's sake, shut up. You are driving me insane with racket. Shut up. We have a baby in there. And you've just woke him up. Where's your parents?'

I couldn't help myself: laughter came crashing out of me. It was liberating. I couldn't stop, the alcohol didn't help. It was so boring to hear these complaints over and over. For once, I didn't care.

We needed to solve the noise problem before the council would get involved. It was only a matter of time, but no one could ruin this moment

It was as if Matt could read my mind,

'I know this bloke; he has an empty cellar under his record shop in Kentish Town. He wants to rent it out. It's not big, but...it's big enough. One hundred quid a month. He likes me, you see, he wants me to start a band.'

The situation with the neighbours was a ticking time bomb and soon the police would be coming around, and that was the last thing we needed. The £9,000 in the bank popped into my head and knew that I could cover the rent as well as a rehearsal space.

'Let's take a look at it after work tomorrow?'

We played for a couple of hours more, trying not hard enough to keep the noise down. Matt smoked weed, so I tried that for the first time. I liked it, I guess. Steve was already a stoner and he and Matt clicked instantly. A match made in hell I'd say.

The rest of the night passed in a daze, the marijuana making me hungry and dizzy. I did make a mental note that Ben was sitting in the kitchen doing his homework again. Crazy–where did that gene come from?

I hit the sack and dreamt of the beautiful, perfect Veronica.

The next day, after work, Matt took me to Rick's place. In my mind I had painted a picture and straightaway I knew it was even better than I'd imagined. The outside was grubby, with metal grilles covering the shop front. The sign was missing the R, so it read 'ick's Records'.

The place stank of weed and there were a few Rastas sitting around on red velvet sofas, talking, smoking or playing dominos.

Rick jumped up and hugged Matt, he looked me up and down and I introduced myself, I think I probably went bright red. You had to walk through the shop, pass the till and down some stairs to get to the basement. A strong damp smell welcomed us. The cellar was already soundproofed and it had a small PA that apparently worked.

'We used to jam 'er for hours back in the day.' Said Rick.

I couldn't speak, it was that perfect. We could start up properly here; the band could make noise all night long. All we needed to do was bring our gear there and plug in.

The shop sold mostly reggae records and the music blasting from the speakers was the kind that made you sway, feel relaxed, a feeling I hadn't had for a long time.

'It's perfect.' I managed to say.

Rick was laidback and when I tried to be efficient he told me to relax. He also offered his beaten-up Volvo to transport our equipment over. Matt and I stayed for a while, answering questions about our band, we didn't have many answers but at least we tried. This place felt like home.

'I want to hear three songs by the end of next month.' Said Rick.

'You're young, you have time…but goals are good.' He handed me a joint, I accepted and sat back and enjoyed the throbbing bass coming from the rickety speakers.

I went home and animatedly told the boys. I dramatically announced how Bus 31 would now be our shared humble carriage on a daily basis because that was how often we would practice, until our fingers bled, until our bodies ached and our eyes had to be held open by matchsticks. We had to work hard, harder than anyone else, if we were going to succeed.

I hugged Fred and told him everything was going to be all right, he'd see, we were going all the way to the top. I was filled with happiness and that strange phenomenon…hope.

On the bus home Matt told me in his own nonchalant way that he liked our playing and that he wanted to join the band. He was excited about it, Steve's voice was the best he had ever heard, we had something, he said.

'Man, that's great.' I said even though I had assumed he already was.

Things were officially 'going great', we had to celebrate. Now all we needed was a name, a band name that would end up in the rock'n'roll hall of fame . I always felt it would when the time was right. Steve had ideas, most of them shit but some acceptable.

And then, just as things were coming together, Christmas was only a few days away. I had to speak to the brothers about it, see what they thought would be the best way spend it. I talked to Matt at work and he suggested we'd go to his nan's house. He'd told her about us and she wanted to meet us. Feeding waifs and strays was all part of her tradition, apparently, so we would fit right in. Not having to be at home felt like the right thing to do. Staying busy had always worked before, so I wasn't about to change my method.

I had two days off, Christmas Day and Boxing Day. I wanted to spend most of my spare time getting the rehearsal space ready, so there wasn't that much time.

The boys were at home when I got in. I told them about Rick's place and they were excited, more importantly, thrilled that Matt wanted to join our band. The good news geared me up to talk about things that were harder to think about. At dinnertime I took a deep breath and blurted it out.

' Matt says we can spend Christmas Day at his. I mean, I can't cook a bleeding turkey and the first Christmas without Mum is going to be hard. What do you think? His Nan is apparently a good cook.' I spoke way too fast.

They all looked as if they didn't know what Christmas was.

'I think it's a good idea. We could invite Linda over in the morning and then go to Matt's. Sounds good to me.'

'Yeah, I'm in.' Steve liked Matt, so no problem there.

Fred looked unsure.

'Alright, If you all think so…I mean…'

'Fred, if it doesn't feel right we can do something else.' I said as he looked like he was about to cry.

'I kinda wanted to go and leave some fresh flowers on Mum's grave, you know, tell her we're doing good and that. And auntie Linda?' Fred's face changed expression. He had aged a lot since Mum had died. He looked older than his thirteen years.

What about Auntie Linda? She's frickin' useless. I thought as quickly as I could and said,

'Course we have to do that too.' I paused and then I remembered something else.

'I don't think there is a stone there yet, I'm saving up, they're expensive, but she's in there, next to Dad.'

'I know, I went there yesterday.' Said Fred and the sentence felt like a cold shower.
Ben put his arms around his shoulder.

'You did? What's it like?'

'Not great but it doesn't matter. I like going there to think.'

Perhaps my strategy of looking ahead and ignoring the pain wasn't right for all of us. It was apparent that all of us apart from Steve *had* thought about Christmas.

'So, it's gonna be great at Rick's place, I just know it,' I said to change the conversation.

'I know. Let's paint it or something… Tell us about it, what's it like?' Said Ben.

'Well, there's a bunch of stoned Rastas upstairs in the shop, sitting around smoking weed while the shop speakers blare out Peter Tosh records.'

'I hate Peter Tosh.' Steve was half asleep.

'You are obviously not smoking enough ganja.' Fred giggled and we were all relieved the serious moment passed.

'Anyhow, it's amazing downstairs. The room is soundproof. There is lots of power points and we could even get a fridge and a kettle there. I love it. No one will hear us.'

'Are you sure we can afford it?' Only Ben would ask this question.

'Yep. Matt has got me the best deal. Rick loves him.'

'It sounds brilliant!' Fred looked happier, I threw a lager can at him, which he caught.

'It is, I swear, it's too good to be true. We can be there whenever we want.'

Finding Rick's place was the little bit of luck that we needed. I looked around and the guys were excited and happy. It made me feel better. But there were other things that weighed heavily on my young shoulders.

I hadn't seen my girl since that night. Veronica. I went to sleep thinking about her, worrying about what might have happened to her, imagining all sorts of scenarios. The worry kept me awake until my eyes were unable to stay open. I had vivid dreams most nights about girls and guitars. Tonight was no different. Sleeping with my brain was paradise. Waking up was another matter. It was hard.

Steve felt inspired, life was different now and he was taller, nicer and it felt good. Finally, he understood why his mum died, everything made sense to him now. Life has paths and each person has their purpose. He now realised that the Henderson brothers were meant to start a fucking rock'n'roll band and take over the world. If his mum had been still alive, nothing would have happened, they would have carried on. It was as if she planned her death so that they could make something of themselves.

Ben and Fred were getting good at their instruments. Ed's song writing was incredible and his voice was perfect for the band. Ed's mate Matt had joined and again, it was like lady luck had knocked on the door: delivery from Sue Henderson, straight from the grave. Spending time at the estate didn't seem so tempting now; being shitfaced at home jamming with the band was what he lived for, and he felt better, different.

He was trying things with his voice and every day he was getting better. Kurt Cobain was a great singer, he liked the guy from REM too, but they lacked the British rawness. No one in England was taking on the Americans, making an English version of that Seattle scene. He wanted the band to be called The Dead Henderson's but Ed didn't like it. He had put together a mix tape for Ed with all the bands he liked and highlighted the names. Perhaps that would persuade him that AC/DC wasn't the best band name ever.

He had bought an album called *Bleach*; it was freaky good. He was going to play it for Ed when he got in. He was also obsessively listening to Helmet; the lead singer shouted so loud it pierced through your ears. It was raw: it was how he wanted to sound, but more British. And Billy Corgan from this new band called The Smashing Pumpkins, he was great. In England people were listening to Tears for Fears; they were nice enough but they weren't angry. There was something fresher about the sound coming from America. He was smoking a lot of weed, listening to lots of music, eating KitKats. Sometimes, he would even go to school to get them off his back.

Another thing that was brewing at home was Christmas. He never liked fucking Christmas anyway– what was there to celebrate? Family or even more ridiculous, Jesus? Sitting around a table eating a grey chicken pretending it was turkey, all the adults far too pissed and some lame presents from the High Road that no one wanted. What was so fucking great about that? When he thought about Christmas he felt sick. This year would be by far the worst. What good could come from pretending everything was fine?

Ed would never leave him alone. He always looked really concerned when he looked at him, his eyes intense like an abandoned disappointed puppy dog. Ben was getting on his nerves; he was such a goody two shoes. He looked clean and he was always bleeding studying. It was crazy. Fred was cool though –he just tagged along. Didn't say much but he was a good lad. He would take part in Christmas for Fred's sake. He was little and he looked sad when Ed spoke about it. Perhaps he missed Mum more than he let on.

Last night he had been at a mate's house, helping him sort out lots of stuff he'd nicked from the shop and he felt a bit dirty, he wanted to be able to buy stuff, with money not steal shit. Then they watched horror movies. It was scary as hell but he still watched because he was scared of nothing. Nothing could touch him. He was invincible.

Chapter 8:
Saving the Day

It was fucking freezing, four in the morning to be precise, the house was a fridge and my jacket was far too thin to manage the bitter bite of a December morning. There was only one tactic that worked and that was to keep moving. The store was busy–holiday rush–and Matt and I were stacking shelves like a couple of robots on speed. There was less talking. We had Iggy Pop on full blast before the others turned up. We discovered *Lust for Life* was a great motivator. The others started to drop in at eight and we put on the radio, churning out rubbish pop. I found myself sometimes tapping my foot to the chirpiest of songs. I hated synthesisers but sometimes those tunes were so goddamn catchy.

I was busy stacking Christmas puddings when I caught the back of Veronica's head. She was limping slightly but she had no crutches, my heart started beating fast. I was so relieved to see her but I was also scared and shy. I walked towards her and tapped on her shoulder. She flinched and turned around. What I saw was unexpected but undeniably there, right in front of me.

Veronica's lips were swollen and she had the remains of a bruise that must have been delivered by a fist of a giant, leaving the damage only seen in films. It was the worst carnage I had ever seen on a woman. There was a gash on her chin and her nose was bruised.

I tried to stay calm, not let her see that I was upset. I was seething inside, like a steaming pot, lid jumping all over the place. Whoever did this would pay. What the hell had happened? I had a feeling, a bad feeling.

'Hey, where you been? I've been desperate. Didn't know how to get in touch with you. You look…..Who did this to you?' I felt sick, angry and I wanted to punch the wall. I hoped that my face didn't show how shocked I was. My fists clenched as I looked at her, she felt uncomfortable, trying to cover her face with her hands.

'Ed, I really shouldn't be talking to you. I look so ugly. He might be looking. He might be outside the shop. I didn't tell him about you. I can't let him know you work here. He'll kill you.' Her eyes looked desperate and her hands started to shake. She was terrified.

'Who? Your dad? Did your dad do this to you?' It was unthinkable. I had never been hit or hurt by my parents. I didn't know what to think. Then a light came on...

'Because you stayed over at mine? Is it my fault? I should have woken you up.'

'No. How could you have known? I mean, he usually goes mad but he has never done this before. He just really loves me and he gets worried. When he drinks he just can't control his temper. He went too far this time, he knows it.'

I gently pulled her cardigan to one side on her chest and saw a massive bruise. It was fading but it was really big. Her eyes were filling up with tears.

'Stop.'

'I'm sorry, I really am. You should have told me, called me at least, I've been sick with worry. I didn't know how to get a hold of you.'

'He broke some of my ribs and my collarbone so I had to stay in bed. Besides he wouldn't let me out or near a phone. He needs me to work, though. That's why I didn't tell him you worked here. He would beat you up, kill you even. Then I could never see you again. And I...' She fidgeted. 'Stay away from me for now, see you at lunchtime in the smoke room.' She wandered off towards her till.

I was livid, I wanted to find him and beat him up, I wanted to scoop her up and run away, take her away with me. I wanted him to pay for what he had done. Time went in slow motion that morning. I kept on looking over at her and smiling. I had to protect her; tell her everything was going to be fine.

It was nearly twelve o'clock when I headed for the smoke room.

Veronica entered the smokers' room moments after me. I put my arms around her and held her gently.

I stroked her chin and even with her face in a mess she managed to look beautiful.

'What are we going to do? This can't happen again. Tell me again, exactly what happened.' I spoke softly because I felt as if she would break if I didn't.

She wiped her tears off her face, took a breath and started to speak softly.

'I got back at 5:30. He was standing by the door. He grabbed me by the hair, pulled me along the hallway. He kept on asking me where I'd been. I told him I been at my friend's but he already knew I hadn't been there. That made him angrier and he punched me in the face three times. Really hard. Usually he doesn't hit me in the face. Then he kept on asking where I'd been and I made up a boy called Will. Then he… he…' She started to sob hard. I didn't know what to do with my temper that was flaring up, I was so angry. Guys like him should be killed or tortured. My fists clenched.

'Ok, ok, that's enough. You can't go back there; I won't let you. You gotta tell the police he did this to you.' I can't believe I actually said that. I was holding her, I never wanted to let her go.

'Where's your mum? Can she help us?'

'She's scared of him too; I know she thinks he's gone too far but she doesn't want to get hurt.'

'Come live with us. He's dangerous. You have to disappear. There can't be a next time.' I had to keep her safe, protect her.

She was working until six o'clock. She wanted to go back home that night to try and talk to her mum, tell her that she planned to get out. She didn't deserve to not know what had happened to her only child. What if he called her bluff or her mum told her dad? I made her tell me where she lived. I learned her surname, Beaton. Veronica Beaton, I said to myself, this will never happen to you again, over my dead body.

I made sure to tell her that it wasn't a good idea to tell her mum where she was going, I mean, she would probably tell her at some point. I wasn't entirely sure her hiding with us was a good idea. Christmas was coming up in a few days.

Our house was tense, brewing an uncomfortable mood. I could sense it. Things were starting to get to me. Could I really cope with all of this? For once, I wasn't so sure.

Steve was in a right mess. He was surrounded by people who were really desperate. He was in need of stuff. Somehow he felt more in control since Mum had gone. He constantly bumped into people that he knew. He was likeable, he always gave the drunks some skunk and he never fought with anyone like some of the other kids did. He wasn't angry, he was just a waster like the rest of the neighbourhood. He had started to walk with more of a swagger since he had found his voice. It was incredible what it did to him, the singing. People treated him differently now, since he told them he was in a band. There was a chance he might be on *Top of the Pops*. Not that he believed that, but there was something brewing inside of him.

When he walked in from school, he found the house empty. He had bunked the last lesson; it was maths, he fucking hated it. The narrow hallway had marks along it from the boys sliding their jackets along, it really was a dump, he could smell the kitchen. Even he felt it was a bit grubby so he started to wash up, it was his first time and it was alright. If Ben, Fred or Ed saw him they wouldn't believe their eyes. It made him smile. Imagine if Mum saw this. He put the old radio on–it was Mum's, always tuned into GLR, talk radio. He moved the cursor onto Radio 1. Status Quo was on. Guilty pleasure, he thought; those guys could really play. He was singing along at the top of his voice, splashing water all over himself as he scrubbed the dried food off the plates.

Damn, it felt good to be proper. He heard the key in the door and stopped washing up, sat himself down and started to skin up. Ben and Fred walked in, scanned the room to see if anyone else was in there.

'Sit down,' he said.

'You done the washing up?' Ben looked shocked.

'Nah, must have been Ed.'

He offered Ben a toke, which he declined, but Fred wanted some, Ben glared ate Steve as to say WTF?

Being an orphan was all right.

'You hungry?' Steve was in a fine mood.

'Starving.'

The two brothers headed up to the chippy on Quex Road, stoned like hell and laughing about the neighbours three-legged dog, kicking the littered cans along the pavement.

The roads were empty and the only other pedestrians were a couple of Bobbies.

'Evening, officer.' Steve started to giggle hysterically. Fred gave them a nod; the two brothers huddled together in stitches.

The thing was Kilburn had its charms. It was home.

I hung around in Camden after work, picking up some silly gifts for the boys and a Kiss t-shirt for Veronica. I ate dinner at Spud-u-Like, next door to the shop. I then waited to see whether her dad would come to pick her up. I wanted to see what he looked like, a face to the animal who hits girls.

A six-foot man in his late forties stood by the entrance of the store smoking a cigarette. I knew it was him as soon as I set eyes on him. He had dark hair, unshaved and slightly hunched over in his army coat. He looked sullen, cagey as he stared into the shop blankly, impatiently. At precisely six o'clock Veronica appeared beside him and after a brief hello the two of them started to walk away. I wanted to rescue her but I knew I had to be cleverer than that.

I felt so bad for her, she probably loved him unconditionally, and at the same time be that frightened. Any man who hit a woman or a child is the lowest form of human. A real scum an evil monster. It wasn't something I had ever thought about before, but I knew I felt very strongly about it, I could never be that man, I detested him. I started to follow them, making sure I kept a safe distance. They stopped at the fish and chip shop, then they continued towards Kentish Town. I followed them all the way back to their house, pleased that I now knew where they lived. I got on the bus and headed towards home. At least I knew what had happened to her, now I could help her. I wished I could have stopped it from happening and the niggling feeling it was my fault wouldn't go away.

Back home, we'd started to pack up the instruments to move into Rick's. We had accumulated lots of equipment lately; leads, mikes, amps and guitar pedals, most of them bought in second-hand shops for next to nothing. Fred had become obsessed with different rhythm instruments, some bought, some home-made, his collection was impressive but scruffy. I walked into blaring music, beer cans everywhere and general mayhem. They had decided to pack the rest of the gear. I smiled from ear to ear at the sight of the three, in fact four, boys working together. I should have known by the music at far too high volume that Matt was in the house, helping out. We worked together and after a while we turned the music down and tucked into some bread and ketchup. I wanted to tell them my news.

'Veronica was back at work today.'

'Good, you can stop stressing now then.' Steve was so annoying sometimes.

'It' really not that simple. Her dad, he hurt her real bad. She's ok now but it is brutal. Ribs broken and a massive bruise on her face.'

'That's terrible.' Ben looked worried.

'I need to help her; we need to get her out of there.'

Matt piped up. 'I wouldn't get involved in that. Her old man looks scary. He's a weirdo, I can tell.'

'Common, we can't let her stay there. I mean, he could kill her. Can you live with that?' That seemed to work, so I continued speaking. 'I've asked her to come and stay here with us. Her dad doesn't know about me, and she is going to leave work, She'll find somewhere else to work, I mean, so I don't have to support her.' I needed them on my side.

'If she's in trouble, we should help her. She's really nice. And…I mean…I think we should, it's the right thing to do,' said Ben.

'Exactly.' Thank god for Ben.

'Ed, you're right, but…she…shouldn't stay here, it's too hot.' said Matt. 'That man will find out about you two and then…'he cut his throat with his finger. 'You guys don't need that kind of trouble. I'll ask my nan if she can stay with us for a while if you want. As I said before, she likes to be a good Samaritan. She's happy that you four orphans are coming for Christmas, and now a battered girl is joining us as well. She's gonna be in charity heaven.'

Matt looked pleased with himself. The boys all laughed; it was kind of funny in a tragic way.

Even though I wanted Veronica with me, Matt had a point, she was probably safer there, further away from Kentish Town and no links to me whatsoever. People had noticed us together at work and made little comments.

That nigh I was distracted, worrying about Veronica, thinking about how the world was a real crappy place.

What made a man, a father, hit their child with such force?

How come we ended up with no parents?

How come Linda was such a fucking mess?

Why were some people luckier than others?

Why did I constantly have this lump in my throat?

Why did it feel like a bomb was about to explode in my gut at any given time?

Where was safety hidden? There must be a better place somewhere. I drank one beer after the other to try and feel better but it still made no sense.

Lucky today was the last day at work. I was done in, exhausted but I couldn't sleep. Wired like a tightrope. The worry and angst didn't let me go, if only I could get one minute's peace to get some goddamn sleep, all would be better.

Chapter 9:
Merry Crimbo!

I got to work 'bang' on time. Matt and I amused our-selves with singing along to the Christmas songs blaring from the radio.

Nine o'clock came me around fast as there was too much to do. Playing on my mind was Veronica, I was worried she wasn't going to come in or that she wouldn't be allowed to leave her house. Mid stacking of the pasta shelves, I looked up and I could see her arriving, she was outside the main entrance talking to her father. He had her chin in his hand, whilst talking to her intensively. She was listening as if her life depended on it, I tried not to stare and I could feel my heart racing. He let go of her and she hurried towards the staff entrance, he shouted something and she turned around and waved. I stopped what I was doing after I made sure her dad was out of sight.

'Veronica. Hey! How was last night?' I said softly but fast, inside me I was shouting because I was filled with rage. Looking at her I calmed down because she looked like a scared baby bird.

'It wasn't great. I did what you said, I spoke to Mum and she agrees with you, I have to leave, at least until he's changed his ways, stopped drinking as much as he does. She was pleased that you, that you want to help me. She is going to get it so now I'm worried about her.' Her hands were shaking like leaves and then tears appeared in her eyes. It was too much for me, I didn't know how to handle it but I tried my best.

'It's the right thing to do. Don't cry Veronica, you know that you can't live with someone who can hurt you like that. It's not safe, he could kill you.' I never in my life meant anything as much as this. She had to get out of there.

'We're spending Christmas at Matt's nan's house and we want you to be there with us. His Nan is apparently into looking after people that need help, people like us, so Matt offered for you stay there for a while, just in case someone blabs to your dad about us, it's safer that way. It might be a bit risky at mine. I'll come over all the time. I promise.' I wiped her tears with my hand.

'I don't know. I have nothing, all I have is £50 that my mum gave me. I left a note so that dad doesn't start freaking out, you know, calling the cops and shit.'

'Don't worry about money, I'll sort that out. What did the note say?'

'That I needed some time to find myself, grow up. And that I'll be back soon.'

'That's great…good. We'll figure it out but you must leave immediately. Tell Mr Brown you quit today. Explain to him what happened–not in too much detail, in case your dad comes here and tell him a different story. Don't mention my name. Mr Brown is a nice guy; I think he will help… Go to my house. Here…my keys. The boys know you're coming…See you at two o'clock…Everything will be fine, I promise you.' I felt heroic and mature for a second and then I started to shake because I was scared.

Veronica talked to Mr Brown, I could see by his body language that he felt bad for her, I watched him walk off and return with an envelope, hopefully with some money in it.

I waited by the back door until she was ready to leave, she mustered up a faint smile but her tired eyes said it all. 'Thank you, Ed, you are so kind. Has anyone ever told you that?' she stroked my cheek and I blushed like a fool.

'No…you can tell me again later.' Those darn butterflies again, like a mixture of nausea and adrenaline, I was starting to get used to them.

As she left, Mr Brown walked past me and smiled reassuringly. I prayed I was right about him being a good man.

At one o'clock I practically ran out the door, threw myself on to the bus and all the way home my legs twitched with impatience, I might as well have sprinted the distance. Today was the 24th of December, London was wet and the streets empty and grey.

I walked into the house to find the strangest scene: the boys had bought a Christmas tree and they'd decorated the whole house with sparkly things. In the corner of my eye I spotted Aunt Linda, over excited and slightly wobbling on her worn high heeled pumps.

She had brought us all a present and put them under a tree. Veronica and the boys were a bit drunk, which was better news, they all looked happy.

'Hello' I said. They all stared at me and laughed as if I knew the joke or I was a joke. I didn't care.

'I have something to show you.' Veronica grabbed my hand and pulled me towards the stairs.

'One minute, Hello auntie…Linda. I just have to…' I kissed her on the cheek and then followed Veronica up the stairs.

'I just wanted to say thank you…properly' In my room she started to undress and we kissed. I could get used to this.

After a short while, we went back down again and drank far too much; even Ben was drunk. Aunt Linda was in a cheerful mood and I was pleased she agreed to come along to the cemetery in the morning.

Perhaps Christmas was going to be ok after all.

The next morning, it was clear from the moment I opened my eyes that today was not going to be as cheery as the previous night. The mood had changed drastically. Veronica was hungover, worried and wondering what was going on at home. She hadn't slept much and she was twitching like a nervous butterfly, the boys were wary too. I had been determined to hold it together but I felt low, memories kept popping I to my head and I missed her, my mother and my dad, I felt young and it didn't help that I was exhausted. It always threw me when my plan to keep going didn't work out. Linda was still asleep on the sofa and the usual vomit and fag fumes evaporating from her chicken-like body, as if she was rotting from the inside. I couldn't tell her to have a bath but I was hoping she would. I gently shook her, 'Here's a towel, it's clean, in case you want a wash. It's Christmas after all!' She accepted the towel and I felt hopeful.

The plan was to open presents and have a cooked breakfast. I woke the boys up and put a silly Christmas record on, Veronica lit a candle. It was as cosy as it could be and for now, it felt peaceful.

'Boys, I got you a little something, I hope you like it.' Said Linda.

Veronica was sat on the sofa, looking waif-like and apathetic. I walked over and sneaked my arm around her waist. She was wearing my woolly jumper stretched over her knees, her makeup still on from the day before.

I noticed that Ben was in the same state, perhaps even a bit worse. I made a noise

'Right you lot, let's make a proper breakfast. I have bacon, eggs, sausages and beans. Who wants to help?' I tried to sound happy.

Linda stood up like a shot.

'Sit down, young Ed. I wanna make it. Let me look after ya love.'

She disappeared into the kitchen. We didn't have a telly; I couldn't bear the shit they showed and especially as it reminded me of mum and her relentless TV viewing. We sat around and listened to records instead. I gave everyone my silly presents and the mood started to slightly lift.

'Let's head off straight after breakfast. We have to be at Matt's nan at one o'clock.' We were chatting and being stupid, Ben and Fred were wrestling on the floor while Steve had his foot on top of both of them, like a sandwich of brothers. For a minute it felt like a normal family on a Christmas morning.

We ended up in a pile, mis wrestle the doorbell went. The knock was robust and determined, it could only be trouble.. I ran to the kitchen and gave Linda the heads up.. Veronica went pale and started to tremble like a leaf.

'He is going to kill you. Don't answer the door. Please.' She looked petrified. Shit. The knocking was getting louder and more persistent.

Linda started to walk towards the front door. I tried to stop her but she wouldn't let me.

'No, Auntie, he's a nutter.' I whispered.

'Ed love, I've been handling nutters all my life. It's my area of expertise. I am *not* scared of him. Hide the girl and you guys go and sit in the living room and look sad.' Veronica was shaking so much I had to push her up the stairs and into Ben and Fred's room. She hid her under their bed. I went back down again.

'Who is it?' Linda shouted in her raspiest whiskey voice.

'I am looking for my daughter. Your son is a friend of hers. I want to talk to Ed.' His thick French accent resonated through the much to thin front door. His huge shadow threatening on the other side of our front door. One kick was all it would take. Linda opened the door slowly.

'Excuse me, who are you? It's Christmas day you know.'

'I need to talk to an Ed Henderson. My daughter has gone missing and we are very worried. She is only seventeen years old. Apparently they are friends.'

Linda called my name and I stood up, Steve grabbed an empty wine bottle, he held it high, ready to pounce.

I straightened my back walked towards the door, trying to tell myself I was not frightened but I was shitting myself. How do you stand up to a man who hits women and his own child? I'm not scared, I Kept telling myself, but I don't like to fight and I'm weak, arms like spaghetti, and this guy is huge and full of hate and rage.

'Ed love, this man is looking for his daughter. Her name is Veronica. Do you know her?'

I looked him straight in the eye, they were so dark it was hard to make out the colour. Black like coal and out of nowhere I suddenly felt confident.

'Veronica? The girl at the till from work? Yes, she's nice. How is she? She's had that terrible accident.' I heard my own voice and it surprised me, I sounded relaxed but I was freaking out on the inside.

'Yes. She's missing, I have been looking for her since yesterday. Someone said you two were talking a lot.' I noticed his fists were clenched.

'Not more than I talk to anyone else. Plus, she's been off recently, when she came back I was chatting to her about her injuries, I felt bad for her. She looked a right mess. What happened?' I just couldn't help myself.

'Have you seen her since yesterday? Did you work? That is what I need to know. Is she here? Veronica!' he shouted into the house. Linda took a step forward and up close to him. Her head barely reached his chest. She pointed her bony finger right in his face. She gritted her few teeth together and she looked like a little Pitbull.

'Listen, monsieur, I don't know who you think you are, coming here, shouting in our house on Christmas day. We are having a nice morning after the children recently lost their mother. We don't need no crazy Frenchman coming in here looking for some girl my nephew clearly barely knows. Now push off out of our house or I will call the ol' bill!' Linda's mental appearance and whiff was enough to scare anyone off, the raged man took a few steps back and Linda shut the door in his face.

'I will be back.' He shouted from the outside.

The adrenaline was rushing through my veins. I ran upstairs and got Veronica out from her hideout; she was shaking, huddled together like a frightened animal.

'He's never going to leave you or me alone. He will find me. Wherever I go. He's going to kill me. I know it.' She whimpered.

'No…he will not you hear? I will not let him; I can protect you; I promise...'

Downstairs the boys were all sitting round the table, scoffing down breakfast.

'He was a huge guy, really frightening, I mean, massive, shit! Wouldn't wanna bump into him in a dark alley.'

'Shut up, Ben!' I said.

We all ate in silence and I thought about how lucky we were that we never had that kind of parent. Ours were broken and weak but they were kind. Linda was ranting on about what a lunatic Veronica's dad was, how she knew the type and what she would do to him if he turned up again. I wasn't so sure Auntie could handle another encounter with the freaky Frenchman but it was entertaining to watch her.

We all got dressed and left the house at 10.30 am. I checked that the coast was clear and we hurried out the door, heading towards Willesden Lane cemetery.

The streets were empty, the air wet and windy and there wasn't a living soul around. My thoughts wandered to the previous Christmas, not because it was the most perfect of family times, but just because we had a mother then. With every step towards the graveyard our mood darkened. Aunt Linda walked alongside Fred; I could see he was already struggling. I slowed down the pace and put my arm around my brothers' shoulder, squeezed it a little, the way I had become accustom too.

'Don't even know why I care. Never liked Christmas.' Fred's face was stern.

The cemetery was grey; the sky, the stones; even the benches. Dead or wilted flower decorated the beds adding to sombre mood. I knew where to go; I just didn't want to go there; we were just getting better. Fuck Christmas and graveyards, what good did they ever do? We didn't need reminding, not now, not never. Right in front of my eyes was my parents grave, with no actual stone on it, instead there was a small wooden cross pushed into the soil. 'Merry Christmas, Mum,' said Fred in a soft voice. I'd kept it together as much as I could but I wanted to cry so badly until I remembered Veronica was there. She'd kept her distance. So I did cry a little, a discreet little tear trickling down my cheek.

Linda had brought one of those red Christmas plants. She put it down beside the gravestone and Steve pulled out a candle from his jacket pocket.

'You got a light?' I nodded. There was no courage in the world that could stop me crying. Steve put his arm around me and I could see he had red eyes too. The candle struggle to stay lit but somehow it did.

'Christmas is really not my thing. Guess it will never be and that's OK.' I wiped my cheek and took a giant breath. I wanted to get out of there.

It was freezing, bitter air stinging us with sharp, ice-cold gusts so we decided to head off. We were catching the bus to Matt's house and our aunt was off home. It was 11:30 already. I felt exhausted, drained from sadness and the mornings events.

We were all quiet on the bus, it didn't take us long to get there, I sat next to Veronica and held her hand. Her head rested on my shoulder, her large sad eyes gazing out on the grey, empty streets. We fell out of the bus, slouching and dull in the lowest of moods.

We could hear jolly music coming from far away, I soon realised we were heading towards the noise. The house looked like a Christmas tree, red brick and a green door, steel pan drums ringing from the inside, lots of lights inside and out. We picked up the pace and it was clear that Matt's Nan obviously liked Christmas a lot more than we did. Ben and Fred's faces lit up, even Veronica cracked a smirk.

Steve rang the doorbell. The tune of 'Jingle Bells' sounded out from the inside.

'What the hell? That's funny.' I said hoping it was the right house.

Matt opened the door wearing a ridiculous over-sized sweater with a reindeer on it, the vision completed the Christmas mood and I have never been happier see anyone.

'Well, hello ya'll.' Then he whispered and pointed towards his sweater: 'My Christmas present. Must wear or get killed.' I laughed and made a mental note that this was the chattiest I had ever seen him. He clearly liked Christmas too. Matt's nan pushed him out of the way, her spirit was as large as she was, her voice loud and her smile as bright as ice.

'Boy, am I happy you're here. Ed! Let me look at you. I need help with lots of things.' She gave us all a cuddle, our heads disappeared between her enormous breasts.

We then rearranged the furniture and peeled potatoes and carrots. Veronica helped with the decorations and the steel pans were moved to the outside of the house, Nana was a very good player. Matt had made some rum punch; it was sweet and very alcoholic. We all had big gulps and slowly started to forget about our rubbish morning.

'He came to the house you know. Her dad.' Matt looked up from his chores.

'Told you he's a nutter.'

'Yeah. You think Nana will let her stay here for a while then?'

'Should be cool. I'll talk to her.'

It was a Christmas I never experienced ever before. Nana had bought us all silly hats; we ate chicken not turkey; we had plantain, rice 'n' peas; we drank rum; and we danced. It was so different from our usual Christmas celebrations with gravy, grey turkey and shit telly. The last few years Christmas had been a write-off, Mum broken and exhausted. This was closer to the magic you would see in ads. I felt warm and happy.

Nana came up to me and said, 'Come here Ed darlin' boy, let me speak to you. Matt has talked so much about you. I feel me knows you. But me don't.' She gave me another bear hug. 'You need to eat boy, skin and bones. I always have food here; you are welcome anytime. Matt tells me you're looking after your brothers. You're a good boy Ed. God bless you.'

'Thank you. I had to keep the family together, that's all. We didn't have a great morning so being here is…kinda magical.' I gave her another hug because it felt good. She smelt of a sweet perfume, perhaps it was coconut, or strawberry, or a mix of both. Whatever it was, it was OK with me. The old lady went outside and started to play the steel pan again. Suddenly neighbours started to come out of their houses and a small street party was starting to form. Nana had made a huge fruit punch and there was food everywhere. We all danced and laughed, even Veronica had her sparkle back. I mean, perhaps I am telling it like it was a fairy tale, but looking back, it was. It was the happiest time we had shared together in ages. By nine o'clock Nana had had enough.

Matt had spoken to Nana and it was OK for Veronica to stay.

'Everybody out!' she yelled.

I said my goodbyes to Veronica, snogging her, holding her, wanted to do everything to her.

'You are incredible,' I whispered in her ear. The rum punch made me say what I thought about her. 'I love you. I want to be with you forever.'

Her eyes glittered and I knew she felt the same. Walking away from her wasn't easy, I would have given my right leg to spend the night with her. I managed to walk away with the promise of eternal love. Veronica was mine, forever.

We were drunk and loud on the bus. Ben and Fred were laughing, still wearing their hats. Steve was a little too drunk, so I sat with him humming a tune.

'You know, Ed, you're the best big brother in the world.' He was slurring but it did mean a lot.

'Yeah, I know.'

Chapter 10:
It's Happening

I had been daydreaming about how to make the rehearsal space cool. Posters on the wall, instruments everywhere. Another step towards the big dream. I couldn't wait to start making noise.

Rick had donated a little fridge for the room and a kettle appeared that Steve had found on the street. We brought five mugs from our house, a couple of teaspoons and a biscuit tin which I filled up with damaged packets from work. The fridge was full of budget cola and cheap lager and the odd pint of milk.

We pretty much lived on noodles these days to the point that I found myself craving them and then when I had them, I felt sick. The people who hung out around the shop were no fans of rock music but we manage to convince them of our sound and the Rastas became our first audience. Most of the time they were sitting on the grubby old sofa and tapping their feet smoking spliffs. I didn't participate much but I liked the smell, it made the place homely.

We sweated blood and tears down in that basement. It felt great and I never wanted to stop. We were hungry for more, a better life; we lived for the sounds and the songs, our intense music that we believed in more than anything. It was the sound I had been obsessing about since I was a boy: the guitar screeching and the dry sound of the snare hitting my ears in time, every time. The melodies, our melodies, which came straight from the heart, words put together to match the sound. We sounded raw, crunchy, like a perfect apple.

We started to play live for anyone who would have us. We even had a concert in Nana's social club; most of them were half deaf but we had a great time anyway. This meant everything to us and we were insatiable.

Camden became our second home. We played the Monarch, the Barfly and the Electric Ballroom. We started to open up for signed bands, people who they wrote about in *Melody Maker* or *NME*. We rehearsed hard, wrote songs and played them over and over. We didn't look up, we just continued, relentlessly. If something didn't feel right we practised it until it sounded perfect. All of us were focused and we formed a unique sound and it was exciting, I can't even explain it, it moved us, together, like a flock of birds . It wasn't velvety, it was rough, and it was angry but at the same time sweet. It was everything we had gone through; it was our hearts on our sleeves, all of our lives we had been invisible and now everyone should see us.

There was no time for socialising. We spoke as little as we could to people, this was Matt's idea, we were young, and we didn't want people to know how young we were. We wanted people to think we were mysterious and cool. Besides, we didn't need anyone; we had each other and that was enough.

We all grew our hair, long and stripy, apart from Matt, who never changed his look. Industry people were starting to ask questions about us. We didn't say much to them either. We kept cool as instructed by Matt. I was working less and less at the shop and was dipping into the sacred bank account to make ends meet. As we made only the odd £50 from gigs, it was a gamble but this was our only chance. I think Dad would understand and Linda would approve, I was sure of that. This was it, our one chance, and we were working our guts out, wrenching every last bit of energy from our teenage bodies. No distractions, only the instruments and us. That was the unwritten rule and we all kept to it religiously.

One evening, the doorbell went. We were down Rick's place, rehearsing. A smart-looking thirtysomething guy walked in. Short, suntanned, brown hair and clothes straight from the ironing board.

'Hey, I'm Gavin.'

We all burst out laughing. I don't know why. He took this well and started to tell us how he had seen us play four times and that he was a huge fan. He wanted to manage us. We said little but we listened to what he had to say. I liked him; he was from a different world from us. He already managed a couple of known bands, and he knew some people that would like us. Did we have a demo? he asked. We didn't. Did we want to do one? Fuck yeah.

He organised for us to go into a little studio. Some guys he knew, said they were good.

'Can I put this on?' Gavin handed me a CD. I put it on, it sounded good, professional.

'I manage these guys, they have lots of interest, I think you are better than them.' He said casually.

'You mean, you can get us some studio time?' Matt said, forgetting the being cool rule.

Gavin nodded.

'We have no cash,' said Ben

'Don't worry about that. I wanna pay for it. I wanna hear you guys recorded.'

He started to talk about our songs. He remembered them all from the gigs. He had done his research; I'd give him that. I liked how he spoke about our sound too, he got it.

'What's the deal then, if you pay for our demos what do you want in return?' I asked.

'I want to manage you, if I like the demo I want first refusal. I know I can get you signed. I will make you money, I promise…that's if, the demo sounds good. I have a feeling it will.'

He continued: 'Some bands just can't cut it in the studio. They don't have the songs, they sound good and have an image, you guys have everything.'

'Everything? Yeah, we have lots of songs and I think we're ready to record,' I said in my most confident tone.

'What's the name of the band?'

'The Hendersons,' I said, Matt looked at me as if I was mad. 'Matt, over there, is an honorary Henderson, as he is more like my brother than any of this lot.' We all laughed.

It was the best idea yet for a name so no one objected.

Gavin kept his promise and got us time in a little recording studio called Bus space. It was the perfect place for us, rock'n'roll history buried in the walls and the now familiar smell of sweat and fags. We did the recording the old-fashioned way: played like it was a gig with microphones picking up the sound of the different instruments. Steve sang in the control room, the rest of us made a racket in the padded live room. The studio was amazing: it was hard to keep calm, thousands of buttons to press and leads sticking out everywhere; boards that lit up and equipment stacked in piles everywhere. I had officially landed in my idea of a heaven. I felt at home, this was where I belonged. I could sleep here, eat here, this was what I had dreamt of. I asked the recording engineer a million questions. I needed to know what every button did. I wrote it down. I borrowed some magazines and books and studied it when I came home then went over it again in my head. I obsessed about different types of microphones, stands and pedals. I was lapping up the information obsessively.

Our enthusiasm paid off and the demo sounded great, it had something. It sounded like us, but it was fresh and screamed passion. The tunes were catchy. We played the demo over and over again and we were excited as hell.

Gavin loved it too and wanted us to sign to him, so we did, because we thought he was great and a deal was a deal. After the recording session I would have gone anywhere with him, damn it. I would have married him. Veronica shared my enthusiasm and told me to trust Gavin. He was good, he understood us. I don't know why I knew this to be a fact, I guess an element of luck played a part but to be fair; Gavin was the right man for the job.

After that, everything started to happen fast. It's all a bit of a blur to be honest. The Record companies loved our demo, we decided to sign to EMI records, the biggest record company around. They loved us, even more when we told them how young we were. They were practically salivating, they listened to the tape over and over, whilst we sat there, we were the complete package they said. They started to wine and dine us, told us anecdotes about their other artists, our heroes, invited us to events and gigs we never would have got tickets for, backstage passes and after show parties every night if we wanted to, we wanted to rehearse so most of the time we didn't go. When they first saw us live, our A&R man vomited because he got so excited. He said we were the best band he had ever heard, told us how his arm hair stood up straight when we played. He had never signed such an exciting band before. Everyone wanted a piece of us, we were hot stuff…And we were ready to give it to them.

Our signing party was held a trendy London bar called the Atlantic. They rented the whole place and the entire record industry was there, waiting to hear the coolest new thing play live…The Hendersons'. It was then that I had the feeling for the first time; that we were going to get bigger than I could ever imagine, that is was possible that my dreams were going to come true.

All things considered, we kept calm. Before the gig, Matt instructed us wisely; 'Keep cool guys, breathe slowly and look like you don't care.' He kept on telling us to stare at our feet if we didn't know what to say or do. 'Better say nothing than something stupid and don't smile. Especially you Ben.'

I guess he was right, he knew about this sort of thing.

We started playing and the crowd went ballistic, people were trying to grab us, girls practically throwing themselves at our feet. It was hard to focus on playing the songs but we did it, I felt as if the floor was jumping and the ceiling was about to come down as I hit my strings as hard as I could.

After the gig, the president of EMI records presented me with an old vintage Gibson SG guitar that used to belong to Pete Townsend. Holding it, stroking it, knowing who's guitar it used to be was the best feeling I've ever had and when I played it I felt complete. My new baby, with every chord, feelings of euphoria entered my young body. I caught myself smiling then pulling myself together by flicking my hair over my face and staring down.

We got out fairly early and headed over to Rick's. We relaxed and had our own party there, drinking our first bottles of Moët e Chandon.

Gavin Manager turned up, hyper, red faced and acting like a madman, raving about the people he had spoken to and how huge we were going to be. We all listened, only understanding half of what he said, but we got that it was good news. 'Bigger than the Beatles!' he kept shouting.

Our struggle in the basement had not been a struggle, it had been nothing but fun. Starting a band should be a struggle, that's what I read. Getting our sound had even been a smooth ride, I knew it was good but I didn't know that people would like it this much. The response was better than anyone could have wished for. I felt confident and then a little arrogant about it. Clearly I was smarter than I thought.

The party was over and I had to get the boys back home. My adrenaline kept me awake until the next day. This had been the best day of my whole seventeen-year life. So far..

Steve was happy, he felt as if he was in a dream. He had money, lots of it, and was able to just give up the dealing, just like that. See ya later, Kilburn scum! I'm off to be a Rockstar…

The usual story was that once you started dealing you were heading towards time in prison. Not him, not Steve Henderson and not his brothers either. Oh no, they were heading for the big time, all thanks to Ed, not forgetting his own contribution, his voice. People thought he was great and real-life page three models were throwing themselves at his feet. Blondes, brunettes and redheads were all giving him the come-on. They all wanted to suck his cock, teasing him by stroking his chest under his top and fighting over his attention by showing off their perfect bodies. He wanted them all and they were desperate to have him.

It was madness. Gavin, their manager, told him they were going to be bigger than The Beatles and tonight, after the gig, he believed him. The place was heaving; other musicians were patting him on the back, telling him how great he was, inviting him to their houses.

He lapped it up, sat down and enjoyed it all. If tonight ended his life, it was enough happiness to last him a lifetime. Ed, on the other hand, seemed to be a bit on guard, worried, suspicious, unable to enjoy it, as per usual. Steve wasn't going to let his serious mood spoil his fun. Matt was more up for it, he liked girls too and they loved him, they made a good party team. Tonight when they played he felt like he could take over the world, no one could tell him shit. He was someone important, which was something he had never expected to be and he knew it would be super easy to get used to.

Chapter 11:
KENTISH TOWN
7 August 1992

My twentieth birthday. Last night was a hell of a party. Again. I woke up on the sofa in our modest rehearsal space. We had kept it on because we loved it and because it was our second home. I was surrounded by empty bottles, cans and fully loaded ashtrays, pillows strewn all over the floor and rubbish everywhere. There was a random girl asleep on the sofa. I nudged her and mumbled 'Eh…Get out.' Didn't know who she was but she ran out the door pretty swiftly.

It had been a tough six months, touring Europe and Asia. I felt dislocated and nervous. Adjusting back to normal life was always hard, soon as life stood still the jitters started. Touring is fast and furious, and coming back, I always felt out of sync. I longed for a normal existence again, whatever that was. The confusion of feeling content made me drink copious amounts of booze, as if the answer was right there in the bottom of a Chianti bottle.

Veronica and I hadn't seen each other in the whole time we'd been away. She was pregnant with our first child. It wasn't something I had wanted, but now that it had happened I was going with it. She turned up at the party for half an hour last night. I barely spoke to her as I didn't really know what to say to her. She wasn't pressing me, which was nice, but I felt distant and detached. I knew I had to confront how I felt, once I had worked out what that was. Being the way I was, my preferred method was to deal with it later and keep moving.

I didn't belong anywhere anymore. Rick's was the only place that settled my thoughts, where I could be alone and think clearly. Another few days here and I would be fine.

The Hendersons' had taken over and world domination was a fact, just as I had planned it. It had almost been too easy to achieve it. We had faced none of the struggles I had read about in articles about other bands. Success didn't drive me, though, it was the music, and right now I wasn't inspired which made me low and exhausted. I couldn't write or sleep. Worrying about my inner self, how I felt, who I was, if I was happy. I was indulging myself. The great longing of being a musician that had occupied my teenage years had been fulfilled in a flash and now I wanted more…Of what I wasn't sure.

We were hassled by people from all angles, and I had lots of money in the bank, as did the brothers and Matt. I had found out that he and Veronica had had an affair years ago, it accidently came out after too many beers and I couldn't forgive him, he announced as if I wouldn't care, which was hurtful. They both blamed it on too much booze and she begged me to take her back. Which I did because I was still in love with her then. Things had been difficult between Matt and me since then, but we managed to remain in the band…Just.

Matt and Steve were pals and spent most of their time off their heads, shagging groupies. I had no time for that kind of time wasting. I did party, I just didn't like it enough to do it all the time.

Ben, Fred and I stuck together. Our bond was stronger than most brothers' now. Ben and I were especially close. He wasn't buying into the whole rock-star lifestyle either. His feet were firmly on the ground, whereas Fred was more of a chameleon. Wherever his mood took him, he went. They were still young, Veronica and I acted as their parents and they needed us.

I had stayed on in our family house with the younger two. Steve had his own place around the corner. His lifestyle was chaotic, fed by clichés and addiction to fame and all illegal substances. Every time I went to his house he was plonked on the sofa, off his head, holding court like some entitled king. He thought it was great, I didn't get it but that was Steve for you. He collected weirdos, the stranger the better. I was OK with him acting like an idiot as long as he kept singing in tune.

Gavin, our perky manager, who thought the sun shone out of our asses, was finding it difficult to mediate between the two camps, but our brotherly love, saw us through. Steve was crazy but he was my flesh and blood.

Last night I had made an observation, his last girl-of-the-moment might be into the kind of drugs that I didn't approve of: eyes pinned and skin translucently pale. Her relaxed, confident persona impressed Steve; he was like putty in her hand, this kooky aura surrounded her. She moved slowly with her long limbs and her voice was close to a whisper. I could see Matt dancing around her as well. I sensed trouble. I had to speak to Gavin about this. The vibe changed when she was around, and I didn't like it. It was shady and strangely powerful.

I plugged in my sunburst Fender Jazzmaster, made myself a cup of builder's tea. My phone kept on ringing. I could sense the desperation in the ringing tone, I knew it was Veronica. I started strumming my guitar.

Since I'd found out about Matt and her I had the upper hand and it had made me care less about her. I didn't want to become a dad right now; I was twenty years old and I was terrified of messing it up. Other girls had started to look more attractive to me since I had found out about the baby. Anyhow, she'd ruined it, she broke us. I knew it was gonna end sometime. I'd never thought of us like that before, a couple that had an end. Whatever happened, I had made a promise to myself I always look after her, she had no one, like us. Her dad was still in jail, where he belonged. We hoped it was forever but the police said he might be out in a couple of years. He kept on writing to Veronica, begging for forgiveness. Apparently he had turned to God for forgiveness. I imagined God wouldn't be too interested in his pathetic plea; but then again, I wasn't God and didn't believe he existed, so it was all a waste of time anyway. I will never forgive him for what he did to V. I wasn't so sure about her though, she was sometimes nostalgic about her childhood and the bond they used to have. Nothing could ever happen to her again.

We had grown up together and she was in a strange way part of our band, like a mother hen or a sister. I just didn't know how to tell her I wasn't feeling the same way about us anymore. I convinced myself that I would get over it; everything would just go back to normal.

My main love was still music and I had tunnel vision. The baby was arriving in a couple of months but it just didn't seem like it was supposed to happen, so I put it at the back of my brain, in the deal-with-later file.

Ben and Fred looked to her as a mother figure, Veronica was our family. She held it together. She was the glue. What the hell was going to happen to us? I wanted to cry, but I didn't.

I grabbed a bin liner and started to tidy up. Monotonous work, great thinking fodder.

Everything will be OK as long as I Could hang out here with my amps and guitars. We had taken over the shopfloor too and our management had their HQ upstairs. Fans hung out outside and we had a close rapport with them. I had to check myself; I wanted to make sure

I didn't end up like some of the bands I met on tour. They had lost the magic, what made them good. Allowing people to literally wipe their butts, laugh at every boring word that came out of their spoilt little gobs.

After I cleaned up I opened a beer, sat down and listened to the latest Metallica album. It was great, commercial and appealing. I had tried so hard to stay credible, now I wanted to simplify things. Thinking about music made me feel calmer. The phone kept on ringing, I put it on silent. Hours passed, as I got lost in a new song after the other. I Locked at my watch. Fuck, it was three in the afternoon.

I had to pick up the phone.

'Hello.' She was shouting so much I managed to smoke a whole fag without saying a word.

'I'm coming now.'

I grabbed my coat and left. Our driver was outside, waiting to take me home.

'Mike.'

'Ed, you OK?'

'Yeah, Veronica is going bonkers. Need to get back home. Quick... ish'

Mike, the driver, took off, heading towards Fairhurst Gardens.

'I took Steve and Co. back last night. They were unusually wild. Not loud though, wasted.'

'Yeah, did that tall pale bird go with him?'

'Oh yeah, they practically had sex in the back, had to tell them to stop.' The driver seemed amused by my brother's outrageous behaviour.

'Mike, can you keep an eye on her for me, I'm not sure about her.'

'Course.'

Mike had been working for us for two years. I trusted him and he cared for the guys.

I got back, and Fred and Ben were shaking their heads as I walked in the door. 'Not cool, Ed Henderson.'

They only called me Ed Henderson when they were pissed off.

'Where is she?' I was a mess.

Ben gestured towards upstairs. The house had had a complete facelift. We had bought it and spent a silly amount on making it follow what the interior designer had said was the current trend. I preferred it before. Veronica loved it. It was really clean, which I liked.

The room was dark and the bed unmade, Veronica was sat bloated and desperate on the floor. She looked straight at me with sadness in her eyes.

'You just don't love me anymore. I know it. I can feel it. Where were you?'

'You know where I was… at Rick's. The party went on and on and then I crashed on the sofa. Stop crying, it was my birthday and I go drunk. Let's make pancakes?' I was exhausted and hungry.

I sat down next to her, wiped her tears, kissed her forehead. She didn't resist. It was easier to make her happy these days. It was all gonna be fine. Veronica and I, we could work this out. I fell asleep on the floor.

The next day we were due back in the studio, making our third studio album. I had written ten songs but Matt and Steve had been working on some new material too. I knew it was going to be tough, as the end of the tour had nearly pulled us apart. I turned up at Sarm studio all prepared.

Ben, Fred and I got stuck in and started to play around with new sounds. The room had a massive mixing desk, three swivel chairs and a sofa at the back. The recording rooms were full of our instruments. We had so much that sometimes I wondered if we really needed them. My guitar collection was nearing thirty. Fred had two full kits. I had twenty guitar amps and Matt's guitar collection was beyond counting.

I had brought records I liked, sounds that inspired me. We were chatting excitedly about how we wanted the new record to sound.

'I want it to sound like The Carpenters on acid,' said Fred. The thought made me laugh. 'Or, like Bob Marley on speed.' Ben found this hilarious. 'Yeah, all right, I want it to be pop, like The Beatles mixed with a touch of AC\DC. Class.' None of these references made any sense. I guess we already had our sound. I wanted it to be simplified. I had written some great new songs. I had been battling with my feelings and music was my healer. The songs had been pouring out of me recently.

The Hendersons had acquired a big entourage and whatever we did we had people hanging around. I wanted a closed session with only the band, no hangers-on. That way we could get it done quickly.
Gavin got it and thankfully, so did our A&R man.

Five hours later, Matt and Steve and the strange girl turned up. She looked as if someone had dipped her in a barrel of flour. Dressed in a denim mini-skirt, Steve's t-shirt, white Ray bans, a floppy felt hat and some sandals, she was strangely beautiful but her aura was creepy. She was walking bad news. She was holding a peach in her hand, staring at it, stroking it with her long, bony fingers. 'Ed, look at this peach. It's so beautiful and soft.' I looked at her and said,

'Yep, sure, it's peachy.' What a freak. She slumped herself down on the leather couch, still fondling the fruit. It was boring and pretentious. Like I would give a damn about a stupid peach?

I was starting to feel a temper coming on but I knew there was no point. I had to bite the bullet and carry on. Fighting would come to nothing at this stage. I would talk to Steve later. Looking at him, I knew this was not the time. I could tell that she was under their skin. I had to try and be calm. She probably didn't know that we had a closed session. I knew the guys did, because we had spoken about it at length, as the last album was a long party with me trying to make everyone play a decent take. We wasted a lot of time and money. Because of that it wasn't as good as the first album. We all agreed the reason was the number of people that were hanging around. We needed to get back to basics. This was not the start I was hoping for, this was trouble. Trouble's name was Irma, apparently. I wished Irma would piss right off but I had a sneaky suspicion she intended to hang around for a long time.

Steve, Matt and Irma all sat down on the leather sofa and within thirty minutes they were all asleep. All draped over each other, like snakes in a pit.

Fred, Ben and I started to practise parts of a song I'd written. We had dinner, we listened to other bands. Around ten o'clock Steve woke up, looking like death personified. Nicotine-stained hands shaking like leaves, dark circles under his eyes and spots all over his face. I took him outside for a fag. He felt vulnerable, and I could sense it.

'You OK?'

'Yeah.' We both smoked in silence for a while.

'You hungry? Got some good food in the kitchen, think it's curry tonight.'

We walked inside, sat down and ate, in silence at first. Until I blurted out:

'What's the deal with Irma?'

'Ed, before you start, she's my girlfriend, she inspires me.' Fuck, never heard him say that before. I had to go easy.

'Nice, I told V she can't come to the studio, as you know, the closed session. We agreed, remember? We were gonna have a closed session this time. I really wanna make the best album we can. No distractions.' I tried to sound calm. I was seething inside. He looked up at me and his gaze changed to a glare.

'Ed, I want her with me all the time, you hear? I don't want this to be a problem because I will really lose my temper with you and your bossy friggin' ways. You are not my boss. No one is. Irma goes where I go and that's final.'

I stood up and walked out. I called Mike to drive me back home. Ben came back with me and Fred stayed on with the others. It was days like these I really valued having V at home. We knew each other so well; she knew me inside out. I'd worked so hard to keep everything ticking forwards. I wished it hadn't happened, I trusted her and Matt, then they just disregarded me, went behind my back, lied and then lied some more. Ben found out and told me and it felt as if someone had stabbed me right in the heart but Matt acted as if it wasn't a big deal… It took time to repair things, repair being the perfect word because things were still fragile. I didn't want to be a man who couldn't forgive; I want to be able to do that. No one is perfect after all. But something in me broke when I found out, everything changed. I love V and I always will. She is part of our family. Nothing I could do would change overnight but I had become cynical and now there's a new life arriving, a baby conceived when we were trying to work out what to do after her betrayal, *she* destroyed us, not me.

When I got home we sat up and talked for a while. Veronica was good at calming me down. I was drinking and smoking excessively. She was sipping tea and we cuddled on the sofa, I felt closer to her than I had for a long time. Then Fred walked through the door. He looked stoned and upset, a strange combination.

'You good?'

'Ed…We have to talk.' He was trying his hardest to be serious.

He paused a little, took a breath in and said, 'I think… they are doing smack. I think Steve is smoking that dirty brown shit. Do you understand what I'm saying?'

I hated when other people were drunk and trying to make sense. This was an exception, we had always agreed that we should stay away from crack and smack, we made a pact. Other bands we knew were messing up, dropping like flies, not able to play anymore. We had seen what it could do first-hand and I thought all of us had understood that. The band was one thing, but Steve is our brother. He's always been fractious and stupid, but this?

'Why do you say that?' I finally managed to say.

'It smelt like cat piss in the loo, like it did when we played Lollapalooza that time with the grunge dudes. And that girl, she just looks the part. It's written all over her face. And.. I found a teaspoon and some foil in the bin.'

I knew Fred was right but I didn't want him to worry. Ben was still awake and I didn't want him to hear, he hated all drugs–didn't mind boozing but no drugs.

'I hope you're wrong. I will talk to Matt tomorrow.' I tried to sound calm. Damn it. What an idiot he is.

V had stayed quiet through the conversation. Her leg was twitching, she only did that when she was stressed. Fred left the room and we stayed quiet until we heard his bedroom door shut.

'What an idiot,' she ranted. 'After everything we've seen. What a fucking idiot. I could kill him.'

Seeing her swear in her condition was odd. Since the pregnancy she had gone all saintly. My mind kept on wavering between worry and anger. Our lives had never been perfect, I just thought the band could make it better. Perhaps I was wrong, perhaps I messed everything up. Heroin kills, I knew that. This was trouble.

'He wouldn't be that stupid,' she said

'Wouldn't he? He's been acting like an idiot since he met that freak Irma. He's obsessed. He would do whatever she asked him to.'

We cuddled up in front of the fireplace, I massaged her feet.

'I just hope he's OK.' she said.

I curled up and stroked her stomach. Then her face. Her leg stopped and she relaxed.

'Course he is. Maybe he just tried it, you know, so he can say that he has… You know what he's like.' she said.

'That is exactly why I'm worried.'

We dozed off. I felt close to her for the first time since it happened.

The phone rang and woke us up. I looked at my watch, it was two in the morning. Mike the driver was on the other line.

'Ed, sorry to call you at this hour but I think you're right about the skinny one, she's trouble.'

'Yep. Speak first thing.' I put the phone down.

I picked up my guitar and strummed a new song I had written about how shit I felt about Veronica and me. She woke up, think she understood because tears were rolling down her chubby face as I sang the words to her in my softest voice into her ear.

Darling, my first love, how did you think when you fell into his arms.

I trusted you, I trust you know but I feel sad, so sad.

My Darling girl, my sweet. We can try to feel the same.

Because I...

I want you still, if I forget, then we can be perfect.

And now...

We're still together, always together, like this.

I loved Veronica so much my heart ached, I wanted no one else, she was my soul.

Wake up, fall asleep, the two things became one. Steve would party for two days solid then he would pass out for eighteen hours. That was his routine. It seemed to function well, as long as Gavin and Mike made sure he was where he needed to be. Smoking weed was so boring, it did nothing anymore. Uppers, like speed and coke were OK but didn't really suit him. He usually downed an E with breakfast, just to get in a good mood for the day, then he would smoke joint after joint, flushed down with a bottle of champagne and then sometimes vodka cranberry, which was his favourite drink of the moment.

Tea was nice too in between hangovers. His fridge was full of booze, Coca-Cola and a block of cheese, a few sad tomatoes strewn across the bottom shelf. The cheese and tomato were useful to make his favourite meal, toasted sandwiches in his posh sandwich maker he got Mike to pick up for him at John Lewis. He really liked melted cheese. One of those a day would keep him alive. He was skinny but he liked that.

He knew Ed thought he partied too much. He was busy trying to keep his doomed relationship alive. Matt had fucked V, we all knew, and the softie that he is, forgave her, just like that. And now, she was carrying his baby. It was very pathetic but at least Vanessa was still around, he liked her a lot, like a sister. Without her the band would probably fall apart. Irma could be like that, a woman they all loved, she was great, *he* loved her. They were soul mates, forever bonded in this strange vacuum, he needed no one else, the two of them were made for each other.

Chapter 12:
I Wanted to Kill Her

I woke up and got to the studio on time. Ben and Fred came too. We felt deflated by the day before. It was annoying when someone did exactly what you expected them to do. Steve never failed to deliver. Since we started The Hendersons', in fact, even before that, he always chose to be the one who caused us trouble.

It hadn't exactly helped that the whole world seemed to agree with me, he was an absolutely amazing singer. His raspy, needy soulful tone got into everyone's bones, made people shiver and feel stuff. He voice was mesmerising. To think such an empty-headed freak was given that talent seemed unfair. The other thing that worried me was that the more fucked up he got, the better his singing became.

I recorded him singing sober once and then again the same tune when he was off his face and he was better after shitloads of booze and drugs. I knew I was on borrowed time with this method. I could see it was harder and harder for him to stay focused. He was nineteen and had been partying non-stop for five years. He had youth on his side but he was starting to behave like a real asshole. A Kilburn drunk in rock star clothes.

The attention we were receiving was addictive and the fact that we were allowed to get away with just about everything didn't help matters, he believed the hype.

He managed to look good, though, with his long hair and pencil frame, slightly hunched-over shoulders and huge hands and feet. The girls liked him and I lost count of how many he slept with on the tours and then back in London. I used to think that was a bad thing but now I was wishing he was still doing it, shagging around and taking his pick of the girls who were hanging around. The STD's he kept getting was now a minor problem. Anything was better than this. Bring back the groupies, riddle him with genital warts, who cares?

Irma, it turned out, was a model. Not a successful one, as it was hard for her to be anywhere at a specific time. She was a disaster on legs.

She had already moved in with Steve. I called Gavin to try and see if we could talk about the best way of dealing with the problem. I didn't want a huge fuss, just wanted to make a record and for my brother not to be on smack. This record needed to be the best one we've ever made. We knew what we were doing now, we could do it, we just had to stay focused.

Gavin turned up fifteen minutes after I called him. Efficient and syrupy, business like and at the same time trying to do the slimy dad thing. I'd come to dislike that immensely about him, I didn't need him for that, I had a dad once, he was dead but still... The boys liked it, so I let him get on with it, continuing his cheesy pretend act.

Anyhow, the conversation about Steve went a little like this.

Gavin: So Ed... what's the problem with Steve? You seem all stressed out. It's not good.

Me: Yeah... I am, I... It's just, it started so badly yesterday.

Gavin: I got that, but what's up with Steve?

Me: He's with this new chick, Irma. I didn't like her from the start. We think she's doing brown... and obviously...

Gavin: I see. That is worrying... (*Long pause, deep breath.*) Ok. How do you know?

Me: I thought she looked like a smackhead. Then Fred said it smelt like piss after we left last night. I mean, come on, it's Steve. He found foil too. Matt as well. And they are both mad about her. She gives me the creeps.

Gavin: He called this morning, said he sensed you have a problem with her but that he wants her around, that he's mad about her. Blah blah blah... never felt this way about anyone before. I can't think of a plan off hand. You want me here today so I can suss it out?

Me: Yeah, that would be good. Shit, why is everything so friggin' complicated with him?

(Pretend Dad voice) Gavin: It will be OK, you'll see.

I sat down in front of the massive mixing desk and listened to a few of my demos I had been working on. It sounded good, I grabbed my guitar and started to play along. I sent a wish out to the universe of dead parents to make this album great. Make us all unite and make some good fucking music. The only way to achieve that was when everything gelled, when nothing else mattered.

I hadn't noticed that the whole band had arrived and was sitting around in the studio. Gavin had managed to make Irma stay outside the room at least.

'Hi. Didn't hear you come in.' I said.

'Not surprised, it was loud. Good song.'

Matt leaned over and messed up my hair.

'You wanna have a go at it today?' he said.

We all grabbed our instruments and played along to the demo. Time stood still the way it used to, our instruments submerged, we mashed into one synchronised sound. I guess you could call it magic, it was what made us so good.

For about two hours I was in euphoria. We were all working out our parts and Steve was singing the words I had written, he added some of his own and made it better. His voice made the hairs on my arm stand up; he sang it the way I wanted it to be sung. Our studio engineer was starting to record and The Hendersons' were in the zone.

Steve was focused, locked into the moment, lost in the song, brilliant and sensitive. He owned the melody; he knew how it should be delivered. This gift he had was somehow magical, he knew when to sing softly, when to shout, when to slow down and when to rush ahead.

We needed to remember why we started the band. I didn't care about any of the perks, the fame or even the money. All I cared about was moments like these, when it just clicked.

Mid take, Irma entered, she sat herself down on the sofa, today wearing a beige under dress, no bra so you could see her tiny little breast. Her bleached blonde hair was scrunched up. She closed her eyes an nodded along. I lost my concentration.

'This song is great. It's really great.'
I didn't want her opinion. No one was supposed to hear the songs until they were done, that was the deal.

Matt looked over at me, knowing that I wasn't happy. Steve was in the vocal booth singing, so he said,

'Irma, you couldn't go get some beers in, could you? We are just working this song out and I'm real thirsty.'

I looked over at Matt as if to say,
'Thank you.'
Steve stopped singing.
'Where she going?'
'She's just getting some beers.'
The magic was gone. He had lost the vibe.
'You're not telling her to go, are you?'

I assured him I was doing no such thing. I tried to keep him in the moment he was just in but there was no use. It was gone.

'Why don't you have a break and we'll record another take later?' Steve took off his headphones and rushed back into the studio room.

He looked anxious. 'Where is she?' She walked in with some chilled beers. We all had one. I tried to ignore that she was there as there was no use . The song was sounding so good, just how I had imagined it.

Fred was in the booth now, hitting the drumkit hard. He did it in one take, effortless. We decided not to overwork things; we did that on the last album. I wanted to go back to basics. Back to Rick's, where we first started. When no one did crazy drugs and we had no money. All of us surviving on my modest salary from the shop. No freaky yes-sayers laughing at everything we say, creeping around us like a swarm of bees, suffocating my creativity.

I noticed Matt leaving the studio and I discreetly followed him. I grabbed him when he came out of the loo.

'Got a minute?' I said.

'Yeah. Sure. What's up?' Even though he knew what was up.

'Steve got all stressed out. I reminded him of the closed session rule we all spoke about and agreed to. It's not personal, I just want us all to reconnect. It's been so mad recently and I wanted a safe space, that's all.'

'I know what you mean.' Matt was in the right mood for me to get to him.

'He's got it really bad for her, it's like he's obsessed. She's all right you know, Ed, give her a chance. And…She ain't going anywhere for a while so you might as well get to know her.'

'I just want to get the album done. Can you talk to him for me?'

'I'll try.' We both stood still and quiet for a while, swigging our beers.

Matt continued.

'How's V doing?'

'Good,' I answered a bit too quickly.

'Nana wants to see you, and her. I haven't told her about, you know, anything. She misses you guys. *I* miss you guys.'

My brain said. 'You should have thought about that before you shagged my girl, you bastard,' I didn't speak it.

'I'll call her. We'll go and see her. Promise. I miss her too.'

That was the longest conversation the two of us had had since it happened. I wanted to have it out but it was too hard and it would just lead to more emotions that I couldn't handle. Fatherhood was knocking on my door and I needed to feel as if it was a good thing. I was trying my hardest and hanging out with Matt wasn't helping.

I took a walk. The noises from the cars resonated with the chaos in my head. Things were spinning around like a merry-go-round, making me dizzy. I popped to the local pub, sat down with a pint in front of me. Bought some salt and vinegar crisps too, the *Sun* newspaper in hand.

Once again I felt as if I was about to lose control. Fatherhood, lost love and responsibilities flashing in my brain and now the lurking filthy drug problem Steve was bringing to the table.

Giant placards popped up in my head, disturbing my peace. I knew Steve, stubborn to the point of stupidity. It was seldom, these days, I managed to be on my own. I bought another pint after I pretty much downed the first one.

'Are you that bloke from The Hendersons'?' the barman asked me.

'Yeah, that's me. Cheers.' He didn't seem to care much and let me be.

I took out my notepad and wrote this:

I know you're trying to say you're sorry. Is this how you wanted it to be?
Is this how you thought it would feel
I hear you, lies, I can hear words spitting out of your gravel mouth,

She was my girl. You didn't care did you?
Threw it away like it meant nothing.
We will get over it.
You didn't care
Yeah, we will get over it.
Someday.

I had never written about my friend before. I guess being upset about Veronica had made me forget I had lost my only real friend. He was better off hanging out with Steve, they were more alike. Girls, booze and drugs, the pathetic side of life.

The pub was perfectly smelly: red velvet seats, dark brown stools and a dartboard. If I'm alone in a pub I liked it dirty. I had a problem watching broken people drinking; it reminded me of my family too much.

I needed to think out a way to deal with the Irma situation. I took a step back and to work out the best route forwards. He was already kicking off, so the hard approach was not going to work. I called Gavin on my mobile phone. He answered immediately, he always did.

'I need to talk. Can you come to the pub around the corner? The Kings arms.'

He got there in five minutes, irritatingly efficient as always. He bought us both a pint and sat down. I was getting nicely merry.

'OK, I've done some digging around with the boys. Seems you're right, she does the dark stuff. I think Matt and Steve are dabbling but nothing major.'

Even though I kind of knew it, hearing it confirmed sent a chill down my spine. We had a deal: no manky drugs were allowed.

'I just wonder how they can be so stupid. I mean, they've seen what it does.'

Gavin wasn't much pleased either, he knew what it can do to a band and we were his very lucrative meal ticket.

'Matt said they were just having a bit of fun. Steve got it bad for the girl and he was keeping his eye on it. He knows you're pissed off. The take from this morning sounded great, though, so everyone's buzzing about it back at the studio.'

There was nothing we could change right at this moment. I could try and keep Steve a bit closer. Perhaps starting to hang out more would help. He would never do it around me, so that would help. I would go around his house more.

'I think banning Irma from the studio is going to make it worse. We're going to have to try and get her onside. I will try and get her a job somewhere, modelling. I'll talk to some friends. Get her away for a while.'

'He's thinks he's in love. Never seen him like this. Bring back the groupies, bloody hell.'

We concocted a plan; a strategy was in place. I was going to start hanging around more, even though the timing wasn't great, Veronica was not going to love me hanging around Steve's house with his new drugged-up girlfriend. I didn't care much what she thought. My brothers were too important.

I got back to the studio and everyone was sitting around listening to the mix of the new song and Gavin was right, it was great. It didn't need much doing to it as the first takes of Steve's singing were absolutely brilliant. His job was done for the day and we actually achieved what I wanted, to go back to basics.

'I'm going to get back home, guys. Do your magic.' He couldn't wait to leave.

'Hey Steve, can I pop over to yours later? Feel like getting out of Veronica's crazy hormone prison.'
Irma answered,

'Sure'.
I could tell Steve wasn't pleased.

'I'll just finish off some of the parts, then I'll come over. Let's eat and watch a movie or something. I wanted to play you this new song as well. I need lyrics from you.'
I knew he liked it when I asked him for help.

'All right then, see ya later.'

Mike was parked outside, Steve and Irma fell inside the back of the car and into each other's arms, giggling .

Steve was sitting on the toilet–that's where he did his best thinking–thoughts rushing around about Ed. I mean, yes, he was wild at the minute, everyone knew that. But where was the trust? He kept on thinking, where the fuck was it? Like he was going to become a junkie, shooting up brown and shit. No, it wasn't gonna happen. He was just having a little dabble that's all. And he had found love, his soulmate. Irma was made for him; thin, interesting and smart. She was into the bad stuff but he could handle it. Ed was really pissing him off. Who does he think he is?

The second night they spent together he asked her to move in. She accepted. They couldn't stop staring at each other and he knew that she was the one. To celebrate their love they partied hard, morning till night. Irma would chase the dragon straight after they opened their eyes. Depending what he had to do, the day pretty much continued in a relaxed haze. If he had to be somewhere, Irma would get some coke or speed in. Otherwise it was hard to get off the sofa. It felt nice, all cosy. If he could only explain to Ed then perhaps he would understand but he knew there was no point, he hated hard drugs and he wouldn't understand.

Last night they'd watched French movies all night, in between nodding off and having sex. He couldn't stop admiring her waif-like body. He had an urge to say, 'I want you with me all the time. I want you to never leave my side. Be my wife.' So he did. He had never said anything like this to a girl before. Usually he would fuck them then spend the rest of the night figuring out how to get rid of them.

Irma held his head in her hands, stroked his cheek so gently it nearly made him cry and said, 'Then I will never leave.' Steve took this promise very seriously. He even called up Gavin to make sure that Irma was now his constant companion. Otherwise he would basically leave the band. Gavin was understanding, like he always was, and assured him he was going to deal with Ed, who probably was going to be the only one with a problem with the arrangement. Irma was quiet but when she spoke she told stories from another world. She loved art. Steve knew nothing and he lapped up every word. The smack was strange, it took over his brain pretty much the first time he tried it. It was amazing. He could do it all day and all night. Even the band didn't seem that important. He could handle it, though. He was sure of that.

The hours disappeared when I was in the studio. I got lost in the work that I did. I loved it that much. Everyone stayed on apart from Steve and we had a great day. When I looked at my watch it was a lot later than I thought. I jumped into Mike's car and asked him to take me to Steve's house.

The music was on in the house. They were playing Bob Dylan. I loved Dylan. I rang the doorbell. Nothing. I rang it some more. Still nothing. I called him. He picked up.

'I'm outside.' I heard some shuffling, the door opened. 'Hey.'

He looked relaxed, wearing his boxers.

'Can I come in?' I asked.

'We were sleeping.'

'Yeah, time to wake up little bro.' I held up a bottle of Jack Daniels.

The house was a tip: books strewn on the floor, clothes everywhere. Bowie posters on the wall and some of the walls painted orange. This house looked completely different. Irma was sloped on the sofa, still, like a wilted flower. She could speak because she said. 'Ed…Hi.' 'Mister Tambourine Man' was playing on the stereo and I could smell cat piss. They were definitely doing gear. 'You wanna line?' She said in a half whisper.

'Nah, thanks. Jack and coke for me.'

The kitchen was a tip, food and dirty washing-up scattered all over the place. Lighters, ashtrays and tinfoil out on the chopping surfaces. I had to say something.

'Steve, come here a minute.' Steve made an appearance. I pointed towards the drug paraphernalia.

'You doin' smack now?'

Irma was suddenly standing in the door, looking a little perkier, she'd obviously had a line of coke.

'We're just having fun. We like each other, that's all. We like to chill together. You must remember what that was like?' Steve put his arm around Irma. I wasn't going to react. Not the way he wanted me to.

'Yeah, I see that. I mean. You do what you like, but it's not a good idea, you know that. It never is.'

It was hard not to sound like a prude. I didn't mind him sniffing coke and drinking. That was Steve, it would probably kill him a little earlier but it was OK somehow. But this was trouble. It was hard to control and it always seemed to take over people's lives, I didn't want that. I wanted him to be himself. I had seen people change dramatically on that stuff. We and been plodding along nicely. So I turned around and looked at the cause of the drama, Irma.

'I don't want to tell you what you know, but I really would like you to stop making my brother take stupid fucking drugs. I really like you (lie), but could you please stay away from that grimy stuff.' I was sounding angry, I knew it, but I couldn't stop. I was irate. 'I don't care if you shove a needle up your arm and smoke your weight in the shit but it's not a good idea for Steve. Can you get that into your brain?'

I was far too close to her and talking too loudly. She didn't seem to care much, though.

'I am not making him do shit Ed, he does what he likes. Simmer down, Granddad.'

The frigging little bitch was so relaxed I wanted to hit her, I wanted to pick her up and throw her out of Steve's house. I knew that was not the best of ideas, so I didn't.

Surprisingly, Steve didn't say a word. He just stood there, looking at me calmly. He knew I did it because I cared and he always had liked that.

'Ed, come on, calm down, I'm not gonna fuck up, I promise. Irma, he does this, it's his big brother cares act.'

I was breathing fast. Steve's voice calmed me down.

He handed me a straight JD. I took it and sat down. I pulled myself together and spoke softly.

'I need us all to stay focused, stay together, remember why we have to look out for each other.'

Irma left the kitchen and went back to her original position on the sofa like a little cat, curled up and gormless. Steve got his guitar.

'You said you had a song?'

'Yeah, I do.' I started to play, thankful for the change of conversation.

We sat there for hours, working out the song until it was perfect. My phone was going off in my pocket. I knew it was V. Wanting me to come home and play happy house. I left Steve's at midnight, drunk and confused. That stupid little vermin girl Irma. Why did she have to come along and ruin everything?

Chapter 13:
It's All Good. The Messiah Is Here

I woke up feeling thirsty and hungry. Nausea was lingering everywhere, reminding me that I had drunk too much. V was sitting at the end of the bed, She looked sweet, her belly was enormous, she was enormous.

'You want breakfast?' she said.

I nodded. She stood up and started to walk towards the door.

'You were drunk out of your mind last night. Talking so much gibberish I was trying to make you stop. Do you remember anything?'

I couldn't. Sometimes it was the best way.

'I don't know…Come here.'

She did, she turned around and sat down, I stroked her face and I felt something,

I guess a reminder of how it used to be... so I kissed her, stroked her, and somehow we made love. Afterwards I had another 'It's all gonna be OK' epiphany, through my fucked-up brain. I even mumbled, 'I love you.' Cowardly…Because I wasn't sure I meant it. We laid in bed together on our backs for ages, holding hands.

I felt safe. We dozed off into dream land.

Another day to get to the studio, and after last night at Steve's, I was feeling nervous as hell. Ben and Fred were sitting in the kitchen eating breakfast and chatting. Ben sounded so mature; he was eighteen but looked a few years older. He was mostly quiet and serious, comfortable in his own skin. He never conversed unnecessarily; when he did it was mostly something that made sense. He thought before he spoke. I was very proud of him and I trusted his opinion.. He wanted to go to school and study law, he just finished his A-levels.

He'd managed to fly back for tests and keep up with his schoolwork; he was committed, he felt the need to feed his brain, be stimulated, he said. He was dating a girl from his school called Freda; she was Spanish and she was equally straight. They were cute, completely oblivious to the rock'n'roll circus around the band. I often caught them talking about things I knew nothing about, like politics or human rights. When he walked into a room, he was completely unaware of all the girls falling at his feet, he didn't care. Freda and Ben were proper people, from a different universe, one I never belonged to.

We all relied on Ben for timekeeping and facts that we might need. In new countries he would find out what to see and where to go, not that we ever visited those places. Then he would tell us all about it so that we would come across as vaguely bright in interviews. Steve did most of the talking and due to the briefings from Ben his public image was that of a thinking person, relatively well-read and politically aware. Steve wasn't stupid, he just didn't care about anything or anyone.

Fred and Ben were talking about Steve as I came in.

'I mean, it's just so stupid.' Ben was clearly un-impressed.

'What are we gonna do?' Fred looked at me as I entered the kitchen dressed in my underpants.

'We are going to do nothing, because there is no point,' I made us tea and sat down.. 'I'm hoping it's just a little phase. He is so stubborn.'

My head was throbbing. Felt as if I was on a boat, in a storm. I needed to puke. Oh fuck, here it comes. I ran for the loo and made it just in time.

'You all right there?' Ben and Fred laughed.

'You want some marmite toast? Asked Ben.

'Yeah, thanks… Much better now.'

The doorbell rang. It was Gavin, perky as ever. Fresh out of the shower, smelling of some shit perfume that probably cost him a fortune.

'Man, did you bathe in a brothel this morning? You stink of cheap perfume.' We all laughed and Gavin did too. He laughed at everything we said.

'Yeah, all right boys. I just came by to pick you up and take you to the studio. Mike's at Steve's house. I think we should have a chat on the way to the studio.'

In the car we listened to yesterday's recording, it was brilliant. Considering how bad the beginning had been, this was much better than it deserved to be. Somehow, that's how the band had always been when it came to the music, too easy.

Gavin was excited because he was playing with his keys. He always did that when things were going well. Pound signs flashing in front of his greedy eyes.

'It's just genius.' He kept on saying. Tapping his foot while he was driving. Nodding his head. Singing along. I wished he would calm down a little. He looked stupid.

'Like it always is, Ed. It's always great. You're great.'

I stared out the window, ignoring Gavin, watching Londoners going about their business. Rubbish all over the high road, drunks waking up on street corners, betting shops and pound shops keeping the locals busy with meaningless tasks. Getting them being meaningless through the day.

'Are you hearing it? Listen! You must think it's good?' Gavin turned the music down and looked me in the eye.

'Yeah, it is, it's gonna be great,' I said.

'It's exactly how I wanted the session to sound.' said Fred.

I guess, it was better than I thought it would be at this stage.

I needed to eat. I felt sick.

'Can you stop somewhere? I need to eat or puke.' We stopped and I had a bacon sandwich and a cup of tea.

'Can you try and back off on Steve a bit?' I didn't answer. I felt like telling Gavin to shut up but I didn't. I felt too sick to fight. Ben spoke for me.

'We want him to be happy, we just worry about him losing control. He's always nearly lost it but we always managed to rein him in. Don't know about this time.'

Everyone listened, because when Ben spoke it was always right on the money.

'For fuck's sake.' I said.

I was exhausted, tired from drinking and my brain working overtime.

Looking at all the people hurrying along, I decided there could be worse things. The best way was to go with the flow for now. Try to make the record and assess the situation after it was done. With Ben off to college we needed to have a break before we toured again. If Steve lost the plot I had the time to sort him out.

'Gavin, it's fine. Let's just keep an eye on it. No panicking needed.' I said that, I didn't mean it but I wasn't in the mood.

We pulled up outside the studio, Matt was already there. He looked worse than I did.

'Hey man, you good?'

'Yeah, just going home. Been here all night. I added some guitar to the two tracks. You're gonna like it. I know you will.' He got into Mike's car and drove off.

He was right, I *did* like it. It sounded like a yearning, guitar screeching, drums thumping steadily and that voice; Steve's performance was flawless. He didn't even have to try. It was incredible how it had all come together in no time at all, when all we needed was time together.

The next few days progressed nicely, with everyone getting on fine. Sometimes a good argument makes everyone sit up and appreciate that we are in a good situation. Irma even kept away… most of the time.

Perhaps, I worry too much. I have to learn to cope with situations better, listening to the results, I had to admit defeat and give Steve a break, his performance on the songs made me forgive all bad behaviour.

The whole team's spirits were up and we managed to get through half the album without that many hiccups. Veronica and I were looking at houses so that we would get a bit more space when the baby arrived. I guess you could say we were nesting.

I found a house in Hampstead. It was gothic and huge, it cost an arm and a leg. I had that and more limbs so I could buy it easily. Hampstead, with its leafy streets and massive green spaces, had always been a magical place for me. Somewhere, where proper people lived. I had never imagined that one day I'd be able to afford live there.

Veronica, the brothers and I went to look at the house and we turned into a bunch of kids in the empty mansion. Fred pretended to pee in the kitchen sink and Ben yodelled to check the acoustics. Veronica throwing herself on the beds and having trouble getting up again had us all in stitches. The agent looked slightly nervous but let us get away with it as she knew we could afford the house with our rock-star earnings. We loved it and decided we would paint it black and install a recording studio in the basement. It was too good to be true. I had stayed in some great hotels, but this was much better.

I heard a scream. It was Veronica. I ran, to find her standing in a pool of water, her face had lost all colour. She was howling like a dog in pain. I took me a while to realise what was happening, that the baby was coming. Ben had to point it out to me. I was that removed from the whole thing. She was holding on to the mahogany bannister, cursing like a Kilburn drunk. I really did not know what to do. Ben took charge.

'Call Gavin.' He said.

I did. I told him Veronica was in labour and that she was in pain. He called the ambulance immediately. The estate agent was getting involved too, her being a woman, she started ordering us about to get stuff, towels and water and I wondered why. In amongst all the madness I could hear my name 'Ed'.

She was screaming.

'It really hurts. Help me.'

She looked like she was being tortured from the inside. The chandelier in the hall vibrated with the screams V was letting out. Never knew she had so much volume, her eyes were wild but her body hard and stiff. The ambulance turned up and thankfully they took over. I was relieved as I didn't have a clue what to do. Ben stepped in again, holding V's hand. I was surplus and useless. I needed, wanted, a beer or vodka and preferably run away. The ambulance staff examined her and said,

'She's too far gone. We are going to have to deliver the baby here.' I felt as if I was going to explode. What if something goes wrong? What if the baby dies? Inside I was a mess but on the outside I kept quiet, Veronica was turning into an animal in front of my eyes. Like a lioness, it was incredible, I thought…she's scary. Squirming and screaming. Swearing and growling.

The ambulance people had made a bed but Veronica was still standing up or squatting. Apparently she was ready to push. I never knew it was going to be like this, suddenly I had the urge to get involved. I shouted,

'Pull,' which was completely wrong as everyone stopped what they were doing and looked at me for a second. Then they shouted,

'Push.' I should have read a book or something. Too late now. Ben was coaching her along.

'Come on, V! You can do it!'

Suddenly she stopped her madness, looked over at me, straight in the eye, like she hated me. Her face scrunched up like a nun on acid. She said,

'It was your fault too.' Then she roared louder. It was piercing. Made me shiver.

'It's coming. I can see the head.' Three people were looking up V's legs. I started to make steps towards her. I stood next to Ben, still a spare part. Veronica pushed me away.

'I want Ben,' she said. I didn't care. I would want Ben too if I was her. He was calmer than me, better at this sort of thing. I looked towards her bum area and I could see a hairy head. It was the baby, my baby. She let out another yell and the rest of the little blue creature just flopped out of her alongside blood and gore. The ambulance woman caught the baby with a smile and then he made the sweetest little kitten cry.

Teddy, my son had arrived, a slimy little thing with long fingers and toes. A proper Henderson.

'You want to hold him?' asked the ambulance woman. She handed me Teddy before I could answer. I sat down on the stairs, holding onto the little parcel. Wrapped in a blanket, blue shivering lips, yelping a little louder, his face was…so beautiful.

I fell in love. I started to cry because I everything, every emotion I had ever experienced came at me at once. The tears landed on top of his little head and I felt as if he looked right through me.

Ben and Fred came and sat down next to me.

'He's amazing.' Their eyes were glazed over too.

'Hello, Teddy.' Fred said.

'Teddy looks like me. Poor thing.' I hugged Ben and said,

'Thank you.'

Veronica was suddenly really calm and I heard her normal voice coming from the stretcher they had now made into a bed. She now resembled an angel, not the beast I had just witnessed in action. She was wearing a hospital cloak and her face was flushed, eyes glittering as if she was drunk.

'Come here,' she said.

I walked over, handed her the parcel. Our son. I kissed Veronica and said,

'You were so good at that. I'm so proud of you.' She smiled and we kissed. She then looked down at Ted. Euphoria and peace strewn across her face. I felt like running around the room kissing people, thanking them for helping.

We rode the ambulance together to St Mary's hospital. By this time we were all smiling and calm. We had a boy. I now needed to make sure he was safe at all times.

'We have to buy that house, you know,' Veronica said.

'I know,' I replied.

In the hospital my mind wandered back to the words Veronica said to me in the heat of the moment. My fault? I had never considered I had anything to do with her going off with Matt. Maybe she didn't mean that; perhaps she meant it was my fault she was in pain. I decided I wasn't going to mention it to her. The brothers, Gavin and I, all went to the pub opposite the hospital to wet the baby's head, or more like bathe the baby's head in twenty lagers. We all got completely wasted to celebrate the arrival of the little man. Even Steve went to see him and claimed that he looked just like Ted, our Father. I didn't even mind Irma turning up at the pub, my mood was that good. On the way back to Fairhurst Gardens, drunk as a skunk, my mind kept on going back to that comment. I felt guilty and I didn't like it.

I always took Veronica for granted, assumed she felt the same for me as I did for her, like she was supposed to read my mind. I never felt the need to gush. Music consumed me and nothing took first place over that. In fact, the brothers and music always came first, Veronica after them.

Matt and her had become best mates after Veronica had lived at his Nana's house for a couple of years. They got close. It was wrong, my part was being slightly rubbish at showing emotions. All that mattered today was that I was a dad.

Ted's birth had left me feeling soft. I was warm all over.

I woke up far too early in the morning, grabbed my clothes and called Mike, who turned up in ten minutes. We went back to the hospital. Mike was excited and had bought Ted a Teddy. Veronica and the baby were asleep; the whole room was covered in gifts from all over the world. I just sat there for a while, looking at them. She must have sensed I was staring because she opened her eyes. A tired smile opened her mouth and she reached out and touched my hand.

'We have a son,' she said.

'I know, he is beautiful.' She scooted over and I lay down next to her. We fell asleep until we were woken up by the baby. In my daze I could hear the hospital coming to life and people were bursting in and out of our room, taking no notice of our bubble. More flowers arrived. We could have opened a stall for the day.

'I wanna go home' Veronica sat up.

'It's too crazy here.'

She was right. It was manic. The nurses came in and told us we were good to go. Mike came up and packed our things. The three of us walked slowly and gently through the corridors, Ted in Veronica's arms. We made it into the car after a struggle with the baby seat. There were some photographers outside who had caught wind of the birth. I didn't get mad at them. I was happy. We sailed through London streets and made it back home, where there were more people outside. It was a good thing we were moving house, it felt less safe at home. Fred and Ben opened the door and we all sat and stared at the most perfect human I had ever seen.

Steve had found his muse, the reason why he loved singing, the single thought that he needed to sound perfect. Irma, the waif, the warm, smart angel that he could never live without. She smelt like flowers, fresh fields or even fruit. She was his woman; he had found his Veronica. It was a relief, after he had shagged every female who wanted him too and there were plenty of those. Since the band, it was too easy getting laid. He still applied the same tactic his dad taught him, keep quiet.

When he met Irma, after a gig, it took him by surprise how much he liked her. He didn't actually know what to do. She was relaxed, nothing fazed her and it was pretty clear why after they had hung out a few times. She was smoking brown. He always stayed clear of that stuff, as he had seen what it did to people. But now, there was no reason why he would turn out bad. He had too much money, he was young and he could see by looking at Irma that the effects on her were only positive. She looked great and she sounded smart. She was cultured. And she was cosy, warm. He wanted to lie next to her, always. Spooning, kissing. The sex wasn't that important, it was the closeness, he never had that. So, he decided was going to try smack to spend more time with

Irma. He wasn't going to do it a lot or that often but he wanted to try. The scumminess of it appealed to him. The spoon, the foil, the smell. It was perfect. He asked Irma to move in after the second time they hung out. She agreed casually and later that day she turned up with her long-haired white cat called Sid. Placed most days firmly on sofa, stroking her cat, listening to Neil Young or The Band, she was part of the furniture and he loved her, intensely. He could stare at her for hours. Sometimes he undressed her and touched her everywhere. She didn't mind or move. She was like his cat.

Ed didn't take to her. Typical. Ed didn't want Steve to be happy like him. It wasn't negotiable, though. He loved her more than his brothers or the band. The drugs were nice too. It was easy to love that drug, it was moreish. It was what heaven must be like, cocooned in cotton wool without a care in the world. He had never been this content.

Now he had to make the brothers like her. It wasn't going to be easy. Not that it mattered, nothing really did any more.

Chapter 14:
There's Always Something

We moved into our huge rock-star mansion, my little family and I. Ben and Fred were cooing over Ted, Veronica and I getting on better than ever. The album got finished, with Irma firmly positioned on our studio sofa, looking waif-like, uninterested and uninteresting.

It didn't bother me as much as I was on high on fatherhood. Ted was part of me. Responsibility had always been acceptable to me–that wasn't new–it was the blank slate opportunity that got me. He wasn't messed up. He was a little man with no hurt around whatsoever. Everything else suddenly meant less. The feelings I had for Ted had taken me by surprise, slapped me in the face. I would wake up in the night wondering if he was breathing or panicking that someone would take him, kidnap him. My instincts were to protect.

Ted's room had a nautical theme, which made me laugh. Like some little lord of the manor in his ship-themed room. I couldn't help thinking that if he could talk, he would protest.

The house was done up by some lady with pink hair. She was really whacky. I said I wanted the house black so she did that. Mostly.

The house was every working-class kid's dream. The kitchen had every appliance you could think of and that ten bathrooms were just perfectly boring. We had a huge telly, video games for the boys and, downstairs, my studio, my favourite room. All my instruments lined up, huge speakers and a mixing desk. There was a toilet next to it–my request. Every good studio had to have a toilet next to it, so you wouldn't lose the vibe running to have a wee.

The stairs creaked when you walked up them. She had put up some pretentious art on the walls. One had a British flag with a skull print on it. I loved my house. Ted was born here. The garden was designed for people who couldn't look after a garden, and on our doorstep were Hampstead's fields and ponds. Pretty idyllic stuff. I had taken to stay up late at night in my studio so that I could take care of Ted when he first woke up at five in the morning. It was my favourite time of the day. I would take him down to the studio, feed him a bottle and put some Joni Mitchell or Neil Young on. Then I would get him back off to sleep, giving Veronica a break, it was a nice time of our lives.

On the other hand, there was trouble in the camp. Steve was still in his own bubble. Matt was dabbling with the dirty drugs too, but somehow managed to look OK; he always did. Fred was hanging around but didn't participate as far as I could tell. A mysterious, seedy and unreliable atmosphere surrounded them.

Before, I would have spent hours worrying about it now I cared less. It wasn't the best time to stop being so obsessed. Like I said, things had changed. Priorities were very different, my son's pure face consumed me.

Gavin mentioned that he thought Steve was starting to look a bit thin and he was concerned the press was about to catch on that he was taking drugs. The press? Fuck the press. It bothered me that Gavin was worried mostly about our image and not that Steve was on smack. Mike was now working for Steve full-time, babysitting him. And the bad things were reported to Gavin, not to me or the other brothers. For some reason my alarm bells didn't go off, on reflection probably because I was enjoying being with Ted so much.

One bright Sunday, when I had managed to get Mike to transport Steve from his house to ours, it was obvious how bad things had got. I didn't want Steve to touch Ted with his dirty, nicotine-stained hands. His rock-star look had taken a new turn towards tramp.

Steve didn't eat and spent the afternoon singing songs to Ted, hunched over him like an ogre. Ted was blissfully unaware of the stench and the appearance of his uncle. Veronica was pacing around, feeling uncomfortable with him near the baby. Irma was too tired to come over, at least we only had one junkie in the house.

'You look rough.' I said.

'Yeah, feel a bit rough. It's cosy here, guys, all proper family vibes.'

'Go and lie down Steve, in the guest room. I'll run you a bath. You look knackered.' Veronica tried. She grabbed Ted from him and headed upstairs.

'Might take you up on that.' He leaned back and looked as if he was about to pass out.

Veronica was already upstairs by the time he answered. I could hear the water running. Ben, Fred and I watched TV, Steve sat down next to Ben and fell half asleep on his shoulder.

'Ready.' Veronica shouted from upstairs. No answer. Ben nudged him.

It took Steve time to take the instructions in but in the end he was making movements towards the bathroom.

'Can you make sure he doesn't drown?' I said to Mike.

Mike followed Steve. He really was in a bad way. The brothers and I didn't say a word, we were all thinking the same thing. He had changed, he was dirty and careless. Why did he have to take it this far? What was wrong with him?

After his bath he fell asleep. In the morning I was up with Ted when Steve appeared, still eyes half- opened.

'Where's Mike? Gotta get back now.' He looked stressed, scratching his arm vigorously as he spoke impressively fast. It must hurt to scratch that hard, I thought. Steve didn't seem to mind. He wanted to get out.

'Why so fast? Hang out here today. We can listen through the album and do some writing.' I did need to talk to him about the next few months with the band. He didn't listen. He was already somewhere else and he needed to get there quick.

'Later Brother. I gotta go.'

Mike was already standing by the door, used to Steve's erratic behaviour. And just like that, he was gone. I got on the phone to Gavin. I now understood how serious the problem was.

Me: Morning, we have a crisis.

G: We do? What?

Me: Steve. He has gone too far. Way too far.

G: What do you mean? He's been like this for a while.

Me: He was over here last night. We have to do something. It's bad.

G: Like what? Do what?

Me: Rehab or something.

G: That will delay the release.

Me: Fuck the album, Gavin. Fuck everything. I couldn't care less and I'm not prepared to stand on the same stage as a junkie, It isn't gonna happen.

G: OK Ed, I'll look into it.

There was no rivalry between Steve and I at any point; we weren't like that, our bond was solid but we were different, I was trying to let him work out a lifestyle he could handle, it seems like my plan hadn't worked out this time. Plans didn't always, I guess. We needed a new plan, one that was vaguely realistic, one with heroin in it, the one thing we had vouched never to enter our bubble. I kicked a chair because I was pissed off. Fucking Steve.

Looking at myself and my other brothers, we were not exactly squeaky clean, we were all products of our upbringing and the scars were showing in different ways. Steve was always trouble, in your face, with his smack habit and super-skinny skeletal body and weird girlfriend. Lack of caring what anyone thought of him didn't help. It was clichéd. We had seen other artists behaving like that; it just angered me that he was turning out like them. I thought he understood how bad it was. The worst thing was people were buying it: he was all over the press, pictures in the papers with him sticking up his fingers at people and behaving like a prime prat.

Ben thought it was pathetic, the real Steve wasn't like this, but I wasn't so sure. This was just some rock-star carbon copy thought up by the media, and Steve was buying into it, taking to it like duck to water. 'He just seems so stupid.' Ben kept on ranting about how he embarrassed the family was by his gallivanting around, thinking he was the shit. Ben was basically the opposite of Steve the Diva. Sometimes I felt as if we were back at home, with Mum, bickering.

I wasn't convinced about Ben's theory. Steve was already boozing and smoking weed before Mum died. He was always in trouble and the fact that the band was a success made it seem more acceptable. It gave him permission to behave however he wanted. He had the cash and fame to do it. People loved him whatever he did. It enabled him to use hard drugs without being a criminal. I always imagined that he might have been dead or in prison if things would have turned out differently. Who knows? And then there was the voice, that voice he and no one else had been blessed with. By whom I do not know. Sometimes I feared it was the devil himself.

Being a Father had made my old feelings for Veronica return. I admired her so much after what she did, how she gave birth, just like that. I was impressed with what she was capable of. She was a good mother and I liked the security of our safe family unit.

Fred had become a nice young man, handsome and sensitive. As he aged his long brown hair, green eyes and sticky-out ears became more prominent. He wasn't as self-assured as Ben, so I kept my eyes on him, to make sure he wasn't too influenced by Matt and Steve. He was still young, and like all of us he'd had to grow up far too quickly. He had four girlfriends at the moment. It was getting harder to cover for him, and Veronica wasn't pleased when they started to ask her questions. They all had brown hair and blue eyes, big boobs and olive skin. They looked the same which made it even harder. I resorted to calling them all 'Babe'. They didn't seem to mind as they were fans and blushed every time I spoke to them.

The whole lifestyle was becoming more and more weird, like a B-movie or a crappy soap opera. It was starting to get me down. It was hard to have a decent conversation with anybody as most people started to act like idiots around us, apart from Veronica and the boys, that is.

Ted was floating in the middle of our circus like an innocent angel. Veronica was starting to look like herself again and we hired a nanny to help us look after the boy. Gavin had sorted it out. She was a nice enough girl, from Scandinavia. She looked like a chubby member of Abba and seemed reliable. She moved in with us and became someone that we trusted and liked.

Steve and I were booked in on a European press tour. We had to do radio gigs and promote the new single. Ben and Fred didn't need to go so they stayed back in London. Ben was in the middle of his law degree and he was enjoying the non-rock star lifestyle. I made sure he was let off as much as possible so that he could focus on what he wanted to do. Fred was happy shagging and drinking, keeping Ted and Veronica company when he was hungover or needed TLC.

Gavin and I spent hours talking about the best way to wean Steve off the smack. We decided we were trying taking him out of his usual environment. Maybe it would make him see how shit it was. On reflection this was not the best of ideas.

I needed to have a straight up conversation with him, brother to brother so I headed over to his house. I rang the doorbell, he answered and to his credit the house was tidier than last time I was there. Then I remembered that Gavin had arranged for a cleaner to come around daily.

'I'm really worried about this press tour. Are you up for it?' I opened up a beer as I spoke.

'Yeah, sure, I am. Gonna be great. Before you say anything, I'm bringing Irma.'

'OK,' I stood up and started to pace, trying to stay calm but not succeeding, literally biting my tongue, I could taste the blood.

'I forgot, gotta head off.' I walked out, probably leaving smoke behind.

A car screeched as I walked out into the road, I apologise to an angry driver. Somehow it calmed me down. I sat down on a bus stop bench wondering what to do next.

I called Gavin, and told him what happened, violently sucking on my B&H, venting words between puffs about how there was

'No way I was gonna share a bus with that slag ', a little voice in my head started saying,

'Stop, It's not her fault!' I continued to rant and walk and the voice kept on saying:

'It's not her, it's Steve. She's not making him. Get that into your thick skull.'

Gavin and I talked all the way until I reached Rick's place in Kentish Town. I didn't stop until I was standing in front of him.

'I need this sorted. I'm not going until it is,' I said.

'OK. I'll make some calls,' he said.

He found a rehab place in Kent, so expensive that they accepted anyone who could afford to pay. The only problem was we had to make him want to go. I suggested that we would get Irma a space too, perhaps then they could help each other. In our defence, we knew nothing about smack and we were making it up as we were going along.

Talking to Gavin, I found out how bad it had got. Mike turning up at the office daily, collecting £600 in cash. I laid into Gavin for not telling me. He pointed out that Steve was an adult and it was his money, that he was just the middleman. I responded with the argument that this was not a normal band, we are family first, and I look out for my brothers, I expected him to do that as well. Clearly, spending that amount of money per day indicated that something was up. I continued to say that if he wasn't happy with our bands ethos he could look for another job. I was really mad, mad at myself for letting things get this bad. This is what happens if you take your eye of the ball.

Finding a rehab clinic and telling Gavin off was easy enough. How the fuck was I going to get Steve to agree to go to rehab? I needed to think this through again, no more mistakes. I called Mike.

'Get over here. I want to know everything.'

I made him a cup of tea and sat down a little too close to him, he looked sheepish.

'It's not great, Ed. I don't want to tell you.' Mike avoided my eyes.

'I need to know, he's my little brother.'

'Ok, here goes. He is not leaving the house much; dealers go in and out as well as some really dodgy people. He's off his nut most hours of the day. He smells. Sometimes I give him a bath. I don't think he is using needles but it's a matter of time. The people he hangs around with are proper dirty junkies. I caught one shooting up in his eye the other day, his fucking eye! Who would do that?' I had to try hard to stay calm. I wanted to shout:

'Why has none told me about this?' But I didn't.

Gavin continued as he had read my mind:

'We didn't want to destroy your special time with your family. We saw how happy you were. You deserved that. Mike and I have been taking about a solution. We didn't want to involve you.'

'And you thought touring was a good idea?'

'It was about getting him out of that godforsaken house. We thought that might open his eyes, you know? Music usually works' Gavin looked genuine.

'And provide him with bundles of cash every day. That was also one of your good ideas? You might as well give him the drugs yourself,' I said.

'That's not fair, it's Steve's money, I can't stop him using it.' A valid but still shit point.

'He is in no fit state to tour,' I said.

'We realise that now.' Gavin looked even more sheepish, if possible.

I heard via Mike that Matt had stopped hanging around Steve. Perhaps Steve would listen to Matt.

I needed him to understand that the band was over if he continued down this path. I called Matt. He seemed in a good place. We decided to meet up in a pub to talk things though. For old time's sake we met up at the Good Mixer–perhaps not the best choice as it was packed with Henderson fans.

Mike was with us and we spent an hour chatting with people, drinking and relaxing. We played pool, had a nice time together. It was really nice to see him. After a couple hours in the pub we realised that it was impossible to have proper chat so we headed off to a local Indian restaurant.

Matt ordered for both of us, knowing exactly what I liked, I missed him. It was still there somewhere, our friendship, which changed my life all those years ago at the supermarket in Camden. The dreams that we made up those early mornings actually came true, that was something no one could take from us.

Matt hadn't changed, he was the same guy and it was easy to like him. He still wore the same clothes, the same hair style. He was cool, I thought to myself. No wonder Veronica went there.

I brushed the dark thoughts away and ordered another beer. I was getting nicely pissed. We spoke about Ted and the album. How great it was, because it was. Our food arrived, vegetable Rogan josh with onion bhaji and pilau rice, nan bread and mango chutney.

It was hard talking about Steve. I didn't want to ruin the moment. We were having fun, dancing around the subject.

After another beer I blurted out:

'I need your help.'

'Yeah, or, I agree, we need to talk about him. Things aren't good.'

'You have to tell me how bad you think it is. Are you still doing it?'

'Ed, I never do anything I can't handle,' he said. Strangely enough, I believed him.

'I had to check myself, it's really nice but I know the dangers, it's not worth it.' At least, he was being honest.

'Steve is a wreck. He won't listen to me or any of the others. What do *you* think we should do?'

He paused.

'I don't think there is much you can do. He's not there yet, he's is in the middle of it. I've seen it before. Irma is getting bad too. Real bad.' He looked at the plate.

'I think she's shooting up. Steve's not…I don't think.'

Mike got a call.

'I've gotta go.' He stood up and left.

'Can you try and talk to him?' I took a deep breath 'Please.'

'I can't work with him like this. No one can. He's become some sort of rock-star cliche. Ben and Fred are freaked out and Veronica is worried sick. We have to do something.'

'I will try, for the band. I'm not so sure it's gonna take. Last time I saw him, he was a blabbering mess. It's all about timing.'

'I can get Mike to call you when he thinks he's communicative.'

'What do you want me to say?'

'I want you to ask him to stop, to get help, before it's too late. For us, for the band and for him.'

Matt agreed to try, a friend's band was playing at the Electric Ballroom. I hadn't been out in ages. I was getting drunk and felt in a good mood so we headed down Parkway towards Camden High Street. For a minute if felt like the old days

We didn't have tickets and we didn't need them. We got given backstage passes at the door and watched the band from the side of the stage. There were lots of people there, friends and fans I hadn't seen in a long time. The hours went by and we stayed on at the after party for hours. I chatted to a pretty girl with a posh accent. I had a few lines of coke and before I knew it, it was five o'clock in the morning. Matt had already bunked off with some chick and I was still talking to the girl, her name was Alice.

She was tall, her hair in a short black bob, pale skin and innocent brown Bambi eyes. She seemed classy. She moved with confidence and used long words, something I wasn't used to, apart from when Ben and his friends spoke. I took her number and when we said goodbye we kissed. Not the friendly kind. Our lips met and they fit together perfectly; her tongue danced round mine, making me tingle everywhere. She was trouble. It was the first time I had liked any other girl apart from V this instantly. I tucked her number in my front jean pocket and jumped in a black cab home. I was pretty drunk, drunker than I thought. The orange streetlights blurred together and I checked I still had her number. Alice. As I pulled up outside I realised Ted was about to wake up. Bollocks. This was not the way I should behave.

Chapter 15:
Steve's Demise

He was standing on stage. His brown, straight, greasy hair covered his spotty face. It was a shame that his voice wasn't a computer, one that you could control, that is. Being in front of the crowd had thrown him, being put on the spot like this. Having spent six months locked in his house learning the art of being a junkie had proved to be less fun than he had thought. He couldn't just give it up, though. It was all he knew. I guess he had always banked on his voice staying the same, no matter how much junk he put in or on it. It wasn't related. Even Ed had told him he sang better off his head. That was a long time ago, though. Here he was, about to sing the new album, and no matter how much he tried, no noise was coming out. He felt like an elephant with a miniature trunk. He went over to the amps and grabbed a beer, making a cutthroat hand signal to Ed. His voice was not in working order. He couldn't do it. At the same time, he felt wobbly. His legs were giving way, he fell over. Like an idiot. He got back up, stumbled across the stage like the street drunks he had left behind in London. He needed more, more drugs in him. Another hit would sort this out. Ed caught on and pushed him out of the way. He looked angry. The roadie ushered him off the stage. He racked a huge line of coke up, snorted it, then the roadie pushed him back out. Yeah, that's better. He roared like a lion and stumbled back onto the stage, throwing his beige dirty Burberry coat on the floor. Under it he wore his mother's sweater, the one that he nabbed the night they packed her stuff away. It was all he had left from her. It was falling apart now. He would wear it as long as it would stick together. Irma had been patching it for him…He swaggered up to the mike and said: 'Hello, everyone!'

The crowd went mental. For a moment, a rare thought that perhaps he had had enough crossed his blurred mind. Then, it was gone. Just like that.

I don't know how they made me go on tour with my brother, who was in the worst shape any human could possibly be in. He was a disaster. I guess, I thought that being with us and the music would sort him out, perhaps remind him what really mattered. I thought we were more important to him than this. I didn't understand what he was going through. Part of me was angry, part of me was sad. The seedy atmosphere had past cool but it didn't really matter because the shit was about to hit the fan. I'd known it would at some point. I let him down, being caught up with my own stuff and allowing him getting as bad as he did. We were on tour and he couldn't do it. Gavin made me go on this tour, and it was not a good idea.

Irma stayed at home. That was the only reason I agreed to do it, because I thought in my naive mind that I could help him if she wasn't around. He didn't want my help, he wanted to be left alone and take drugs, exist as he chose to without any interruptions or judgements. It didn't look fun anymore though. Most of the time he was slurring, his voice was going and we had nearly had to cancel the previous night's gig. He looked like a tramp and his teeth were yellow against his pasty skin. The press was catching on, making comments. It wasn't cool, it was pathetic.

The rest of the band were fed up too. I needed to do something. And I was going to, today.

The touring plan hadn't worked, that was plain to see. At least now I knew that we needed help, from someone who knew what they were doing. After the gig I tried not to be angry. I kind of understood that he was too long gone to care about anything.

I simply said,

'Either you go to a clinic or I'm leaving the band.' I knew he still cared about the band a little. His whole life was based around being in The Hendersons.

We didn't talk about it that night again, we ended up going out and having an alright night. Paris was a great city and we knew lots of people there. Steve was high but he was in a good mood, nearly charming in a Peter Pan way. Matt was grumpy because of the gig and I sent Ben and Fred home.

Being away from the family felt good as my head was acting up after meeting that girl Alice, I felt suffocated at home. She kept on playing on my mind and in my drunken state I called her. She was happy to hear from me, I could tell. I didn't think through what I actually wanted to say. Did I want to meet up? Probably not the best of ideas. We didn't make any plans apart from that I was going to call her again when I came back to London. I felt good thinking about her. I didn't want to cheat on Veronica, it wasn't my style. But this girl kept on creeping into my thoughts, far too often to ignore. It had never happened before, or at least since I'd been with V.

I was standing on the Champs-Elysée with my phone in hand. I had left the club to call her. People everywhere looking cosmopolitan and cool. I liked the French. They just seemed more sophisticated, even if they weren't.

I stood around chain smoking and watching people passing by. I made another call, this time to Gavin.

Moi: Hi, Gavin. Eh, you've probably been told but there are no more plans needed. Just the Priory. That's all I'm gonna say.

Gavin: Look, Ed. I agree with you. It's starting to be a real problem.

Moi: Starting? It *is* a disaster. He is a friggin' time bomb, waiting to go off or die.

Gavin: There are different ways to do this.

Moi: Are there?

Gavin: There's this guy that hooks junkies up to drips, cold turkeys them, he weens them off while they are sedated.

Moi: Ok.

Gavin: It costs a fortune.

Moi: Who cares about that?

Gavin: Thought you'd say that. I'll get on it. I cancelled the rest of the dates. Get him back to London tomorrow.

Moi: Ok. Oh, and pay for Irma to do it as well.

Gavin: Irma? She won't talk to me. She doesn't answer the door or the phone to me.

Moi: I'll get Veronica to go round there tonight.

Gavin: Thought you hated her.

Moi: I don't hate her…I hate the drugs. Gavin, she's not well.

Gavin: Ok.

And that was it, we had a plan. The next phone call was to Veronica. She agreed to go round and see Irma, talk sense to her. She also suggested that Matt's nan could stay with him after the detox, just for a while. Sounded like a good idea but I just didn't know if Steve would go for any of these plans. If Irma agreed, we had a better chance to succeed.

I headed back to the hotel to find Matt. He was sitting in the bar with some girl. He was pretty loaded. Since our night out in London we seemed to have rekindled our friendship. I could nearly say that I had forgiven him. I couldn't help but think that it might be connected to the feeling that I had about Veronica, or the lack of. Perhaps it was just a phase. I wanted to be with V forever but we had both changed. It always surprised me how much I was able to shift between different emotions. It was hard for me to work out what I really felt; my mood switched and so did my feelings. Control didn't come easy and I was desperate for it.

Matt agreed; Steve was a disaster zone and we had to act now. I didn't know much about addiction, what I did know was that it was hard to beat. All true drunks from Kilburn had always got worse, never better. We sat around, drank and talked, forgot about everything, it was fun until Mike delivered Steve home, Mike held him in his arm, there weren't many pounds to him these days, light as a feather and frail like a dried stick. A sorry sight and the sombre mood was back.

Matt disappeared upstairs with the girl and I stayed in the bar on my own, staring into my glass as if the answer was at the bottom of it. It was quiet and calm but a storm was brewing and I could feel it. I knew what had to be done the next day. I wasn't looking forward to it. Running away was my usual method but this time that wasn't going to work. My phone rang. It was Veronica, she just had got back from Irma. She sounded shaken. I ordered another glass of red while I spoke to her, my head slumped on the bar between my elbows as I listened to her story.

Irma had answered the door to V. The place was a tip, paraphernalia and dirty dishes everywhere. Irma was wearing a worn petticoat, making her skeletal body visible. She looked terminally ill. While V was talking to her she kept on nodding off. When Irma heard what had happened on stage she took a little notice. She listened to the idea of the detox, and thought it was a good idea, for Steve. She kept on insisting that she was fine. Yes, she had said, she had a problem, but that she wasn't ready to give up, she had it under control. Veronica stayed with her for an hour, and in the end she reluctantly agreed to give it a go, for Steve's sake. Because she loved him and his singing. Veronica had asked her about her family, if there was anyone in her life that could help her, come visit. Was there anyone that we could call, someone that cared about her apart from Steve? After a few faint vague mentions of people and names V realised then that there was no one. Irma was alone, just like us.

I never told V that they were shooting up, but her visit to the house made it obvious. Needles and spoons everywhere, Irma's arms bruised and skinny.

Veronica had done her part; now it was my turn to sort out Steve. With a heavy head on I made my way to the lift. It was harder to get to sleep then it should have been; my mind was racing. It was all about timing, I had to get him when he was awake, not too desperate for a hit, and not too out of it either. I needed Mike's help; he knew his drug routine better than anyone. I called his room. Told him to take Steve's phone, so that he couldn't speak to Irma. It was two in the morning now and I needed to rest but my brain wouldn't let me; it was torturing me with niggling thoughts, the kind that keeps you awake, the kind that makes you feel like a bad person. My failings as a brother, boyfriend and father was harassing me, I was letting everyone down, not being enough, I am selfish, said the voice within me. The music was my only sanctuary, not measured by success, but how much I loved and cared for it, that was still there, the only constant, reliable part of my life. Eventually I fell asleep.

The phone rang and I sat up as if a bolt of lightning had hit me. It was Gavin.

'What's the plan?' he said. Plan, I thought? Then I was back where I left off last night, just like that.

'You know. The plan is to speak to Steve and get him back to London. Is everything in order on your side?'

'Yep,' he said.

'Good, good, that's great.' I got out of bed and grabbed a bottle of Coke from the mini fridge.

My head was foggy, I needed a cold shower, the icy water whipping my sensitive, clammy skin.
I called Ben and Fred and asked them to come to my room.

'I'm telling him today.'

'Shit, what you gonna say?'

'I'm gonna tell him he has to clean up.'

Fred sighed.

'And you think he's gonna go for that?'
'He has no choice. Otherwise he's out of the
band.'
Ben nodded.
'Good luck Ed, rather you than me.'
Fred was tired, he had been drinking too much recently.
I made a note that I wasn't to let things slip again, get so
far that I had to do this, my hands were shaking with a
combination of hangover and nerves. There was a knock
on the door, it was Mike.
'Heads up. Steve's in a shit mood, really bad, I
don't know if...He needs a fix.'

I was up against a force I probably wouldn't be able to
beat. I decided to ignore Mike's warnings, stick to the
plan. The hotel corridor was closing in on me with its
shitty patterned carpet and flowery wallpaper. I felt like
vomiting. Steve didn't want me, he wanted smack. I
touched my watch like I had started to do when I needed
extra strength. A niggling feeling that no matter how I
approached this, it was going to go wrong. I made a de-
tour to Matt's room. I needed his help. He was still
asleep, I managed to wake him up and convince him to
get rid of the girl from last night–I don't think he remembered her name anyway.
'I need to talk to Ed, babes. Sorry, but I need you
to leave. It's important. Band stuff.'

She got out of bed stark naked and got dressed, she was beautiful. Matt kissed her on the cheek and said,
'Write down your number, babes.' She did.
Matt chucked her number in the bin and got a juice out of the mini bar.
'We've sorted a clinic in London. We need to tell Steve; it's over. He's already pissed off, clucking for gear. I need you.
' Matt was already putting his clothes on, he put his arm around my shoulder and it was what I needed.
'I'm in Ed. Let's do this.'

Steve was awake. His whole body was aching and itching from the inside. He needed a hit so bad. After yesterday's gig he deliberately didn't score as he was shocked that he wasn't able to sing, he always could sing, even if he was twatted. He now knew that was a mistake. His body hurt, all he could think of was smack, he would literally eat poo to get it, suck a dealer's cock, whatever he had to do, he would do it.. He called everyone he knew in Paris, trying to get some. No one picked up because it was ten in the morning. He tried calling Irma. She would have to get on a plane or FedEx some to him. No answer. He called Mike. He did answer–he always did. Mike had made it clear, like he always did, that he would never help him score. They had fought about it many times, but Mike was very stubborn. He begged him, he even cried and pleaded, offering him thousands of pounds if he would do it, just this once.

The roadies were usually helpful, but they were on the bus and their phones were turned off. His skin was so itchy, he scratched it until he drew blood. Damn it! He needed some gear now. He went over to the minibar to get some booze to take the edge off. There was none left. He called room service. 'Can I have a bottle of vodka, please? Actually, two bottles, I need two bottles.' He slammed the phone down.

Chain smoking and pacing up and down in his room, he was trying to think. Why didn't he sort it last night? What an idiot he was.

Fuck the fucking fuckers.

He went to the bathroom and splashed some water in his face. He caught a glimpse of himself and for a moment he didn't recognize his own face. He was white as a sheet, his skin shiny, pasty and spotty.

His hands were sweaty and the dark circles under his eyes had turned into proper black bags. His eyes looked like black holes, like a mentally ill person, his chest was so skinny you could see all the ribs. There was a knock on the door, he put a t-shirt on, it was room service with the vodka. He grabbed the bottles of the trolley, closed the door in the waiter's face, he drank straight from the bottle until his stomach was on fire. It brought some relief but it wasn't enough, he drank more. He needed a fag. Another knock, it wasn't room service, it was Ed and Matt. Shit. He didn't want to deal with them right now.

'What do you want?' He sniggered blocking the entrance. The vodka was definitely making him calm down.

'Can we come in?' Steve got out of the way and they sat down on the little sofa next to each other.

'You want a drink?' He got a couple of glasses out.

'Yeah, all right.' They all drank large gulps and lit a cigarette each. Ed looked nervous. Matt looked aloof. The tension was brewing. Ed spoke up.

'You have to listen to me, listen to us.' He said.

Steve was squirming, fidgeting like he only did when he was uncomfortable. Matt spoke, which was un-usual.

'We want to help you, mate.'

Steve was sweating, a cold sweat, but he didn't speak. Perhaps they were kicking him out of the band? They couldn't do that, they needed him. Or did they? He was tapping his food and shaking his other leg. He couldn't think what to say. Nothing was probably best.

'If this is about last night, I think I have a cold.' Ed was looking at his glass. Then he said,

'It's not about last night. It's about the junk. It's about you. You are scaring us, Ben and Fred too. We are worried about you.'

Matt looked up.

'Yeah man, we're all worried.' For a moment he felt safe. He just needed a hit and he would be good.

Perhaps he had been doing a bit too much recently but he could cut down. He could quit whenever he liked. He was in control.

'The thing is, we are not willing to go on stage with you in this state. It's not cool. We have sorted out this guy in London who can get you off the smack. Irma is in. She spoke to V last night. You can both go. Together.'

Steve knew how much Ed cared. Because he knew, he didn't go mental, like he felt like doing. Instead he said,

'You've cancelled the gigs? Are you mad? The fans, they're expecting us.'

I nearly felt like going out to score some gear for him, that's how bad it looked, as if death was knocking on his door or like he was operated by a faulty battery, making him move erratically.

What did this drug do to people? It must be powerful to make a person behave like this. The only comparable feeling I could think of was being possessed or obsessed. Alice, I thought. Strange how she popped into my head. I called Mike, told him to get to the room as soon as possible. He did. We needed to make a plan that Steve would agree to. Gavin had made arrangements for a private plane to take us back to the UK. Just as things were starting to get completely out of control the news of the private plane made Steve calm down. Probably because he knew it was easier to score in London. Mike packed Steve's things while Matt and I headed back to our rooms to get our bags. There was a lot of stuff we didn't know and perhaps sometimes that's the best way. We managed to get sleeping pills from the crew. Mike didn't think Steve would make it otherwise; he was acting like a crazy person and the pilot wouldn't let him on in this state.

We fed him vodka and Rohypnol all the way to the airport, which was decked out like a cosy living room. We plonked him on the bed at the back of the plane and took turns to sit with him. We all knew Steve had taken it too far and that it was going to be hard to get him back but we would, we had to. The flight took two hours, the slowest one hundred and twenty minutes I can remember. The painful whimpers from the back were torture to listen to. Gavin was waiting at City airport with a car. When the plane touched the ground I asked Ben and Fred to leave the plane and I sat down next to a comatose Steve.

'I need you to trust me, Steve.' I kept calm. He was searching for his phone.

'Irma,' he said.

'Irma is at the place already. I know you don't think I care about her, but I do. I care about you. Fuck the band, fuck music. I need you to get clean so we can hang out and be brothers, ride bikes, write songs and talk shit.'

When you relax, shit like this happens. I thought it would be ok. I didn't notice that Ben was standing behind me. He sat down and put his arm around me.

'It's not your fault Ed. you know, you're not responsible for us. I know you think you are, but you're not. Steve will be fine , come on, let's go home and get him sorted.'

Chapter 16:
Whatever it takes, brother!

In the car back to the house we hardly said a word. We didn't need to. We all knew that Steve was going in protesting, something we had heard was not the best way. In order to succeed you need a willing candidate. We had the money, just not the patient. I spoke to Gavin and we were not allowed to visit or speak to Steve for the next few days. I was relieved to be back home, with my son.

Driving up Hampstead High Street past the ponds and the Heath, I felt lucky, euphoric and strangely calm. A new feeling was brewing inside me. Calm before the explosion. Family and Veronica was what I needed but never what I wanted these days. I felt like I wanted to run away and never come back, get a job in a bar in the sun, sing for my supper, write songs about stupid things like the way to the shop.

Getting lost, getting found out.

I was tired of all the problems I kept on having, tired of being in charge of everyone else's life. I wanted to curl up and be left alone. When we arrived at the house, the shiny black gates felt boring, the pebbled stone driveway made me feel like a visitor and the doorbell, shaped like a lion didn't humour me one bit. I wanted to go home and this was home…I guess.

Ted and Veronica greeted us at the door, Ted stretched out his arms towards me and I buried my face in his little chest. Fred and Ben hugged V. I wanted to be alone because I felt lost. Usually I just got on with life but somehow this last turn of events had got to me, badly. My heart was beating fast, it was hard to breathe; sweat was pouring down my face from my temples. I felt sick; Shit, puke was coming up in my mouth. I made into our perfect bathroom and vomited my guts out just in time. Veronica found me slumped in front of the loo, holding onto the wooden seat, white as a sheet. She sat on the floor down next to me. She understood. We didn't have to speak much.

'Why don't you get into bed?' she stroked my forehead.

'Where's Ted?' I managed to say

'Don't worry about Ted. Just get into bed and have a rest. I'll bring you tea and toast.' She helped me up and over to the bed.

'My heart's really racing. What's the matter with me?'

'You need to rest, that's all.' She was right, I was exhausted. I fell asleep.

I finally woke up twelve hours later. It was nice to be home. I picked Ted up from his cot and went down-stairs, it was five in the morning, my favourite time of the day or night. Hanging out with Ted was simple. I caught my reflection in the mirror and didn't like what I saw, dirty nails, spotty skin and greasy, mousey brown hair. Dark circles under my eyes and I looked skinny, far too skinny. I smoked a fag and considered opening a lager but I felt sick; the nausea was still there. I waited until seven o'clock to call Gavin, see how things were going. He didn't answer. I called Mike; Mike always answered.

'Morning,' he said.

'Hey man, how is he? I mean, how are they…'

Mike was always trying to protect me from the truth. This time he realised I didn't want him to go easy. He told me how Steve had gone insane when they'd arrived at the guy's place instead of his house. He was frantically trying to call Irma. When Mike told him she was already inside he calmed down a little. He screamed and shouted that he needed a fix and that he had already started to turkey. He was shitting himself and shivering as if he was stuck in a freezer. He vomited on the floor as they walked into the room and tried to escape through a bathroom window, he was that desperate. The guy gave him a shot of something to calm him down, explained that he was going to wean him off smack slowly for a couple of days and then turkey him, as he was in a really bad way.

He described the house; it was in Kent to be precise. A small old house but they had a separate building in the garden that could take two patients. After he had calmed Steve down with the injection and got him off to bed, Mike had stayed for a good while, chatting to the guy about Steve, what he was like and how it had gotten this bad. None of us was allowed to visit for a whole week, that's how long it would take to wean them off physically. After that it was all about staying off the gear.

He had suggested another clinic that Steve and Irma should go to for at least six weeks, though six months was the recommended time. But if we got them a private 'babysitter' he should be good to go.

'Whatever it takes, there's no rush.' I said.

Ted was smiling at me while I spoke, oblivious to what was going on with his uncle. I walked around the living room bouncing him around.

Ben and Fred came down early, we spoke about the best way to handle things. The doorbell rang, it was Gavin. Today he had really excelled himself, doing the rock manager look to perfection: balding head, long hair at the back, white shirt and jean jacket with some black jeans. Nice watch–didn't know the brand but it looked expensive.

'Guys, how are we?' He always managed to sound so goddam perky.

'I'm good, spoke to Mike, things are under control.'

'Yeah, it's all good. He'll be back to his old self in seven weeks. I've rescheduled the European dates and hired a private bouncer for him, to work with Mike, to make sure he doesn't fall off the wagon. Sorted.' He looked pleased with himself as if he just repaired a car or something.

Ben, Fred and I were seduced by the 'everything's gonna be OK' charade but I wasn't going to let myself be persuaded so easily this time. I was ready to stand my ground.

'You know, Gavin, Steve is a person, a very wilful person. I don't know if six weeks is enough. The guy at the clinic recommended six months, you know, for him to be proper good.' I needed to be sure we did the right thing. Ben was pacing around the room like he does when he's thinking.

'It just doesn't feel right, going back on the road is a bad idea, at least for a while. He could have died. He still can. I mean, I don't care about the tour, I want Steve to be well. Right now, Gavin, we cannot be making that sort of decision. We simply can't.'

How I love Ben. It was obscene that Gavin was even talking about a tour when we all saw Steve's state on that plane yesterday. This wasn't something that would just go away, this was a real problem. We knew we were close to losing him forever and we were all scared. We had to make him it our priority.

'Gavin, until Steve is well, I don't want to talk about the band. No tour dates are being confirmed and I need Steve to know that too. No pressure on anyone.'

I was politely trying to tell him to F off. I was so sick of being sucked up to by this slimy guy who didn't give a fuck about our family. He just wanted to bleed us dry. I went back upstairs and fell back asleep, dreaming about a vampire hanging off my throat.

I woke up, covered in sweat with a naked Veronica next to me. We didn't speak much but we cuddled, gently. I held her for a while and then we gently made love. I was lying in bed thinking that being in the band hadn't turned out to be such a good thing. I was a terrible boyfriend, I wanted someone else, Alice; I thought about her while I had sex with V, imagined it was her. My brother was a full-on junkie. Dark thoughts were racing around in my head and my whole world was closing in. The thoughts were so intense, too many of them. My heart was racing, clammy hands and a feeling as if I was falling. I ran for the loo and once again I was sick.

Veronica caught me naked with my head in the toilet.

'That's it, I'm calling a doctor. You're freakin' me out.'

I actually don't know what happened. I was very ill, I knew that. The doctor came and said I had had an anxiety attack, gave me some Diazepam and a number for a shrink. I binned the number but downed a sleeper, or two. I managed to eat five pancakes and then I fell asleep again, not waking up until the next day. My first thought was Steve so I called Mike.

'I wanna see him. I want him to know that we are right behind him, that we haven't just dumped him in some clinic.'

Mike had spoken to the guy who told him that Steve was still asleep, put under in order to be weaned off.

'OK, I wanna be there when he wakes up.'

Being in a band, being famous was useful when you wanted something. I could stamp my feet and usually someone made it happen. We left Ted with the Swedish nanny, who was now sleeping with Fred, which sucked, because we probably had to sack her soon. The car drive was long but the countryside relaxed my head. Mike had sorted out a cottage nearby to the clinic for us to stay in. I wanted to be there when Steve woke up, even if we didn't speak, I knew that it was important.

All the way there we listened to Mike ramble on, he clearly had been talking to Gavin and probably got a telling off for telling me about the six-month programme. Gavin wanted us back on the road.

'Yeah, he's doing really well.' Mike tried to sound cheery. I couldn't be bothered to reply.

Veronica wasn't having any of it.

'How do you mean? He was put under anaesthetic to go cold turkey. How can that be classed as 'doing well?''

'Let's see what he's like when he wakes up, shall we?'

'Doing well doesn't usually include fucking going cold turkey in a clinic. Sorry Mike, I just have a hard time understanding how it got to this?' Mike didn't reply and that was probably for the best.

The small country roads wrapped in curved trees calmed the mood down. There was no point fighting anymore. Looking out the window, I thought about when we were kids. Mum and Dad use to rent a caravan in Camber Sands. Steve and I running on the beach, throwing stones in the water, wrestling in the sand, driving our parents insane with our constant bickering and fist fighting. Steve would always take it too far and throw sand in my eyes. The caravan was cool, we thought, with seventies thick carpet that Mum found a toenail in. Fred was a baby and Ben was quietly watching the madness. Life wasn't all bad then, at least I had those memories.

We got to the cottage and waited for the call. It didn't take long before they rang.

Ben, Fred and I would visit Steve, and V would talk to Irma. I wanted to have a proper chat with the people from the clinic, make sure that we were doing all the right things, not edited by Gavin. Mike cared about us but he was controlled by Gavin, he answered to him.

'Mike, I want you to tell me if Gavin tries to see Steve. I don't want him around at the moment. We need family time; the band is on hold.'

'Will do.' Mike looked sincere but I wasn't sure.

We arranged for a meeting at our cottage as Steve and Irma were still under. The doctor guy was nice enough, Peter Smith was his name. He told us how our brother was doing, how his habit must have been excessive as the weaning off had taken a lot longer than it usually does. There is nothing worse for a junkie then an unlimited flow of funds. He and his pals had probably smoked and injected the price of a terraced house in Kilburn. It was madness. The good news was that he could afford it and he was still alive.

Him and Irma being together was not the best of ideas, as it would only take one of them to come up with the idea of using drugs and it would be all over. It was hard to stay off heroin, that's basically what he told us, it was harder than any other drug.

It sank in and we prepared ourselves for a rocky ride. I knew was I wasn't ready to organise Steve's funeral without putting up a fight. Beating myself up over the fact that I had let him get this bad, I started to feel the panic rise once again. I took another Diazepam to calm down. What if he had died? I would never have forgiven myself.

Walking into the room, I felt apprehensive and scared. I mean, I wouldn't blame him if he told me to fuck off. I had driven myself mad pondering how to tell him that I cared about him without pissing him off. I knew he wasn't up for hearing some drivel about how I loved him. I needed to try to be honest and calm. He was quiet and still, his bony chest moving with his timid breaths. It was hard to tell if he was sleeping or not.

'Steve,' I whispered. 'It's me, Ed. Just to let you know. We are here. All of us.'

Nothing, not a sound. So, I sat down, next to his bed on a chair.

'I heard this track on the radio. You would love it. Actually, the singer tries to sound like you, he nearly gets it, not quite. Have you heard it?' I started to hum the tune. His eyelids half opened. He knew I was there, I continued speaking. 'It's hot in here. You know, we are close to the beach, where we used to go with mum. Camber…and dad, remember?'

He still didn't make a sound. Still no reaction, so I kept my mouth shut.

After an hour of silence he said, 'Ed, it's ok, I'm not angry with you. Stop acting like you've done something wrong.'

'Nothing matters Steve. I don't care. I just want you to get better.'

'Where's Irma? Can I see her?'

'Course.' I had accepted her; I was not to be judgemental.

I left the room and grabbed the nurse, told her that he was awake and…that he wanted to see Irma. Peter Smith was called in and he said that they could see each other under supervision. Apparently, this was a crucial stage: the physical dependence was gone but the brain was another matter, not as easy to control. We knew that Steve didn't care much about himself; he always been using whatever he liked whenever he liked. It was hard to tell whether stopping was something he wanted to do at this stage. And if Steve didn't want to stop, we were in big trouble.

Veronica had been to see Irma, who was feeling rough but seemed to speak sense, at least she said she wanted to give up the drugs I decided to visit her. The best thing would be for them to be separated for a while, at least until they were both in a good head space to cope with being clean around each other.

I knocked on her door, gently. 'Hey, Irma, it's Ed.'

'Come in,' she said softly.

'I just wanted to check in on you.' She looked better; her cheeks had a faint pink colour. Still, thin as a rake.

'Thanks,' she said.

'You're looking good. How you feeling'?' I sat myself down, it was strangely calm in her room. She didn't answer me so I just sat there for a while.

'He wants to see you.' She turned around and faced me.

'I don't think that is a very good idea.' It was not the answer I expected so it took me by surprise. She continued, 'I love him but we are no good for each other. When we're together we don't need anyone else, just us

and the drugs. We will die. I am not so sure I want that.'
She turned to the other side again.

'What shall I tell him?' I asked her.

'I wrote him a note. I'll give it to Veronica; I just need to finish it.'

It's strange, when things go the way you want, somehow, it's not as satisfying as you thought it would be. I felt for Irma; she looked fragile and heartbroken, she had no friends or family around to root for her.

'Peter mentioned some clinic. Do you wanna go?'

'Yes, I think so.'

'That's really good. It's gonna be all right you know.'

I stood up and gently squeezed her hand.

'You're going to be OK. We are here for you.'

The next step was to tell Steve that Irma didn't want to see him. This might set us back a bit. I thought Veronica could tell him, she had a good way with Steve. He couldn't get as angry with her for some reason.

Irma wanted to be clean, now we needed to convince Steve. I had a feeling he was not going to have the same insight.

Veronica was apprehensive, walking into the room where Steve was, I told her I'd wait outside so I could listen in. She knew that he was more aware than he had been for a while. She'd seen Irma, she knew they were coming back into reality, at least physically. It was painful to see their frail bodies, so weak and ill, what did this drug do to people? The withdrawal I witnessed was horrific. Squirming, sweating, puking, pissing and shitting. Like a person possessed by the devil.

Steve was sleeping. She decided to sit and wait until he woke up. The room was interesting: flaky paint and posters with flowery themes. One of the posters had girls dancing in a field. Weird picture, she thought. They were wearing white dresses.

'Weird, isn't it?' Steve was awake.

'Yeah, very odd.' She turned to face him. 'I mean, who would do that? Makes no sense.'

'Lock me up in a room to stare at a poster with some virgins prancing around in a field, why don't you? Great.' At least he sounded like himself.

'How's Ted?' he said.

'Ted's good, funny and annoying. A little like you.'

Time stood still; she didn't want to take this conversation any further. She saw that Steve was better, wasn't that enough? It wasn't.

'You look better, I've missed you. I wanted to speak to you about something. It's Irma… doesn't want to see you just yet. She's going off to rehab and needs some space to figure stuff out.'

'What? Ed sent you, didn't he?' Steve was breathing a bit faster than before.

'Yeah, he did. He wanted you to understand.'

Veronica moved her chair closer to the bed, leaned over and grabbed his arms, both of them, and said, 'Ed was the one that insisted that we looked after Irma too, that she got the treatment. It is for the best. I know you don't think so right now, but it is. When you're well again, you can meet.' She stroked his cheek gently. 'For Ted, I need you to trust that you need to focus on yourself. Then, maybe later, Irma can come back.' She loved Steve like a brother and I felt my heart ache a little.

'I will try, V, I will try. I love her, though, and…I love Mum as well, I feel so..guilty, I was so bad.. and my brothers, you. Shit V, I've really fucked up.' Steve was crying, huge man tears rolling down his bony chest. Grief was gushing out of him. Finally. Veronica held him as close as she could.

'It's gonna be ok. I promise.' She reached for her pocket and pulled out the note. 'She wrote you a note.'

'Not so sure I want to read that. She's not thinking straight.'

But Steve couldn't resist the urge to read it. It wasn't what he expected. It was short and sweet:

See you on the other side lover, Irma

Chapter 17:
Doing Alice

The Hendersons were number one. I was surprised how little I cared about the success this time around. I had thought it would be sweeter, like summer rain or Jack and coke. I found myself walking around, restless and indifferent.

The success we had was the stuff that dreams are made of and enabled me to make more records, play my guitar. That part was good. I couldn't help feeling suspicious the whole time. People acted strange around me; it was confusing and very irritating. Adoration and weirdos approaching you wasn't as good as I thought it would be, sometimes it was scary. Strangers that new more about me than I did.

'Morning.' Steve was up earlier than I. Weird. It took some getting used to this new persona my brother had.

'Hey, you're early.' I made a coffee and lit a Benson.

'Yeah, been thinking. I think I'm ready. I feel like singing,' he said.

'Singing? You really think you're ready? If I tell Gavin he will start planning a t our this second. He is desperate for us to start back up. You know what the road is like...'

'Yep, I do. I miss it and I don't want to use; I feel like that is behind me.' He looked like he meant it. I guess I missed the band too and playing live was what we lived for.

As soon as I made that phone call, the machine that was The Hendersons would start rolling. The album was doing great even though we had done no promotion whatsoever. Gavin was waiting… impatiently. There was lots of money to be made and we were just sitting back, letting it happen. It irritated him greatly that the album was doing so well just on its own, without him working it.

Steve's drug abuse and recovery had been all over the press. The fans kept sending messages and Steve lapped it up. He was clean but he was still Steve. He liked the attention, he liked being a rock star, reading the stories, lapping them up like a thirsty dog. Having the four of us at home had been healing too.

When the other two woke up, we talked about what to do next. Ben was honest, leaning over the breakfast table, staring Steve straight in the eye.

'Are you sure? There are going to be people literally waiting for you to screw up so that they can write a story about it. Piranhas wanting your blood, girls wanting your body, and you can't party with them. You can't drink. Are you sure you can handle that yet?'

'Ben, try and remember that I am your *older* brother. I have had some problems but they are sorted now. I wanna sing, I miss it, I'll start drinking if I have to walk around this house another day doing fuck all, forever.' He paused and caught his breath and in a littler voice he said, 'I can't promise I will never use again but I will die if I can't sing. I'm going to have to do it at some point and if it's too much you will be the first to know.'

Steve looked fine. Fuck it, let's play.

'Why don't we go to Rick's today and have a jam, just a little jam? I'll call Matt.' My leg was twitching and I was talking a little too fast. I felt excited.

Matt had enjoyed the time off. He'd made a psychedelic solo album and was getting married to some model with red hair and milky skin.

There was a spring in our steps as we got ready to leave. I decided not to call Mike, as he would go straight on the blower to Gavin.

We'd never rehearsed the new album. We had recorded it and played a few small gigs, but then everything went wrong. We never spent time getting it right. I knew we could play some festivals if we wanted too. I wondered how Steve would sound without any substances in his body. He'd never been on a microphone sober. I knew he got courage from the booze or the drugs. Singing was for brave people, and booze had sorted that out for him. I knew he could do it. It was a Sunday, so the office was closed. I'd made sure I always had a key.

Walking into the office felt surreal. For some reason I always expected it to be the same as it was back in 1988: reggae music, waifs and strays hanging out, stinking of weed and sweat. Now it was corporate, oozing success and world domination. Desks after desks were covered with phones, piles of papers, letters and band merchandise. Walls covered in awards and gold and platinum records with our names on them, life-size pictures of each one of us looking better than we ever had in reality.

On my instructions, downstairs was left nearly the same, apart from better equipment and more stuff to make noise with. The kettle was the same, the posters, the black walls. The shitty old sofa that I had slept on a thousand nights. The floor was hoovered, I didn't like that; I wanted it to stay exactly the same.

'Such a perfect pigsty.' Fred smiled a wide grin. Steve plonked himself on the grimy sofa.

'Smells great in here.'

'It could do with a new bleeding sofa.' Ben was not as nostalgic. Now he was a law student, the rock'n'roll lifestyle was not that appealing. I needed to have a chat. Soon, I thought, not today.

'It's fucking perfect.' I was walking around turning everything on when Matt walked in.

'Hello, assholes!' I'd almost forgotten how cool he always looked, with his skinny legs, worn-out t-shirt and grey Vans. He could even get away with jewellery.

Anyhow, he walked over to the well-stacked fridge and opened a can of beer.

I nearly gave him a stern look when Steve said, 'Chill out, Granddad. I have to learn how to cope with other people drinking.'

He was right, we were in a rock band, surrounded by booze and drugs. He had to learn to cope. We couldn't protect him. He had a sponsor, someone who he could talk to, it was a girl. I didn't know what the rules were, and I think they were sleeping together, it didn't seem like the best of ideas. I had to let him manage his business, I had been told, by the experts. I was not responsible for him. Besides, Steve was an adult and he was doing well, a lot better than expected. So far, he had not spoken about Irma. He seemed to be at ease with himself, confident and caring. It was a little spooky how great he was. I had been waiting for him to mention her but he didn't. I knew it was for the best.

The PA and guitars were plugged in, the mikes were on. No one made a move towards them. We all sat around and looked at the stuff.

'We have so much stuff.' Steve said. 'Do we really need all this?'

Matt answered.

'Yes, dear singer, we do, there is no such thing as too many guitars, pedals or amps. That concept does not exist.' He continued looking pleased with himself.

'In fact, I was down in Denny Street before I came here and purchased a new Fender Strat from 1962, best buy ever.' We all cracked up laughing, which made him continue.

'I'm going to spend all my royalties on bleeding guitars. I'll have to buy a warehouse I think, just got the new royalty cheque and I can afford shit loads of guitars. Every fucking guitar in the world will be mine. Joining this band was the best decision of my life. Apart from drinking this beer, that is.' This made us laugh even more, as Matt very rarely spoke, and he was on a roll. It was great to hang out.

'It was really big, that cheque. I don't know what to do with it,' Fred continued. 'It's scary. I could probably buy an island or something.'

Ben stopped laughing.

'Let me help you, I have a plan. We have to be responsible.' That made us laugh even more. I threw a pillow at him. 'Cut it out, Ed.' Ben laughed and threw it back at me.

We were still so young, but we were richer than footballers and most people born into wealth.

'I wanna buy a fat house.' Steve looked serious.

'I know, I'm working on it for you,' I said.

Steve looked away and caught a breath and said. 'Thanks for helping but I've got this, I'm moving to the countryside. Ed, I don't wanna be in London. Freaks me out here.'

'You sure? I want you close by. There's a house further down on the....'

Steve didn't look impressed and Ben gave me a stern look. He was probably right: London was a dangerous place for him.

'OK, not too far. Don't move too far away.' The mood nearly changed.

'Fuck it, let's play.'

We all walked towards our instruments, plugged in our things. Fred started a beat on the kit, Ben added a bass line and then we all joined in, we played for hours until we had exhausted our bodies and brains. Steve's voice ripped a hole in my heart as always; the pain was there, the longing, the rawness. It was better than before and I wanted to kiss him. Even more in tune, more Steve, more heart, more everything.

'You are really great at this.' I said to him because I meant it; he was the best.

The record was itching to be played and sung. After all we'd been through, we had come out stronger than ever, more focused, more soul and with our feet firmly on the ground. After six hours we took a break. We ate some Indian food and I relaxed and had some beers. Ben and Steve went back home. Matt, Fred and I headed for Camden Town. We were in great spirits, we sounded great, we had Steve back, everything was going to be fine after all, The Hendersons were back in business. The plan had worked out and I felt lighter, happier and hopeful.

We had made it as far as Camden High Street when my phone rang. It was Gavin. He was so excited he could barely get a word out. The security guards at the studio had informed him about the rehearsal. I cut him off mid-sentence. I intended to make him stew; I was still pissed off about his handling of Steve. But the fact was that we needed him if we were going to get back out there. He made us a lot of money and kept things ticking along. I didn't have to like him to work with him. Or, as Veronica had pointed out, he worked for us and better the devil you know.

We ended up in the Good Mixer, playing pool with fans. I had learnt that was wiser to call home and warn V, so that's what I did. As I was speaking to Veronica someone tapped me on the shoulder. I knew who it was before I turned around; I could smell her, Alice. I quickly ended my phone call. She was prettier than I remembered, her eyes more sparkly than the ones that I dreamt of. She smiled.

'Hello, Ed.'. My body tingled just looking at her., I didn't remember her being this pretty. She'd cut her hair shorter; her long neck was showing and all I could think of was kissing it while she chatted to me. It had been hard resisting calling her for the last few months. I had nearly forgotten about her–nearly…

'What happened, stranger? You stopped calling.' She tilted her head.

'Yeah, sorry about that, I lost my phone.' Matt was calling me back to the pool table. I ignored him. I had to pull myself together.

'You want a drink?' That's better Ed.

'Yes, gin and tonic, please.' I ordered her a double.

The rest of the night I talked to Alice, avoiding the evil glances from Fred, fans and groupies. I could have been anywhere. She was telling me how her art degree was harder work then she thought it would be and how her flatmate had a drinking problem. She told me her mother was insane and that her dream was to move to the sea. I didn't say much, I didn't want to, in case I would ruin it. We were in a bubble. It was getting late; the others had already left. I asked Alice to take a walk with me. We strolled up to Primrose Hill, all the way to the top. I'd bought a bottle of Champagne in the off-licence.

'The BT tower looks so cool,' she said and laughed and I laughed too but I don't know why.

We sat down on a park bench, ignoring the view, we were staring at each other instead. Like teens, like fools. I touched her hand, her leg, we kissed. I felt as if I could tell her everything. I was drunker than I thought, she made me feel carefree, passionate, uninhibited and greedy. I knew I was going too far, but I couldn't stop. Her body was warm and willing and I was ridden with lust. I needed more of her. This was trouble. The kind of trouble I wanted to get into.

In the taxi home, I smelt her on my hands. Windows opened and deep breathing. I had to try to pretend that nothing had happened. I wasn't a good liar; I was hoping she would be asleep. Veronica, that is. I sneaked carefully up the path, put the key gently in the lock and tiptoed in like a burglar. I headed straight for the bathroom, cleaned myself up, brushed my teeth, threw my clothes in the wash basket.

Alice…sweet, addictive and insatiable. I went downstairs to my studio and started to play. I stayed for hours. I wrote a song about her. I was trying to work out if I felt guilty. I thought it over for a while: I didn't, or was I confusing guilt with regret?

I didn't regret being with her, or what we did for one second. It was confusing, like romantic love always is. I wasn't so sure V would ever understand this. In fact, I was pretty sure she never would. How could I convince her that we were better off as friends? I didn't want Ted to leave the house, I didn't want to lose my son. But I needed to be with Alice again, desperately. I knew that I didn't want to be dishonest. I drank red wine until the morning arrived. I needed to figure out what was the right thing to do. Battling with my conscience was hell, especially as I felt ecstatic after my night underneath the stars. Alice… you ruined everything.

These days Steve felt great. The birds were singing and he could hear them clearly, the rain was falling and he noticed without the haze of drugs clouding his mind. Being straight was great; the people at the clinic didn't make that part up. Living at Ed and V's wasn't the best; he never felt like he was part of that gang. They all pussyfooted around him like he had cancer; it was irritating as hell. Just because he'd got sober didn't make him a completely different person. He needed to get out of there. Sell that stinky drug den he used to live in and start a new life. He missed singing, standing on stage, being adored by fans. Even though the thought slightly terrified him, he was desperate to get back out there. He was the same person. He was ready. He was restless, he needed hobbies and fast, otherwise he would call a dealer; his old life was only a phone call away. He'd thought about the country. His mate from the rooms that he liked wanted to move out to the green trees and fields and that was what he wanted too.

Weirdly enough, the thought of Irma terrified him. He kept on dreaming about her and her waif-like body; she looked dead in the dreams. Perhaps she was dead. He didn't want to know. He wanted to move on, start his own life. He felt new, a huge amount of money in his account and endless possibilities. He was starting to plot his new life. Steve Henderson was a proper person. The most surprising thing was that he really liked himself like this. It never occurred to him that being straight might feel nice. But it did.

Chapter 18:
Being a Dirty Dog

The machine was in full swing. Tour dates, TV performances, interviews and videos. The lot. We were being picked up at eight every morning and did not finish until well into the small hours. It was hectic and I enjoyed it, more this time than I ever had. Our world tour was going to start in a few months and I wouldn't be at home that much. I put my plan to speak to Veronica on hold. Ted and V would be in London and I would be travelling around the world. I was being a two-timing asshole but I couldn't stop. I was scared to hurt V and terrified to lose Ted. I needed to work this out so that Veronica would be spared any unnecessary pain. Hurting Veronica wasn't something I wanted to do. Thinking about betraying her was painful but I felt as if I didn't have a choice.

It was strange with Alice. I couldn't help myself with her. I wanted her all the time and I had her all the time. In loos, buses, TV studio dressing rooms and in the recording studio. She never asked any questions; she was easy-going and fun. I couldn't get enough, there wasn't enough of her; I wanted more. We drank a lot together, partied, enjoyed the perks of being famous. I had never taken part in before and it was fun, really fun. The drunk people I used to avoid were now my friends. Being with

Alice made life carefree, something I never had experienced before. She would whisper challenges in my ear, make me steal stuff in shops, touch my privates under the table, making my body feel as if it was loaded with electricity.

She never asked me about Veronica and Ted and I never mentioned them, which made it easy for me to keep the two lives separate. She was hanging around a lot and I knew it was getting obvious to everyone what was going on. We were in love and it showed. Steve and Matt were oblivious but Fred and Ben were starting to give me and her dirty looks. They use to like Alice, there wasn't anything to dislike about her, but they loved V and were protective of her.

'Ed, man, cut it out.' Ben hissed as I was in mid snog with Alice.

'Show some fucking respect.' He stormed out of the dressing room.

'Go after him. He's upset.' Alice demanded; I wasn't used to that.

'You gotta talk to him.'

'What do you know?' I asked.

'I know he's upset because we spoke about it a couple of days ago. I made it clear that it was your business. You never talk about your family so I assumed you were single. If you wanna be with me then you have to sort out your problems. It's not my business. I'm only with you, I don't have a family holed up at home somewhere. You do. Your problem.'

'You know that I live with V and we have a son.' It was hard to say this to her as I had separated the two just beautifully in my mind. Two completely separate things. I tried to calm down.

'It's not your fault Alice, I know, it's. It's hard my problem. V, the boys and I grew up together. We're family. And I really love my son and I don't want to lose him.'

'You and I are different. I'm mad about you, I wanna rip your clothes off now and always, I laugh at stupid things with you, you make me feel better.'

We locked eyes and then lips and I was putty in her hands. I had to talk to Ben but the thought of facing up to this was unbearable to think of. I stood up and left to find Ben; a good place to start to clean up my mess.

'Ben. I don't know what to say.'

'What's wrong with you and your head sometimes.'

'It's not as easy as that. Things are different with V and me after, you know…' I mumbled.

'I knew you were going to blame that. That ship has sailed. It doesn't give *you carte blanche* to be a complete wanker. What about Ted?'

I couldn't think what to say, he was right. The press was whispering about Alice and me. V was going to find any day soon one way or another. In fact, she probably already knew. She'd been acting odd recently, putting lipstick on, wearing clothes she knew I liked. Plus, she probably knew something was up because I avoided being alone in bed with her.

'I'm going to talk to her. I'm mad for Alice that's all. I can't help myself. I didn't plan it. It just happened.'

Ben looked indifferent.

'I don't care, just sort it. It's out of order. You have to be honest.'

I decided to walk home, so I could figure out how what to do. I ended up in a pub. I ordered a bottle of red wine and some crisps. I got a pen and paper out and started to write a letter.

Veronica
I have met another girl and I think I'm in love with her.

Rubbish, I started again

Veronica
My feelings for you have changed and I think I need some space. I will always look after you and Ted and we will always be a family.

Fuck.

This letter is very hard for me to write. Sorry Veronica, I can't do this anymore. I haven't been honest with you, not for a long time. I've met someone else and been seeing her behind your back. She is not the only reason I want to end it. It hasn't been the same for a long time. You and Ted are everything to me, I mean that, but somehow, we've grown apart. There are no excuses for how I've behaved and I hope you can forgive me. I want to be friends as I will always love you.

That would do. There was nothing I could write that would make this excusable. Writing this stupid letter was a start. I was too scared to face her; the words wouldn't come out. This way she would know and then we could talk.

I made it back to Hampstead, I had drunk too much, I stumbled up the walkway. The key wouldn't go in the door. In the end Veronica opened it for me.

'Hey. Oh…you're pissed. Surprise, surprise…' She didn't look angry. I wanted her to look angry so that I could get angry. She looked sweet and disappointed. Loyal, pure and safe. This was not the time to tell her or give her a stupid letter so I passed her and made my way towards the stairs.

'I need to sleep.' I stumbled up to our bedroom and passed out.

As I opened my eyes, still in my clothes, no shoes though, it took a while to process what had happened last night. A heavy feeling was suddenly upon me. I was too tired to do this anymore. The bands schedule was frantic plus my double life was stressful as hell.

I had to do the right thing, I remembered the letter and started to look for the piece of paper but couldn't find it anywhere. Where was my jacket? Shit. My jeans pocket, no, not there either. I could hear Ted crying downstairs. There was someone scuffling about. Fuck. In the jacket, must be in the jacket, where is it? I stood up and made it to the bathroom and looked myself in the eye. I was a mess, dark circles and greasy hair, my breath sour.

Not good. I brushed my teeth and splashed some water in my face, I had to find the letter. I must have dropped it. I wasn't ready to tell her. Not today, I had to feel stronger, I was too weak. I needed a fag and some liquid. My bloodshot eyes looked back at me in the mirror as if to say, 'You're a real idiot, Ed, a real prime idiot.'

Ted was now screaming. He never cried like that. I decided to go downstairs, I sensed trouble and I knew it was too late to run away, which would be my preferred way to cope.

Ted was sitting in his highchair so I picked him up. He calmed down and said, 'Dada.' I was looking around for my jacket.

'Hey, little man,' I cuddled my son, I could sense Veronica's presence behind me.

'Looking for this?' She was holding the letter.

'I found it in your pocket.' She stared right at me, steely-eyed and stern.

I wanted to tell her it was a mistake, lie more, just to get out of this. Ted was quiet, resting his chin on my shoulder. Veronica took Ted from my arms.

'I know, it's really crap, I know that. I don't know what to say...I'm sorry.'

'Yes, it is crap, it's crap because *you* are sleeping with somebody else. Don't you think I've noticed?'

'Why didn't you ask me? If you knew.'

'I was waiting for you to tell me. I know I did wrong before. But now, with Ted, us, the family, how could you do this to *us*?'

'V, we are always going to be a family. I've changed, you've changed, that's all. We were kids.'

'I haven't changed. You've just become a wanker, that's all. A Cocaine talking vacuous asshole. I never thought I'd see the day your feet left the ground. You think your hot stuff.'

I wanted her to be angrier, crazier, slap my face, throw a vase at the wall, scream wicked insults. It was worse, she was dignified and cool. I felt like a dick, it was all my fault, but somehow I had managed to ignore that.

'I want to move out. Ted and I will move out. To-day.' She tried to look strong but her bottom lip was quiv-ering.

'No, no, you don't have to do that. This is your house, I will go, I'll move out.' I meant it.

'You can have the house. I don't care about this place, and Ted was born here. It's yours.'

'Perfect, sorted… so you can go and live with that slut, feeling all generous and full of yourself?'

'No, so that we can have some time apart to work out how we are gonna do this. There's Ben and Fred to think about as well.'

'You have changed for the worst and it's a little fucking late to pretend to be considerate. Now be so kind and fuck off out of my face.' She was about to lose it and when V lost it there was unhinged wildness exploding, it was animalistic and scary, so I decided to do as I was told. I felt scared and a little relieved. I practically ran out the door.

'Leave, you fucking loser,' she snapped.

I ran up the stairs, put a t-shirt on and practically ran out the door, adrenaline pumping through me. I went to Hampstead Heath. I wanted to call someone who would be on my side. I couldn't think of anyone.

I went to the pub and ordered a bottle of Chianti and drank it on my own, my brain switched off. I fell in with some local pissheads and ended up talking rubbish with them. It was getting dark and I genuinely did not know what to do with myself. I was too drunk, sitting in a pub with drunk strangers. Perhaps I was becoming a proper Henderson, a fuck-up. I needed a friend, a real friend. I couldn't call Alice, it felt wrong, disrespectful. The only person I could think of was Matt.

I reached for my phone, which had thirty missed calls from various people I didn't want to talk to.

'Hey, mate.' I was relieved he picked up, he sounded sleepy but he was my only hope.

'Hey, I'm in a pub by the ponds in Hampstead. Can you come over here?'

'What's up mate? You sound pissed.'

'Hammered.'

'Oh, you're OK?'

'No'

'What's happened?'

'Veronica, she found out… about Alice, she's real mad.' The line went quiet.

'Where are you? I'm coming.'

I gave him my whereabouts, sat back and sipped my third or maybe fourth bottle of Chianti. For some reason it didn't hit the sides with all the adrenaline that was pumping through my veins.

By the time Matt got to me I was leaning up against the wall to stay upright. I was drunker than ever, I was slurring, a sorry sight. My brain was not thinking straight. I wanted to see Alice and I wanted to go home to my house with V and Ted waiting for me with open arms. I wanted it all the way it was. This wasn't an option anymore, my heart was beating fast and I felt lost, I wanted to cry. Everyone kept on telling me I was a genius. It's hard to admit that I was affected; I was clearly was as I thought I could behave the way I had, I felt like an idiot.

Matt arrived and took one look at my sorry ass and got me a pint of water. He sat down next to me with pint of lager and said, 'So, the shit hit the fan?'

'Yep, it's been coming for a while, I really messed up.'

'Why do you always give yourself such a hard time? You're twenty-three, not forty-five. People break up. Relax, it'll be fine. You want a line? In fact, you need a line, you are drunk my friend.'

I accepted., desperate to sober up. I went off to the loo and snorted a massive line. It felt good. I could speak again. On my way back to the seat I grabbed another bottle of red and sat down next to Matt.

'In a way, I'm relieved. Lying is hard, it's exhausting.'

I was surprised how sober I felt, and chatty. Perhaps drugs weren't so bad after all.

We stayed until closing time. If I could just feel exactly like this forever, then all would be just fine. I could just stay here with my glass and my fast-beating heart and the urge to speak too much forever. It was perfect. Time flew by, I never needed to sleep, I was awake.

Matt took charge as we were getting chucked out of the pub. It was midnight. I didn't have anywhere to go, nowhere appropriate, so I started ranting about hotels.

'Even a Holiday Inn would do. We could raid the minibar.'

'Come and stay at mine. We can drink more there.'

Mike turned up as if by magic, he took us to Matt's new Gothic mansion in Haverstock Hill. His pretty wife took one look at us then left us to it, we drank and snorted coke till the sun came up. In the end I collapsed on the sofa; I don't think I have ever talked as much shit as I did that night.

'Ed Henderson, you are losing it,' was the thought that swayed past my brain as I started to doze off as the sweet Rohypnol kicked in, making me feel tired even though my heart was beating fast and hard.

Chapter 19:
Turning into an idiot.

Being a twat came easier to me then I had hoped for. I was taking to it like a duck to water. Me being in love with Alice, me leaving Veronica and feeling relieved about it. Me… It was all about fucking me. I was obsessed with my personal life, I never thought that would happen, but it did. I kept on having out-of-body experiences while I was talking to people. I had opinions on things I knew nothing about and people took it as gospel, I felt important.

Everything I had disliked about Steve was now who I was turning in to. Not the heroin thing, but everything else. Fame was the worst drug. It was making me do things I never thought I'd do and Alice liked it. My confidence was disgustingly good. Somewhere deep inside I was shivering with embarrassment, usually for about twenty minutes after I woke up, then I was back in the carousel, making plans with Alice, desperate to please her.

Alice and I became a pair of media darlings; everything we did was reported in the tabloids, they were camped outside our place around the clock. It wasn't Alice's fault; she was a good time girl with an impressionable brain. She liked the attention; she was used to it but not on this scale and it was making her want more and more . I was madly in love with her and anything she wanted I would have gone along with. Not that she was a bad person, she was nice but she swam on the surface and did so with grace.

The grounding that Veronica and Ted provided was no longer there so I had *carte blanche* to conveniently forget the important things, stuff that had mattered most to me up until I'd met Alice. I did see Ted, every week, if we weren't touring. He was now three years old. He was the only grounding I had in my now very shallow life. Looking at him made me happy, he was perfect. He looked just like me and I guess that felt good. To my credit, I was always there for him, I didn't mess that up, not yet.. I had made a promise to give him the good upbringing I had never had and I intended to keep to that.

Veronica, Ted and the boys had stayed on in Hampstead; I had never felt that at home there so I guess it was for the best. Ted had a full-time nanny who ferried him between V and me. She managed the communication between us and for now that was the best solution. V hated Alice and she still thought I was the biggest prick in the world.

Alice and I had moved into a place in Primrose Hill. It was tall and narrow, rickety and full of characters, with red walls and seventies interiors bought in Camden market by an extravagant French dude that Alice hired. It was hip and my girl was good at making it look cool.

She'd purchased large David Bowie prints and Egg chairs, fluffy rugs and chandeliers. We had a walk-in wardrobe leading to the en-suite bathroom, which was massive, the bath had a scull tiled into the bottom and we installed a steam room shower too, I had never been in such a cool house before and now I lived in it. Ted had a huge bedroom and a ridiculously kitted-out playroom. Alice liked Ted, which was pretty much a deal breaker. That being said, she never looked after him, as I spent every minute I could with him. I didn't even need the nanny who was hired to tend to his every need, I really loved being with my son. Saying that, It was probably a good thing to have the nanny, as the parties escalated most evenings from a quiet drink to a full-on all-nighter. The mornings were tough but I got up to hang with Ted. We were young so we could handle it, I guess. We made lots of new friends, most of them were successful trendy people, just like us. We were having fun, drinking and taking cocaine and popping pills like there was no tomorrow. There was a tomorrow, though, there always was, and I coped with it fine. Like I always did.

Fred and Ben had accepted Alice and liked her enough now to come and hang out. It had taken some time but now we were back on track. We were all getting on with it. Ben had dumped his nerdy girlfriend and was starting to hang around with us. I was happy about that; I had missed him. After the break-up they refused to talk to me for six months. They sided with V, but after a while there was no side to take as Veronica and I had broken up and there was no going back on that. I had given her the house and plenty of money. Financially I had behaved like a gentleman. One day I hoped Veronica and I could be friends. I missed her, the familiarity, her smell and laugh. I reached for the phone to call and explain myself but I knew she could never truly forgive me. She was never going to be the same Veronica. I had lost her and it was all my fault.

Alice, on the other hand, with her easy-going personality and fun-loving ways, had opened a whole new life for me, one where I could forget that I was an orphan from Kilburn. Perhaps music wasn't the only thing that mattered; perhaps sometimes you could just not give a shit about anything or anyone. The world was not weighing down on your shoulders and laughing at stupid things was in fact fine.

Every morning I would wake up first and make it down to our basement kitchen. I made Alice a cup of Earl Grey tea with one sugar and a piece of toast with marmite. The mornings offered the silence and the scope for thinking. I had my moments. If Ted wasn't there I would miss him terribly. I would think about what he would be like when he grew up.

This particular morning I found Ben on the large brown kitchen sofa, fast asleep. I gently nudged him and handed him a cuppa.

'Morning dude.'

'Man, don't wake me up. Just fell asleep'

'Have some tea, it's ten you fool.'

I sat myself down next to him. Slowly he made awake movements and started to sip some tea.

'Now that was a good party, you guys know how to throw a party.' he said.

'Yeah, it was all right.' I handed him an Alka-Seltzer. 'Drink this, it will sort you out.'

I felt forgiven and it felt good, like we were back on track. I respected Ben, if he disapproved I knew I had messed up. He had managed to stay focused through all the shit without cracking up; it was impressive.

He was about to graduate, actually becoming a proper lawyer. He had done all this while the band had been in full swing. I had no idea what the plan was with his studies. We never spoke about it; he kept it separate to the band and the family. Perhaps he felt he would hurt my feelings if he said he wanted to hang up his bass guitar and be a normal person. I respected him because I knew he would tell me when he was ready. He was way smarter than any of us; it was strange to think he was born into the same family as the rest of us.

'So, can I throw you a graduation party? Alice and I could do it here.'

'Yeah, that would be great. It's in a couple of months, you know.' Then he went quiet.

'Actually Ed, perhaps it's not a good idea. I would have to invite Veronica. I mean, I don't have to, but I want her there. She's been amazing, helping me study and encouraging me the whole way. Without her I couldn't have finished the course.'

'Why don't I talk to her? Perhaps we could do it somewhere else and we could all be there. I mean, we are going to have to be able to see each other. What if Ted got married?'

We laughed.

'Nah, don't worry about that, he's gay.'

'Fuck off.' I threw a pillow on his face.

'Like his dad.' I threw another pillow at him.

'Fuck right off.'

Alice walked in, wearing her vintage silk robe, she looked fresh, even though she went to bed at five.

'What's so funny?'

'Ben is saying that Ted is gay.'

Alice smiled, I was defenceless when she smiled, and I would do anything to see it over and over again. Why was she so addictive? It amazed me how she managed to always look so perfect without even trying after a big night, she was supernatural. She did things to my brain I didn't think I was capable of. I wanted to grab her and take her right back to bed. I reached for her arm and pulled her down on my lap, holding onto her, smelling her back like a freak. She wasn't like any other human; Alice just smelt like Alice, and I was obsessed with her.

Today would be another day with my girl, where we would do something that she suggested, usually check out an art gallery or go shopping followed by a lunch in a pub with some of our friends. She handled all the social engagements. I was ferried along like some sort of prized possession. I did enjoy it; I was with her and I didn't have to think about anything, she even told me what to wear. It was all fun, fun and more frigging fun. Gavin would liaise with her if there were any work I needed to do. I was their puppet. Today was no different: our local pub, some actors, our regular coke dealer. who had become more like a mate. He cashed in thousands a week on our party lifestyle.

The previous night he had left early, one in the morning to be precise. A couple of hours later we had run out of coke and wanted some more. There were ten people in the house and we were talking shit and listening to records. There was no reason to break up the party, so Alice called the guy, knowing he would happily get out of bed to accommodate our every wish, bring us more talking powder. And we were desperate, it was very moreish.

'You're not going to believe this.' Alice appeared in the living room with a massive grin on her face. Like she'd won the lottery or something.

'What baby?' She looked so pleased with herself I was eager to find out what happened.

'He's only gone and hidden some grams in the hallway.'

We all started to cheer and clap, high fiving each other, man hugging.

'He's so great, he knew we would be calling so he prepared by hiding three grams by the front door on the third shelf to save himself the journey over. What a genius. I just love that guy.' She was now waving the three grams in front of my face.

'Now, that's a professional if ever I've met one. What an amazing guy.'

I grabbed a gram and started to crush the rock with my bankcard. I used a twenty-pound note to pulverise the little rocks, then I chopped lines out on the glass table with brass corners in our front room. Alice rolled up a note and I chopped away on the little rocks to make sure we had a smooth powder. It was good stuff. I took a deep breath as I snorted it deep into my nasal passage.

The party got back into full swing. We listened to the whole of *Dark Side of the Moon* and a few of us discussed it until the early hours of the morning.

This drug made me come out of my shell, talking to people and making new friends every night. There was no end to how much we could get, I was a rock star and everyone wanted to be my mate. I was trying to see how far I could take it and I discovered that it was a lot further than I thought anyone would be prepared to go. I never behaved like that and I didn't understand why anyone would but they did. It was enjoyable to feel power. I was flirting with arrogance. People were impressed by our success. To me, it was work and I was enjoying the perks. That's what I kept telling myself anyhow.

The night ended when the coke was finished and we necked a Diazepam or two each. We slept like logs after some weird sex that I couldn't get enough of. I recalled it involved red lips and stockings, spanking and a few toys. I got hard thinking about it the day after. More. I wanted much more of everything.

I sat up straight as a ramrod, realising that it was the afternoon; Ted was coming around and the house was a minefield of empty booze bottles and drug paraphernalia. I called Gavin and he arranged for a cleaner to come. In a few hours it looked like nothing happened, like it did every ordinary day. Alice had booked a massage and some guy came around and made us some kale juice and some healthy food. I wanted a bacon sarnie and a fizzy drink but Alice probably knew best. Ted arrived and suddenly it felt like we were a normal family again. Perhaps tonight we could watch a film and chill. Just the three of us.

'Alice let's watch a film after Ted's gone to bed and have an early night. I'm knackered.'

She smiled at me, that irresistible smile.

'I would love that, but, I don't know Ed, I've been invited out. You want to hang with Ted right? You don't mind...do you? I feel so great after that juice we had.

Rejuvenated even.' She was dancing around the room and I wondered where she got the energy from.

I started to fidget. I didn't want her to go out without me.

'Course, cool, where you going?' I asked

She started to tell me about some awards ceremony for a magazine that I never read. She was going with her best friend, whom I was starting to dislike as she was always around or on the other end of the telephone or on her way to our house. I wished she would clear off, leave us alone. It was that green-eyed monster again.

The American tour was coming up and we were starting rehearsals in Camden in a few weeks. We had rented a massive warehouse. Roadies, soundmen, tea getters and bum wipers were on hand 24/7. It was our first major American arena tour, so there was a lot of money and high expectations riding on it. We nearly had a sensible band now. Matt and his wife were expecting a baby and he was completely devoted to her. Steve was staying clean. Ben and Fred were the same, and then there was me, Ed, the ex-goody-two-shoes turned shallow party guy. It was getting close to another collision with myself, another confrontation with the real me.

I was scared I would lose Alice if the parties stopped. She loved it, she loved all our celebrity friends and she scanned the papers every day to see if were in them. I didn't want to push her away so I didn't stop her.

I was worried about the tour too; she had started to say she wanted to stay in London for some of it and fly out and join me now and again. Give me some space, she said, I didn't want fucking space. I didn't feel comfortable with her in London. I wanted her with me.

The thought of losing her made me feel anxious, and far too often I felt close to panic and I calmed myself with beer. Not that she did anything to make me feel like that. It was all me. She made me feel vulnerable, on the edge of losing control because I couldn't control her. If she was in the room I would always know where, as I would keep her movement in the corner of my eye. Other girls tried to get my attention regularly but there was no room in my screwed-up head for anyone else. I guess I was like that with Veronica, before the Matt thing. The difference was that Veronica and I weren't as physical as Alice and I were, and Alice was not as available. Her body drove me insane, I wanted her constantly.

She didn't have the same thirst for me as I did for her; she was cooler, at least these days. Alice wasn't screwed up; she came from a nice secure family, nice married living parents. She didn't understand why anyone would feel scared or abandoned. She was confident; there was no reason why she wouldn't chat with other men, she was with me and she had no intention of leaving me. She didn't get why I felt lost, like Veronica used to. We never really talked about why or how I was orphaned or where I came from. We mostly spoke about her and her perfect life, which intrigued me greatly, I thought that was the kind of life that existed in the movies. Clearly not. Alice wasn't messed up and it fascinated me. She was pure, no strange hidden agendas or wounded anxiety. This is what I wanted for Ted; to be liberated from all the pain that the boys and I had endured. In a drunk state I asked myself if had I finally started to mourn my childhood and my mother? I had never stopped to think about it before. The drink and the drugs made me, they made me dwell on things, and dig into my murky past. About the days when I looked after the boys and pretended I was their parent. I kept on going, working towards my goal. The party life made me feel vulnerable and emotional and I questioned my life whereas before I had accepted it. I found myself talking to strangers at parties about how I looked after my family when I was a teen and the next morning feeling dirty as I revealed too much. I'd always been a private person, someone who didn't share much. Now I would tell people my darkest deepest secrets at the drop of a hat. Part of me loved it, it was like therapy, I guess. It felt good talking about it. At the same time, it was no one's goddamn business and it wasn't my style. Confusing as it was, it was what was going on, my life seemed to be spiralling into a brand-new direction and I wasn't sure it was the right one.

The tour was just around the corner. I was picked up every morning to the rehearsal space, I was always last to arrive and usually the only one with a raging hangover, shaky hands and stinking breath. Steve was always there first, perky and enthusiastic. Fred was there early too, warming up his Ludwig kit, pleased with the purple-blue colour. He was so into playing these days; drumming had become even more what he lived for. He reminded me of how I use to feel about my guitar before I met Alice, he'd started to sing too and he was alright. We were getting close to the end of the rehearsals, and our tour started in a few weeks. I was deep into thinking about the set list when Ben turned up.

'Hello there. Let me look at that.' He snatched it from me.

'Hey.' I felt grumpy, glared at him.

'That isn't right. Let me fix it. You're not thinking straight, as per usual these days.' I didn't protest. It was always my job to decide what order we played the songs in. I couldn't even do that right. He finished it and made it better.

'I graduate tomorrow,' he said.

'You what?'

Damn, I knew about this. I'd forgotten. Shit. I jumped up on stage, grabbed the mike

'Listen up everybody. Tomorrow, Ben Henderson, my little brother, will become an actual man of the law. Not a copper because that would be wrong but, a lawyer.' Everyone stopped what they were doing and gathered round Ben, who was grinning from ear to ear. I could tell most of them knew about it but even so they let me take the lead. I continued my charade and pretended to be an interviewer.

' Ben, come up here…What did you get?'

'A fucking first.' Ben smiled. And everyone roared.

I grabbed my guitar and did a ridiculous guitar sole a 'la, Yngwie Malmsteen style, and everyone was in stitches.

'We have to celebrate,' I said and hugged him.

Ben was clearly amused and calmly said,

'We need to practise, and the graduation is tomorrow. I wanted to know if you wanted to come and get me. Fred, Ben, Matt, Steve and Veronica are all coming. Then we are having lunch. So rehearsals will start a bit later.'

'Fuck rehearsal. We have to celebrate that you are the first Henderson to ever have become anything proper. I think it is called an academic, a word very rarely uttered in our humble tribe.' I was on form, like a clown, entertaining the troops. Everyone laughed, even Steve.

We all played together and as per the norm the band gelled and everything made sense. Music was so simple, a relationship I could handle, one that never faltered. Even in hard times, as soon as we had our instruments in hand we didn't need to speak, we knew. My addled soul was currently hard to reach but when we played I felt the happiest.

It was the graduation morning and Alice had just come home from the previous night's party. I had Ted so I didn't go out plus I was tired. She fell asleep, fully clothed on our bed. Last night I had Spoken to Veronica and we had decided that it was time to finally get over the past and move forward. It had made me so happy that she was willing to give me a chance. She even said for me to bring Alice along. The lunch started in two hours and Alice was completely gone. I blasted Positively 4th Street on the speakers the loudest I could.

This time I sang along the loudest I could. She woke up and came down the stairs looking half asleep.

'Ed, what the fuck? I'm trying to sleep.'

I turned the music down, tilted my head to one side and glared at her. Took a minute to check out my girlfriends' state, with her make-up still on from last night, breath like a brewery. For the first time she looked not so hot.

'I've been trying to wake you up. We are going to Ben's graduation; we have to be there in one hour. Get your skates on.' I tried hard not to sound angry, because it wasn't my style.

She started to dance to the music, miming the lyrics and slowly taking her clothes off, she was still drunk.

She was naked and moving towards me and I forgot about the bad makeup and the stinky breath.

'We really need to leave soon.' I tried to sound strict but my voice failed me. I tried my hardest not to get drawn in by her charms. It was impossible. I started to smirk. Damn it. I cleared my throat.

'Seriously Alice, we need to go.' It was pointless; I was hers to do what she pleased with.

We had sex on the kitchen worktop and it was explosive because I was irritated with her. I quickly pulled my trousers up, looked at my watch. 'Shit, we're supposed to be there now, we're going to miss it.' I called for the nanny, who hesitantly walked into the kitchen, having probably seen something she shouldn't have.

'Where's Ted?' I cried.

'He's ready and waiting.' She said ,sounding unamused.

'Let's go.'

I looked at Alice. She was in no state to meet Veronica.

'See you later, babe. Get some rest.' She was already half asleep.

The college was in Hanover Square, and the driver stepped on it, we got there just as Ben came out wearing a silly gown and hat. I thought he looked cool but Fred kept on wolf whistling like a kid. Ben was grinning from ear to ear; he could not give a shit what anyone thought of him. He had achieved a rock star lifestyle alongside academic success. Something I could never do.

Veronica looked beautiful, fresh and classy, like she always did. Ted was in heaven hanging out with the both of us and for a minute I imagined what life could have been like. The boys, Ted, Veronica and I, all one happy family

Matt was there too, with his new-born baby and wife, and Nana of course. Gavin, Mike and everyone else in The Hendersons' gang. I looked around and I felt happy, happier in a different way from how my current life made me feel.

Veronica had arranged a feast at a nearby French restaurant, Nana had her steel drums set up, and the mix was silly and put as all in a celebratory mood. Fred and Nana had a steelpan off and we all cheered, it was a great time. I tried to call Alice to say to come down but she didn't answer. I told V that she was ill.

We had an amazing evening and I learnt a lot about Ben's and his secret life, how hard he had worked for this. I asked him the question I had wanted to ask him for the last ten years, since he first started to study with the goal of becoming a lawyer.

'What's the plan? You know, with the lawyer thing.' The table went a little quieter. The million-dollar question.

'You mean if I'm leaving the band?'

'I guess,' I said, trying to sound cool.

'It's hard. I want to do both.' Everyone started to clap, then we all stood up cheered like bunch of freaks.

'Thank fuck for that.' Matt was hugging him.

'I was worried this was like a leaving do, all serious and shit.' He went over and hugged Nana, who had had far too much champagne and was now letting out little snoring sounds, she's fallen asleep on her chair.

'I love The Hendersons, I couldn't live without music, this is my back-up plan,' Ben explained.

Everyone started to chant:

'Speech! Speech! Speech!' Ben stood up reluctantly.

'I just want to thank all of you, especially Veronica. She's been a great support and I guess you are the closest thing to a mum I have. A fucking hot one I'd liked to add. Also, I wanted to announce another achievement. I passed my driving test, first ever Henderson to do so. (Everyone cheered.) I have also bought my first house. In Camber Sands, on the beach. And…I am flying to the moon and you are all invited! That's all. Oh, and The Hendersons are number one… again.' Everyone clapped.

'Camber, really?'

'Yep, Camber. I found a beach house there. It's bought.'

'One of the ones on the actual beach?' I said.

'Yep, the ones we use to walk past and dream of. It's like a boy-from-Kilburn done good, kinda thing.' We smiled because I knew exactly what he meant.

'You've done more than good. It's like a fucking miracle more like.'

It was the perfect afternoon. Veronica took Ted off me and I got into a car; headed to Primrose hill and for the first time I wondered whether I had done the right thing, leaving V.

Chapter 20:
Oh, How the Tables Have Turned!

Steve was living in the countryside, clean and living with the sponsor girl he had met in rehab. She was sweet-looking, a blonde with a raspy voice and high cheek-bones. When she spoke she always said, 'don't you think?' after every sentence. He had tried to reach Irma after the six months that she asked him for. She wasn't interested and neither was he.

She'd gone and lived in a Christian community, learnt the accordion and played with her Church band, spreading the word. They were called 'Jesus Angels'. Quite funny, he thought. Irma had moved on, she had a new vice, the Lord, and he was more addictive then rock'n'roll and the brown junk. It couldn't have worked out better for the two addicts; together they could only make trouble, without each other they had a better chance for a life worth living.

The new girl, Gloria, was sweet, an ex-cokehead and alcoholic, never a junkie, so the temptation wasn't there to use heroin. They had bought some chickens and the egg laying had become Steve's new obsession. The names and breed and how many eggs they would produce would be the regular topic of their conversation. He had a chart in his chicken den and it was incredibly precise.

'How many chickens did Laila lay?' he would shout to Gloria.

'Only three. I'm worried for her. She always lays six.'

Steve would log the laying and so it continued. The house was cosy and manor like.

He was into eating organic produce so he grew his own veg, he'd also started running, six miles per day at least; he was fit. The change was miraculous and resulted in a movie star image. His voice was greater than ever too. On the odd occasion he would come up to London, meet up with Ed at Mildred's, a vegan restaurant in Soho. They would drink green juice and eat lentil curry, Ed hated it but he still came along. Steve knew it freaked the brothers out so he would exaggerate his lifestyle in front of them as it amused him. He *was* transformed, he had started drinking and smoking when he was a kid so no one ever knew what he was really like. It turned out he liked being straight, he was a square guy these days. He's started to talk about their mother a lot, remind Ben and Fred and Ed about her, of the sacrifices she had made, he even surprised himself with how much he remembered about her. Steve had taken the time to work out why he was messed up, the deaths, the depression and the struggle their poor mother had to face all on her own, his guilt over his own behaviour. Now that he was

out on the other side, an aura of calm surrounded him
and he was soothing to be around. He had made a proper
life that he loved.

He observed Ed sitting opposite him, the messy
one of the brothers these days, partying like a prime idiot.
Steve wanted to tell him what he saw, he wanted to shake
him, but there was no use, not yet. It was weird to think
this was how he must have looked when he was off the
rails. Ed was not ready but it was obvious the shoe was
on the other foot now. He made a note to be there for him
when the time came. It wasn't far off now; he was in a
real bad way, close to rock bottom.

I was forgetting the important things that had always kept me grounded and inspired. My drug of choice
was killing my creativity and every day was the same. It
was like black was no longer black, more like grey, and
white had turned into a dull cream.

It didn't matter much though, on the outside I was
coping fine, my job was organised by various people, I
had money on the bank and when it really mattered, I was
always there, a carbon copy of myself. Ted had the Swedish nanny, I kept to all the arrangements I made with V
but I was finding it harder to cope with him without help.
I was functioning at an acceptable level.

I was constantly obsessing about Alice and her
social calendar. I guess it was my social scene too but I
always felt a bit more like an accessory or an outsider.

She was comfortable talking to anyone and spent her time working the room away from me. I was a paranoid mess who got high and then shared information with strangers that was no business of theirs.

The parties kept happening and I was shuffled around, with a drink in my hand and a nose full of cocaine. There was a small chunk left of the old me, this part would come out when I was hanging out with Ted. The brothers and Matt weren't around anymore because I felt embarrassed of my constant hangover or being too high to care about them. I was that wrapped up in my vacuous life; myself and Alice's. The surroundings were closing in on me and I was becoming paranoid, stressing about everything and thinking about stuff I had never cared about before. Intrigues between people and gossip would regularly occupy my mind. It was different.

My brain would function a bit like this after opening my eyes.

My head hurts,

Where's my fags?

Is Alice home?

I'm gonna relax.

Food, no. I feel sick.

Where's the paper?

I want a beer but is it too early?.

Not yet. Fuck it.

Sit down for two minutes.

I don't feel good.

Where's Alice?
Call Gavin to find out.
Is Alice fucking Pete? (Probably not, but worth thinking about.)
Fuck it, I'll have a line.
Call Mike.
Put the telly on.
No… put music on.
 Aliiiiiice!
Pour her a glass of wine, actually champagne.
Put the telly on again.
NO. Music on.
Jesus fucking Christ. Neil Diamond.
Get the fuck out of here.
More beer. That's better.
Another line. 'Aliiiiice!'
Where's my keys?
Let's go, I feel better.
'Aliice!'

I was starting to freak out, the American tour was looming. Alice was not budging on her decision to stay back. She said that she trusted me and thought it was best for me to concentrate on the band. The problem was that I didn't trust her. I needed her with me. Rehearsals went ; we sounded like the well-oiled band we were and with lots of hits under our belts it was going to be easy. Fred and Ben were sounding so tight and Steve's voice was incredible and Matt was Matt, consistent and edgy. I felt on the outside for the first time. My guitar was in my hands but it wasn't on fire and luckily it didn't matter. It was playing the correct notes but I wasn't feeling it. My mind kept on wandering to Alice...The tour was planned and happening in a week's time and I had no choice in the matter.

We had thirty dates over three months in the States. All I needed to do was play the songs right; everything else was sorted out for me. Most of the time we would be on a private plane, sometimes we would travel by bus–not the usual kind, but one with four double bedrooms with tellies, separate bathrooms and a well-stocked bar and kitchen. The tour was a big deal and today was the last practice, we were ready.

Gavin came along and we had a meeting to make sure that we knew what was going on. Ben was adamant that we would come across like a band that cared about people and the world. He had prepared a document on all the cities that we were visiting and a couple on pages on American politics that might be relevant, Steve glazed over the pages and put them in his bag.

My gallivanting around in the tabloid press circuit was a sore point, we had always stayed away from private scrutiny but Alice and mine relationship had changed all that. I knew that Ben wanted to make sure America would be spared the Ed and Alice circus. He had been hinting about it. I pretended I didn't hear. Gavin wasn't as worried as he quite like the press hysteria.

'Guys. so were leaving in a few days. You packed?' I had to take a deep breath not to get annoyed with Gavin's' perkiness.

'Nope,' I said swigging a beer.

'Well, get packing. Shall I send someone over to help?' Perk off. I didn't reply.

'I'll send someone round to help you later.' Gavin was serious. I didn't protest.

He continued to go through the schedule, which was ridiculously busy. Radio stations, TV shows and magazine interviews crammed in between stadium gigs would be hard to keep up with. I wasn't near enough fit for this tempo.

'I have taken the liberty of bringing a team of well-being experts on the tour,' Gavin continued. 'Massage, raw food, yoga, the lot. Thought you might like that, Steve.' Steve looked pleased and inspected the Itinerary.

'That's great, I will need it. This is a very full-on schedule.'

I was zoning out, then, feeling impatient. I needed to ask about Alice's tickets.

'Have you booked Alice's tickets?' I interrupted Gavin and spoke a bit too loud.

'I keep on calling her re dates but she never gets back to me. Can you speak to her this evening and let me know. Obviously we will sort it.'

'I know she wants to be there for New York, LA and San Fran–'

Ben blurted out, 'I'm not being funny, Ed, this is a meeting about the tour and the bands schedule I couldn't give a monkey when your or anyone else's girlfriend flies out. You can do that later with Gav.' Ben was irritated.

'OK, Gavin, can we speak about this later?' I said. Fuck Ben.

'Sure thing, Ed. Anyhow, back to business. In NY, we play Letterman straight after the gig so try and not get too drunk.' He pointed his pen at Matt, Ben, Fred and me.

'Steve, decaffeinated brew only.' No one laughed.

The meeting went on for two hours. We had a mean feat ahead of us but the excitement I usually felt wasn't there. I was wrapped up in my London life and stressing about how was I going to convince Alice to come with me. If only she did then everything would be fine. I felt deflated after the meeting and when Ben asked me to go to the pub I said yes reluctantly. I knew he wanted to lecture me and I figured I'd better endure it, clear the air before the tour. Start off on the right foot and all that.

'That's gonna be tough. The schedule is insane.' Ben was sipping his ale.

'I mean, it's too much. We are going to be knackered.'

I tried to pretend like I cared, so I said.

'It's gonna be full on, mate. NY sounds fun though.'

'About that, Ed... I know you are an adult and my older brother but...could you tone down your celebrity partying, please? It's embarrassing and we decided we weren't gonna do all that.' I couldn't believe what I heard.

'What do you mean?'

'You're in the *Sun* practically every day, at the opening of an envelope, sticking your fingers up. Is it really that much fun?'

We had been out a lot, Alice would drag me to stupid things, but I mostly didn't even know what they were about. Just another party, I guess.

'Ben, I have been partying a bit, it's nice for me. I've spent my whole life indoors, guitar in hand, worrying about everyone. This is my time to have fun. Besides, some of my friends are famous, that's alright isn't it?'

I tried to sound unaffected by his comment but it was hard and I drank my pint far too fast.

'By all means, enjoy yourself. I just don't like the tabloid thing, that's all. It's a bit naff, and I don't like you to be part of it. It's rubbish.'

I knew he was right and that made me even angrier.

'I'm gonna go. Before I say anything I regret.' I stood up, put my biker jacket on and walked out the door. Mike was there, ready to take me home. There was drink in the car, so I downed another lager and called Alice.

'Meet me at the Queen's in five.'

I walked into the pub at the same moment as Alice, we got our usual table by the cosy fireplace. We ordered a bottle of red wine and some chips. I was starving. I never ate much these days–the last few days I had had a couple of packets of crisps all day and I was skinny as a rake. The booze hit the spot earlier than it should and I instantly felt relaxed and confident.

'Gavin said he tried to call you a few times,' I said.

'Did he?' She looked genuine. 'What did he want?'

'He needs to book your tickets for the tour. We're leaving next week and he needs to know when you're coming.' I tried to look casual.

'He wants to chill out. I'll book them myself when I fancy it. I'm trying to get on with my life, my acting, I think it will be good to do it while you're away. Less distractions.'

I felt heat rising, panic. The pub walls felt closer and I could even feel sweat trickling down my face. I tried to breathe more slowly, but it was no good.

It was clearly obvious, as Alice said, 'Stop freakin'out, Granddad, I'll be there. I'm gonna probably miss you after a couple of days and jump on a flight. Let's call Franklin. I want to party.'

She had that naughty look in her face, like a stubborn child. I relaxed a bit more with every drink and waited patiently for the coke dealer to arrive. Perhaps things were going to be fine after all. The night progressed the way they always did. We crashed around three o'clock after talking about the tour and our plans together, Alice in an amazing mood and me gazing at her in admiration. She was effortlessly carefree and confident, an amazing person, an alien from another planet. Her reasonings were simple; the way she presented her arguments was free of any judgments or fear, clear and precise. I'd never met anyone like her before. I could listen to her talk shit for hours and then we'd get naked. I could never get enough of her, never.

Chapter 21:
The US of A

The tour started in Chicago. When we landed on American soil the circus was already in full swing. We were all nervous, for different reasons.

Me, well, I was nervous because... I hated myself when I was hungover or not drunk, which was all the time. I was obsessed with my flimsy girlfriend. I lost my urge to play the guitar, which never happened to me before. It felt as if someone had taken away my soul, I lost a piece of myself, the only piece that use to matter. I found myself more often than never staring into nothing, thinking about nothing, tired and fed up. Then I would get a surge of energy, grab a beer and things seemed brighter. I tossed the nervous feelings to the side.

I was treated like royalty at the hotels we stayed in, given the best suites and lavish gifts by the management and the local record company. Then, there was my rider that I, or actually, Alice had thought up during one of our late-night sessions. It was funny at the time but the reality of sitting on my own in a posh suite loaded with champagne, strawberries, red roses, Pellegrino water, mangoes, Mars bars, pistachio nuts, Jack Daniels, blue roses, marmite, Maryland cookies, white lilies, cashmere blankets, cashmere socks and copious amounts of ice and lemons, was slightly embarrassing. The room looked like somewhere Elvis was going to stay the night, not Ed from Kilburn. I picked up the phone and called Gavin.

'Get rid of all the diva shit from my room, please. I'll call room service if I need any of this stuff.'

I popped the Dom Perignon open and poured myself a glass. It tasted good. OK, they could take everything apart from the vintage champagne.

Then I called Alice. She didn't answer. She was coming tomorrow which made the day better. We had a show in about ten hours. I called Ben and asked him over, I felt anxious about the gig. He was doing what I should be doing, resting. He took pity on me and came on over. Ben made me feel calm, reminded me of who I was. And who was that?

I stared out the window at the Chicago skyline. The answer wasn't there, it was inside me, and I knew I needed to change, but I wasn't ready yet, it was her, she had me jailed. I could vaguely see my reflection in the glass and the person I saw was not someone I knew. My life was cocooned, service and solutions from all directions. I felt untouchable. My personal drug intake was not that severe but it was constant these days. The doorbell on my suite went. Ding fucking doing. It was Ben, wearing his most charming of smiles.

'Hey, holy shit, this room is pimped.'

'Alice's idea of a joke. She filled in the rider form,' I said.

'I had PG Tips on mine. Next time I'll consult Alice.' That broke the ice.

'I usually have tea and crisps. It didn't make it on the form this time. But, we have plenty of this!' I held up a bottle of Dom Perignon.

'Let's have some, sit down.' He did and we both went quiet.

'How are you?' Ben looked straight at me, squeezed my shoulder with his hand. 'You're not yourself these days, you're all stressed and shit.' He mimicked an American accent.

He'd caught me off guard. Don't. Don't say that Ben. I'm not ready. I don't want to talk about it. It will pass. I need to figure this out.

'I'm fine, just a bit worried about the tour, I guess. And…'

'Could have fooled me. Seems like you don't give a fuck about the tour.'

I should tell him how lost I feel. How I wasn't able to get peace of mind. How I don't know who I am any more. The anxiety driving me mad and I want it to stop. But I didn't. Instead I said, 'It's Alice. Women, who needs them? Cheers, man of the law! I have to stop worrying about my woman. Can you sue her?'

We had a nice afternoon, drinking champagne and talking about the tour and catching up about the brothers. I felt relaxed for the first time in ages, the phone rang and we were told to be in the lobby in twenty minutes for sound check.

'Let's do this.' We were comfortably woozy.

'Nice to hang with you.' I hugged him and had a moment of 'this is going to be fine.'

Fred, Matt and Steve were already in the lobby and the five of us got into a large black limousine. The huge car was decked out with shiny leather seats, a drinks cabinet, a phone, a massive television. I don't think I had realised until this moment was happening. The Hendersons touring the States, playing to millions. It used to be my dream, when I was a teenager at Fairhurst Gardens, in my room, dreaming of exactly this. And now, I was here but it didn't feel as good as I thought it would.

Then, a pang of excitement. There it is, I thought. The guys and me, in Chicago, in a limo on our way to our first American arena live tour date. It was good, it was great, wasn't it? Surely this must be the ultimate goal achieved.

The limo was, I stroked the leather. It was plush. All of us apart from Gavin looked as if we had no place in a vehicle like this; we were lifestyle hijackers. It made it more fun, to feel like an intruder. It started to feel punk rock. I opened a beer and took a swig from the bottle. 'The Ace of Spades' was playing on the stereo and I felt better.

We arrived at the huge venue; the sound check went smoothly. The machine was well oiled, my roadie was a pro, he knew what I liked, so there was little for me to do. My monitors sounded prefect before I even touched my guitar and everything was exactly the way I liked it.

We played a couple of songs and it sounded great, the buzz I use to get was nearly there, this was the closest to happy I felt for a while. Our dressing rooms were comfortable and we huddled together after the sound check, sat down in the velvet sofas that had been especially flown in to mirror our rehearsal space in London.

Everything was done to make sure we felt comfortable. Steve was in a fine mood; he had his girl with him. I could sense he was nervous; it was a long time since we played such an important gig. He was sipping tea and sucking on Fishermen's Friends even though he was absolutely fine. Fred was drumming on a pillow and Ben was reading the news.

'Guys, we have two hours until the show. What do you wanna do?' said Gavin.

'Guess we should eat. Get some Indian,' I said.

'You can't eat Indian food in America. It sucks here.' Ben was right, of course.

'Let's get ribs. Chicago is known for the best ribs.'

Within thirty minutes we had the best ribs Chicago could offer, the local record company people dropped in, meeting and greeting, time flew by.

'You're on in twenty minutes,' someone said and I felt a pang of panic.

'Shit,' I said. Ben handed me the set list. I glanced over it and it was perfect. I wasn't needed so much these days for anything. I'd written some good songs in the past; now I was someone who couldn't even organise a set list. I could hear the murmur of crowds though the door. Chanting, clapping, the sound of adrenaline and expectations, I thought about how much Alice would like this.

The arena was heaving, every single seat sold. Steve had arranged for a local band he liked to open for us and they sounded great. Everything was perfect and I had nothing to do with it. The crowd was getting louder. I was frantically trying to call home. Alice wasn't answering. I didn't want her playing on my mind while we were on. It was late in London; she was probably out. I was strumming on my Martin acoustic guitar; I was playing 'Mr Tambourine Man'. The song made me sad. 'Let me forget about the day until tomorrow.' Damn. I wanted to find out what she was up to. I called a few other friends. Gavin knocked on the door. 'In a minute!' I said. No one had answered.

It was time to go on. I checked myself in the mirror. Who was this desperate person? I looked myself in the eye and said out loud, 'Fuck her, you're going on stage to play to 25,000 people that love your music. Now smile, motherfucker!' It felt good. I fixed my flat hair, rubbed my teeth with my index finger, took a deep breath and walked out.

Everyone was already standing side stage and I knew we were about to have a great time. The crowd was clapping and cheering, the atmosphere was that of a 'Let's do this'.

Fred went out first, followed by Ben. The crowd went mad. Matt and I went on together and we started to play. The lights were low, spotlight in the middle, waiting for Steve to walk on. He did after about five minutes. It was impossible to hear a thing as the crowd went ballistic. Steve was a star. He was so good at it: handsome, talented and incredibly charismatic. The spotty fucked-up teen, now a fully-fledged rock god. I looked at him and I felt jealous. He was sorted now, clean, talented and sensitive. He got the messy bit out of the way and he came out the other side. He was the man Alice would want now. He was the best he could be. He was what she deserved. Not me, this quiver of a needy idiot that begged for her attention. It was humiliating. I needed to play, so I did. I could always play guitar, that was a given, at least no one could take that away from me.

The gig was a roaring success and by the end of it I was pretty drunk as my roadie, on my request, kept feeding me beers and the odd line. I played well—we all did—and it was a great gig. We played three encores and the audience went wild, the tour had started, and I could tell it was going to be a massive success.

Afterwards, we headed back to the dressing room, where the post-gig party went on for hours. Different-coloured passes for different levels of importance. Hangers-on and record company people wanted to see us and we were all in good spirits. Pretty girls everywhere, staring back at us with hungry eyes if we gave them the slightest glance. Even Steve stayed for a few hours. When everyone got too tanked up he slipped out. I stayed with the others, and later we went on to a local club. Ben, Matt, Fred and I were seated at the VIP area, where people were desperate to hang out with us, I forgot what it was like on the road, life in London was nearly normal now, I wanted Alice to see this so badly, that would make her want me more. Beautiful girls were trying to get my attention; the best-looking ones did, and they were then ushered over to our table.

There was coke around and we were snorting and drinking until the early hours. We talked to people who loved our band. I was offered blowjobs in the toilet four times that I declined. The music was good, the gig was a hit, our tour had got off to a good start and I should be happy.

I got back to the hotel room at five in the morning. Wired as hell, there was no way I was going to get to sleep. I opened a brandy miniature and downed it, hoping it would take the edge off. It didn't do the trick. My heart was beating fast through my t-shirt. I put on the porn channel and had a wank. That didn't help either. I was even more awake. Opened another brandy; it burnt my throat, I didn't mind. In the end I woke Gavin up, asked him for a sleeper, which he dutifully delivered half sleep-walking. He would probably sell his mother if I asked him to. The Diazepam did the trick and I relaxed into a cotton-like cocooned sleep. I was woken up at ten by the phone. It was next to me; I didn't turn it off in case she called. It was her. Alice.

Alice: Hi, baby, I know it's early. Sorry. Were you sleeping?

Me: Yeah, I was, but it's OK. Nice to hear your voice.

Alice: How was last night?

Me: Great. Aren't you supposed to be on a plane?

Alice: I missed it. I overslept, such an idiot, I'm back at home now.

Me (*sat bolt upright*): You missed the flight? Alice, get to the airport and jump on the next one. I'm missing you. (*I wanted to say, I'm desperate, but I stopped myself.*)

Alice: I'm too tired; I'll come in a couple of days. I don't feel like flying now. It was really stressful missing the flight.

Me: I'll get Gavin to call you now to arrange. Love you. It's great here. People are going wild. You would like it. Promise (*I was practically begging.*)

I put the phone down, I felt weird, dirty. Something wasn't right.

I picked up the phone and dialled Gavin. He insisted he'd come over so I let him. He brought me a cup of PG.

'Morning, dude.'

'Hey, fucking Alice has gone and missed her flight. You need to book her on a flight tomorrow. Can you get her collected next time so she gets there on time? I want her here with us, I want her to see us.'

Gavin looked a bit nervous, not his usual self. Perhaps he was tired after I woke him up at 5.30 in the morning.

'You ok? Sorry I woke you up. I was too wired, impossible to sleep. The American gear is so strong.'

'Sit down, Ed.' He was asking me to sit down. What the fuck was up? Was it Ted? I was starting to feel nervous.

'What's up? You're freaking me out.'

'It's Alice. We, or you, have a problem.' He handed me a fax; it was the cover of the *Sun* newspaper. There was a picture of Alice snogging Tom Price, a famous actor who we hang out with, on the front cover. The headline read: 'Where's Ed?' My heart started to beat, adrenaline pumping through my veins.

'I just spoke to her. She didn't say anything.' I stood up and started pacing the room. I stopped at the minibar and opened a beer. 'I mean, let me look at that again.'

There was no doubt that the two of them were kissing.

'Can you leave please? I have to work this out.'

Gavin was relieved. He wasn't comfortable in awkward situations like this. He needed me to be functioning for the next day, so he said,

'It might not be as bad as it looks. You want me to speak to her?'

This comment made me mad.

'I thought you knew that under no circumstances do I ever want you to interfere in my personal affairs. Ever. Do you get that?'

He got the message and left. I was standing holding onto the fax when the phone rang. It was a journalist wanting a comment. I called downstairs and barred all calls to my room. My mobile phone started to ring and I didn't answer. I called Matt.

He didn't answer. Still asleep. I called Ben. He did pick up.

I couldn't bring myself to tell him so I asked him if he would wake Matt up for me.

'Is everything OK?' he said.

'Not really. Could you come over when you're up?'

'Yep, sure.'

I dialled Alice's number. Everything was ruined.

Alice: Hello.

Me: Hi, did you forget to tell me something?

Alice: So you've seen it then, I was hoping…

Me: That I wasn't going to see it.

Alice: It's pretty shit.

Me: It's on the fucking front cover. What's going on?

Alice: I'm just confused. I mean, I been feeling a bit like this for a while.

Me: How? What do you mean?

Alice: I haven't felt the same about, you know, us.

Me: I have.

Alice: I know you have, but I haven't, and then I met Tom.

Me: What do you mean by 'met'? We know him, we met him, he's our friend.

Alice: He gets me, that's all.

Me: And here's me thinking you were going to apologise…

Alice: I am sorry.

I put the phone down, there was a knock on the door, it was Matt. He knew… I could tell by the sheepish smile on his face, Gavin must have sent him.

'Women, fucking slags,' he said.

My body started shaking because I think what just happened was that I just got dumped, for Tom Price, Tom Price cunt. I wanted to hit someone, instead I threw something, I think it was a vase, against the wall. It smashed into little pieces. I saw red, then black, I sat down on the floor and started to laugh. Matt was looking at me as if I'd gone mad. He sat down next to me on the floor, passed me a fag and handed me another Budweiser.

'That's really ugly, I trusted her.' I finally said.

'What a bitch.' Matt said.

'I know what I'm going to do tonight, I'm going to get laid,' I finally said.

'That's my boy.' We drank together in silence, like we always did in difficult times.

The tabloids back home were having an absolute field day with our break-up. I hated the lame attention the papers accumulated. Alice, on the other hand, was being interviewed everywhere and making the most out of the naff exposure. Her every move being papped, I imagined her talking to her friends, revelling in the attention.

She moved out that day and moved in with Tom Price cunt. It transpired that their affair had been going on for a while. I was heartbroken and it hurt. I threw myself into the tour and one-night stands. I had never done that before; I had always been with someone that I liked. It didn't matter how pretty they were because I was still in love with Alice. I found myself looking for girls who reminded me of her. The tour was hard work and I was in a right state, only sober for a few hours a day. Gavin was baby-sitting me and the poor guy was looking worse for wear. Matt and I were a force to be reckoned with, partying like never before, enjoying being rock stars properly for the first time. It was easy to get lost because there was no end to the nights or the days, the drugs, the drink and the girls. Minders and management dealt with any trouble that might appear. I was too drunk to care or know. The ride was smooth and I rode it perfectly. New York was coming up and we knew it was going to be a crazy few nights. On the bus I was trying to rest to save up some much-needed energy but it was hard to switch the brain off. My phone rang. I Stopped breathing when I Say who it was.

Alice: Ed?

Me: Yep, it's me.

Alice: Just wanted to see how you were. We haven't spoken and I wanted to talk to you.

Me: About what?

Alice: I don't know. I miss you…a lot.

Me: Could have fooled me.

Alice: I really messed up; I know that now. I want to see you, so I can explain. Can I come to NY?

Me: What for?

Alice: I don't know. I want to see you. I miss you Ed.

Me:…I… You know Alice, perhaps it's better we do that after the tour, I need to work.

Alice: Yeah, I guess you're probably right. I am sorry, Ed.

Me: I'm sorry too.

The bus was quite tonight and I gazed out on the flat, dusty landscape, I felt a calm after hearing her voice.

Part of me was happy that she'd called; another part wished she would disappear forever. I was coping fine, the booze, coke and the willing groupies helped. I didn't want to be reminded of her; her smell, her laugh, everything that I was desperate for but not getting. The gigs were going well and the guys and I were back being a proper band. If I saw her now, I would fall apart and so would the band, she had to wait until London. I couldn't handle it now.

Ted and Veronica were flying out to the New York gig. I'd made sure a fuss was made of them. Ben and Fred were excited to see them too and I wanted to hang out with my little man. Up until the phone call from Alice I had been excited about them coming, now, my brain was obsessing about Alice, my heart was telling me to get her on a plane but my head knew it was a bad idea.

The roads in America were relentless, like my thoughts about the careless Alice, who I knew deep inside, didn't give a flying fuck about me. My love for her was more like infatuation and it didn't make sense, I was powerless with her. We stopped at a diner and stuffed our faces with fatty burgers that left my hands greasy and stomach wanting more. We were nearing New York City and the roads were starting to change; they felt narrower, houses fencing them in. I loved New York; it was one of my favourite cities. The steam rising from the streets, the yellow cabs, the pulse and the adventure that might happen at any time.

Inside, I was nervous, anxious. I didn't know who I was any more, being in New York it felt like a good thing: it was the perfect city to lose yourself in. I didn't know if I liked anything that much anymore, I didn't feel passion for my music or the care for my family that had always followed me. I was removed from my life, as if I was stuck in a Perspex box, viewing everything remotely, without any emotion or care. I soldiered on with our schedule, like a robot. I didn't feel anything, I was numb. I'd slept with so many chicks, I'd lost count. I had talked to people I didn't care about for hours. This would have been acceptable for most people but I wasn't that type of person before I met Alice. It was the drugs, the coke and the drink; they made me someone else, made me cover up the fact that I was lost as hell. Perhaps I was finally mourning my mother and my father but even that felt like a sorry excuse.

In my mind, I kept going back to the music. It had always been my dream. I had achieved that over and beyond any childhood expectations. I didn't need to fight for that, but I was a fighter; what could I fight for now? Alice? That was infected, but I wanted it because I felt as if I didn't deserve anything. I wanted to be with her but I knew it was my ego, my stupid ego that was rearing its ugly face. I had had sex with so many women on this tour I'd forgotten that it was supposed to be intimate, not just a thrust into some nameless girl I'd met an hour ago. This tour was crazy, it could kill me and the scary truth was that I didn't care.

Chapter 22:
Ed Crashes.

My face is looking back at me in the mirror, bloated and blotchy. I have four yellow spots on my forehead, dry skin and a cold sore on my top lip. I'd looked better. It was midday, I opened my eyes in my suite at the Royalton Hotel New York city. I woke up because someone was banging on the door. I could hear a child's laughter. It was Ted.

I looked around the room, it was trashed. Full of bottles, fag butts and rolled-up notes. There was a girl next to me. A brunette, she was naked, I noted her long legs and perfect breasts and vaguely remembered the night before.

I put on a robe because I couldn't find my clothes. I didn't smell good and this was not how I was supposed to be when I met Ted. I opened the door and asked V for ten minutes with some lame excuse she didn't believe. I didn't get to see them last night, as I was too busy after the show. I hadn't seen my son for three months and I missed him and this is how I behave? I shouted, 'Hold on a minute Tedson!' I threw off the robe and quickly located some clean clothes, brushed my teeth and splashed my face with cold water. Found the door key.

'Daddy! Daddy! It's me.'

'Hello, my little man!' I flung the door open and held onto him a little longer than normal.

'Let's get some breakfast.' I avoided Veronica's eyes; she was standing right behind him. She looked me up and down and said,

'You look like shit.' I ignored her comment.

Then Ted said,

'Where's Alice?'

I ruffled his hair and said,

'I'm starving.' Veronica started to walk away.

'You wanna come?'

She hesitated. Ted started jumping up and down and said, 'Mummy, come on, let's have pancakes together!'

'Ok, let's do this.' We all held hand hands; I wasn't wearing any shoes. No one seemed to mind.

'And after breakfast we are going to the world's coolest toyshop and you, my friend, can have whatever you wish for.' Ted threw his tiny arms around me a held on like his life depended on it. A tear appeared in the corner of my eye.

'I missed you so much.' I said and I meant it more than ever before. Veronica even softened up after that and the three of us had a perfect time. I called Gavin.

'Gavin, can you see that my room is cleaned up? I'm with Ted, it's dirty in there, and there's some chick in my bed. I need to go back there after breakfast. Please?'

'I will sort it. What's her name?'

'I have no idea.' I should really try and remember names.

It was a long time since I felt this happy. Even if my hands were shaking and I had a hangover created by the devil. The brothers started to turn up and we all made a fuss of Ted. Ben was taking him to museums after the toyshop, as Steve and I needed to do interviews.

I was smiling from ear to ear. I scooted over to V and said,

'Don't go tomorrow, stay for the rest of the tour, I need you guys here. This feels so good, all of us together.'

Veronica was nearly convinced by the good atmosphere.

'Ed I know you're in a state. I get it, it's written all over your face. In fact, I don't recognise you. There's only two weeks left. Come back afterwards and let's talk. I'm here for you, but Ted needs routine. It's too crazy on this tour.'

She was right, I wasn't thinking about them, I was in no shape to look after Ted or hang around with Veronica. Playing happy families was not going to work right now. It felt good, though. When I returned to my room it was empty and clean. Being a rock star made it a lot easier to behave like an absolute dick. It was easy to pretend everything was OK when everything around you were not falling apart. Inside, I was a mess, but who cares? It was only my mess, my brain, which I managed to completely screw up, all by myself.

We had a great time and as we had a night off I spent it with Ted, in my room. We built Lego, watched a movie and had room service. The brothers popped in. Steve stayed and watched *Toy Story* with us. I managed to stay sober but it was hard. All I needed was my family around me and everything would be OK. In the middle of the film I noticed that Steve was staring at me.

'What you looking at?'

'You.' He smiled a pearly white smile. 'I just never thought I'd see the day when you got this messed up. You look like a proper junkie my friend.'

Ted was snoring on my lap. I carried him gently into the bed.

'Steve, with all due respect, I might be partying a bit too much but I am not a junkie.'

'Whatever you say. Your hands are trembling. Have a drink, you'll feel better.' He started walking towards the door.

'Perhaps I am partying a bit too much. Got to get this tour out of the way, then I'll sort it.' I realised I sounded like a loser but it felt good to say it.

'Let me know if you want help. You helped me once, it's time I returned the favour.' The door closed behind him. I opened a bottle of red, contemplated whether to call Alice or not. I decided against it.

I was tired so I was relieved to hit the pillow, I passed out next to my son.

'Dad! Daaad.' I woke up. Ted was jumping on the bed.

'Oh, Ted, it's seven in the morning, man. Put the TV on.' My previous love for early mornings had long gone. I was always exhausted, drained. I ordered up some breakfast and we chatted about school. He was a big five-year-old, smart too. Veronica had been teaching him how to read and he could actually do it. The door went, it was V, all sweet and familiar.

'Hey! Come in. This guy woke up early.'

'Kids do that Ed, remember? Our flight's midday. You gotta say your goodbyes.' Ted ran over to me and held onto my leg.

'Daddy, fly with us. Please Daddy.'

'Daddy has to work Ted. I'll be back before you know it. '

The warm safety of the two of them was something I really needed. Back home loomed the infected situation involving Alice, and I knew it was going to be hard to go to the house and be in London without her in it. I knew it was going to be nearly impossible to resist calling her.

The rest of the day was going to be busy; we had a show that night, the day was jam packed with interviews, mostly with magazines. They all wanted Steve and I, so we had five hours of solid speaking ahead of us. We had been answering the same questions now for weeks and it was getting boring. It had been doing the trick though, the record was selling millions of copies; we were a huge success.

The door went. It was Ben, knowing that I'd be sad, he hugged me and I exhaustedly hugged him back.

'Hey, I promised Ted to take him to Camber Sands. I've been telling him all about it. He wants to go and then it occurred to me he is always being chauffeured. Not healthy. Uncle Ben is taking him in his new car. Oh yes. It is a Mercedes.'

I was vaguely listening to his rant.

'Yeah, Camber sounds good, can I come?' I mumbled.

'Might do you some good. The sea is healing, ask Steve…' We both laughed.

'Yeah, sounds perfect.' I meant it, it sounded like bliss. Away from London, from Alice. Camber Sands and its dunes, some happy childhood memories.

The last two weeks of the tour continued in the same crazy way. The temporary thinking break from when V was in New York was long forgotten. The tempo was back high again. Drink, drugs, women and gigs. There were some good moments; in Utah, for instance, in Red Rocks, the sun came down as we played, I connected with the music the way I use to, a glimmer of hope reappeared.

I met a girl after the gig called Alice who looked like Alice. Only her American accent gave her away. I wanted her to shut up; the whiny accent was messing with my head. She blew me in the back of the bus. I closed my eyes. Then it turned dark, I got rid of the girl and did the worst, I called London, told Alice what had happened with the lookalike. I was slurring but she got the gist. I wanted her to hurt. When I woke up in the morning I had a raging hangover. I vaguely remembered what I'd done. I did it again, got her back on the phone, she didn't seem to mind, laughed it off, continued her quest to get me back 'to come back home', as she called it. I heard whispers from London that Tom Price idiot dickhead had dumped her and that she had nowhere to live. He had tried to call me to apologise, saying it wasn't a big deal. It was a big deal for me. I would never forgive him. He wasn't even a real friend to start with, so his apology didn't matter much.

The very last gig was in Los Angeles, a star-studded affair with beautiful people everywhere talking pleasant rubbish. All I could think about was Alice and how much she would love this, the city reminded me of her, easy-going, young, shallow and fun. Full of promises and people with dreams. It wasn't damaged goods, I decided I liked it.

I woke up with two girls in my bed, it was the last day of the tour. I was many things; a stud was not one of them, without my guitar I would never had found myself in this predicament. All my tour conquests had happened because the girls had made it easy. I scanned the hotel room, the Chateau Marmont was perfect with its bohemian rock'n'roll interiors. There were clothes, bottles, glasses, cigarette butts and rolled-up notes scattered across the room. The room stank, I got up and opened the window. Images of the night before started to pop up in my head. The two girls in my bed dancing, taking their clothes off whilst play fighting. Matt was here too but clearly he left at some point. I remember them sitting on my lap starting to undress me, my scrawny pale body on the massive bed. Both of them all over me like in my own personal German porn movie. One brunette, the other one a blonde. Their American drawl, which I was now used to, talking dirty words to me. It was easy to it , giving into pleasure. For some reason it didn't feel as sexy with a raging hangover. I put the telly on, nudged one of the girls. Fuck! What were their names? I made up a lame excuse. 'Hey, babe, I've gotta go, I'm doing an interview. I called room service; pancakes are on the way. Here's my number if you ever get to London.'

I gave the number for the office–I always did.

'Thank you, Edward. ' She replied, flashing her breast.

She looked nice; she was so beautiful, why did she want *me*? It always played on my mind why people turned out the way they did. There was always a story. I had no clue who this person was that I had licked, kissed, squeezed, penetrated and stroked. I was a single man; I liked women, willing ones that made sex easy when I was drunk. I hadn't wanted to be that sort of man, but now I was. My brain wandered back to the previous night with the two girls kissing and I felt a twitch in my trousers.

I knocked on Ben's room, I collapsed on his bed and we had breakfast. He'd already been for a swim, had a shower, packed his suitcase as he went to bed early. He was excited, telling me about his new car which was now waiting for him in Hampstead. A Mercedes, a silver one; the classic colour apparently. I could barely concentrate on the words that came out of his mouth. I fell asleep on his bed like a child. Gavin sorted my room out, even packed my bag for me. I had a long shower and borrowed some clean clothes off Ben. I scrubbed myself hard thinking there was no soap in the world that could clean this smuttiness away.

The flight home in first class was pleasant until I started to think about what I was going home to. Primrose Hill without Alice, her things gone. I was going to be all on my own in that soulless house.

'Ben, can I come back with you to Hampstead? I wanna see Ted.'

'Course. I'll warn V. Will she be ok with that?' I didn't know the answer to that.

'You want me to come to Primrose Hill with you? Might be weird without Alice there.' He finally said.

'Is it that obvious?'

'Yep.'

Touching down in London, I felt apprehensive. The drive back from the airport didn't give me that usual warm feeling, instead I was worried and stressed. My brain and body were still recovering from all the partying and my emotions were vulnerable and unsteady. I felt myself staring into nothing, a heavy burden hanging over me. I felt as if I didn't know what to do with myself. I was anxious and nervous because I knew what was going to happen.

My phone rang.

It was Alice.

Alice (*forever chirpy*): Hey, you're back!

Me: Yep, just now. What do you want?

Alice: Just wanted to say hi. Also, I still have some stuff at home.

Me: Really? Why?

Alice: Just couldn't get it all into one cab.

Me: I need some time, Alice, to sort shit out. I need to see Ted. Can we speak later?

Alice: Yes, of course.

Ben looked over at me with one raised eyebrow; he always did that when he was scanning someone.

'Alice, huh?'

'Yeah, she wants me back.'

'Really? You're not gonna, I hope?'

'Nah, I still like her but I don't think it will work, not after what she did.'

'She's all right, Ed. She's not your girl, though. She's too dumb. Take the hit now and find someone else.'

He was right of course but I wasn't so sure I could stay away from her. I wasn't strong enough. What else was there for me? An empty house and friends I didn't care about. I liked being surrounded by people without having to actually talk to them. I never handled solitude very well. This was probably not the time to start.

Primrose Hill looked the same as when we left and it dawned on me that I was the same too. The tour seemed like a dream, the kind you wake up from slightly stressed and wonder what the hell happened. Walking into the house I felt fearful and unprepared for the memories that came flooding back, memories of Alice and I. Casually I threw my keys on the kitchen table, pretending I was comfortable. I put the telly on.

'Wicked, Carol Vorderman. I love *Countdown*.' Ben sat down on the sofa.

'Beer?'

'No thanks.'

We hung out for a couple of hours, both of us feeling sketchy, I could sense that Ben wanted to leave.

'I have to go to Hampstead. You wanna come?'

'I'd better not. I've arranged to see Ted tomorrow. I need to sleep. I'll be fine. Veronica doesn't want me hanging around.'

'She'll be OK. She's just French, that's all. I'd ignore that. She'll be pleased to see you.'

'I don't think so. I have to deal with this situation. Can't just run away the whole time.'

Ben left and all I could do was think about the phone and whether I should call Alice. I was bored; I wanted to go the pub. Doesn't mean I'll go back with her, it's a drink, that's all. Fuck it, I dialled her number. She answered before the first ringtone.

'I'm going to the pub. You wanna come?'

Alice squealed with delight and said she'd be there in 15 minutes. I left my house and practically ran to the pub

The landlord welcomed me like a soldier back from the war. The regulars all shook my hand and I got my usual table by the open fire, I felt more at home in the pub then I did in my own house.

Then… She walked in. My heart sank. I could smell her, the familiarity. I knew as soon as I set eyes on her that here was nothing in the world that could stop me from having her.

'Hiya stranger,' she said in ger usual cool manner. She looked good, really good.

'Hello there Alice.' I hugged her a little too long and decided I had forgiven her that instance.

I had my revenge over and over in America with all the nameless girls I had slept with. I got my own back on her. Guess it was even stevens, so I gave in to her just like that.

The warm feeling I was missing was suddenly there in the instant she entered the pub. It took about five minutes before the coke dealer was called, our friends turned up and the party was in full swing. My jet lag hit me around eight o'clock and I had to head home.

Alice noticed.

'You need to rest, Ed, you look exhausted. Let's get out of here.'

I wasn't going to protest; I was desperate to get her into bed.

The morning came quickly; I woke up after a twelve-hour sleep, remembering I had to get Ted. Alice was gently snoring next to me. She looked sweet. I got into the shower and felt better than I had for ages. In my head I reasoned that now Alice and I were back together everything would be OK.

Obviously, I was wrong.

Chapter 23:
Hare Krishna…ish

Steve couldn't stand seeing Ed like this, his big brother who saved him when he was in a bad way was going down the same dark path that he had. The only problem was Ed was a stubborn fucker and he saw himself as the head of the family and the band on top of that. That emotional persistence and leader-like determination was not the easiest combination to break. Looking at him, it was apparent he used to be a lot of things. Now he was a dirty addict. Functioning badly. Looking like he felt on the inside. Even his guitar playing had lost his magic, it was dull and mechanical. The soul was drained out of him and he was scouring around the edges, holding onto what was left of the old Ed. The one who saved their family. The one who pulled the brothers together after they had lost their mum. Steve knew he had to do something, it was his turn to step up and he was ready for it. It would have been easier to ignore Ed but it was getting painful to watch him. Even sitting next to him was difficult, as he was trying hard to act his old big brother persona. He wanted to say, 'Chill Ed, it's obvious you don't want to talk, play or do anything apart from snort coke and drink. Stop pretending. It's painful to watch.' But he didn't.

Steve never got that drug, so much shit was said about coke and users turned into absolute assholes. At least with smack people would be mellow and shut the fuck up. With Ed being a lost cause, Steve had taken over the father figure role of the band and there was lots of shit going down in the Henderson camp, stuff he didn't want to deal with, so he needed Ed back on his feet again in his rightful place. In fact, it felt as if the band's future was in jeopardy and Steve didn't want them to split.

The band was his life, how *he* kept clean. Without Ed they were nothing, and Ed was dangerously close to the edge. He had got in touch with some mates from his rehab and they had suggested this really strange place. They were having some success with cokeheads. It was a hippie slash Hare Krishna compound. It was spiritual yet hard core. It sounded good, Steve and Mike took the car to have a look at it and as soon as they entered he knew it was perfect. Afterwards, they visited Ed and what happened there wasn't pretty, it was time to get better. He was definitely at rock bottom or possibly the stage after that. Steve thought to himself that Ed would never had let him go this far and with that he got the strength to take him to the rehab.

Hertfordshire

Steve finally did it, he told me I was a fucking mess, and I was ready to listen. Here I was, chanting away, giving in to giving up. The meditation was interesting, it suited me. Yoga was all right as well.

What really made me want to change in the end was the fact that I lost contact with Ted. I knew I was someone I didn't like. I felt very lost.

The nights I spent pissed confiding in strangers became one long continuous evening that meant nothing; they never did. Most of the time I couldn't remember the night before, so what was the point of it all?

I missed being with Ted, I missed my old life with Veronica and sometimes I ended up calling her drunk, begging her to take me back. It was getting pathetic and my friends' and family's empathy was starting to run low. Steve came to my rescue one morning. He found me strewn across my bed, fully clothed, the house looking like a bomb had hit it. The cleaners were already there to make it look as if nothing had happened, like they always did. They'd let Steve in. He made me a cup of PG and sat down next to me. He smelt clean, like he had just stepped out of a shower. I sat up like a bolt when realised he was in my room. He always made me feel as if I needed to be on my best behaviour, trying my hardest to disguise the state I was in, but there was nowhere to hide.

Steve looked around, looked at me and said.`

'Ed, it's time. I can't watch you do this to yourself any longer.'

'What do you mean?'

'You're an asshole. This look, this lifestyle, it doesn't suit you.'

I was trying to think of something witty to say but words failed me so I simply answered,

'Ok. I can't argue with that.' I held back tears.

'I've been wanting to talk to you for a while. I've found you this hippy place, fake monks run it. You need to spend a few weeks there, then I'll take you to meetings if you want. It works, I promise. '

I was too hung over to protest, so I agreed. We packed a bag. Mike was outside. I was ready. I can almost say it was a relief to drive to this strange place in Hertfordshire. Driving through the lush countryside, I rested my head on the car window, staring into nothing, and I thought of nothing because there was nothing inside my brain. The only thing I could think was 'Get me there, get me out of this hell hole.'

A bald man with brown, kind eyes met us by the main gate. He was tall and thin, wearing an orange cloak. I was thrown a bit by the fact that they looked like a bunch of Hare Krishna cult members. I made a snap decision not to protest or question, just to go with the flow.

The building was vast, well-manicured and welcoming. There were cloak bearers kneeling down around the bushes, pruning and weeding the boarders. This place was well taken care of.

'You must be Ed,' said the brown-eyed guy.

'Yeah, hi.'

'I'm Brother Daniel.'

'Nice.' I didn't know what to say to that but I wanted to kill my real brother, Steve, who I think was wearing a smile at this point. He kept walking behind me.

'Where are your things?'

Mike handed Daniel my black sports bag.

Steve and Mike made a quick exit, left me there with the freaks.

'I need my guitar.' I desperately whispered.
The car had already sped off. Daniel put his hand on my shoulder.

'Don't worry, we have plenty of instruments here.'

Now I was worried, I was fucking worried. This was not what I had expected. Perhaps I should just run now. I wondered whether they would hold me down, lock me in. My heart was beating fast and my face was going red. My body was getting stressed. Get me the fuck out of here! I need a pint.

There air was clean and I realised that I was tired so I followed the weird guy wherever he was taking me. There were no locks on the doors and the front door was wide open. A sign read: WELCOME TO FREEDOM.

My room was more like a prison cell; it had a sink in it, a single bed with one pillow and a shitty blanket on top of it. I sat down on the bed and instantly started to feel restless. There was no TV, no speakers, no nothing, just me and nothing. I lay down on the itchy blanket for a minute. I stood up, I decided I couldn't bear to be in there so I walked out the door. I bumped into another orange dude.

'How are you?' he said.

'Pretty shit.' Summed it up.

'Come with me friend, I'll make you a tea.'

I followed him because I didn't know what else to do and apparently we were friends. I was regretting my decision to come here increasingly by every minute that passed.

'Do you know what the plan is? When can I leave?'

'There is a gathering in ten minutes. Go along to it and you'll start your journey. You can leave whenever you want. It's not a prison.'

That's what I did. I went along to the nut nut meeting, where I met some other non-cloak wearers. They were also nice. I learnt to chant. I said my name countless times. It didn't seem to help. I hated the Ed that I was, and I never liked people who referred to themselves in the third person. I voiced my problems with the method and was met with faint smiles and reassurances that I would see the light if I was patient and gave in, I had to surrender. 'I am Ed. I am real.'

There were now five of us in a row. All chanting. The men in orange cloaks walking around us, spreading serenity. I wasn't ready yet, I wanted to give up the drink and the coke because it wasn't fun anymore and this was the place that could help me, apparently. Steve had found it, he believed it was the right place for me. It wasn't a rehab, as such, he'd said, it was somewhere you could rediscover who you were and who was I? I liked this question. I didn't have a clue. I hated being here but at the same time I felt safer than at home. I had another go at chanting because I had decided to try.

'I am Ed. I am real.' I repeated.

I was encouraged to touch myself, squeeze my skin. Stroke my arms. Be kind to myself. I had been here for a week and for what it was worth, I didn't hate it. I found it a bit comical but it was a nice change from my usual groundhog day loop of parties and drugs. I was given a mantra, I repeated it with my eyes closed and slowly something was happening, I saw a light in the darkness and it felt relaxing.

After a week of no drink or drugs I felt better. The thing was, that stuff just didn't suit me, the coke. I didn't drink because I needed it, but more to disguise how I feel. All the layers I had been stacking up and hiding inside while I soldiered on, worked and functioned, anything not to feel the pain. Alcoholism was in my genes. I couldn't think of an older Henderson who wasn't a complete gin head, apart from Mum. She was weak, too weak to drink properly. It was strange that it had taken me this long. Weighing things up, the clean lifestyle appealed to me better. I missed actually being creative, not pretending to be artistic while high. Actually connecting on the level I used to be at when I started out. I was changing slowly and I felt better.

The orange men made me laugh. Today we were all going to learn how to knit. Having guitar hands, I imagined it was going to be easy. I often thought about Alice, I finally mustered up the courage to tell her to piss off. Her perky vacuous personality had finally drained me and I wanted out. She wasn't so hot these days either; she'd lost the spark in her eyes. Instead there was a dull sense of desperation surrounding her. I felt lonely in her company. The walls would close in on me, I would be dripping in sweat, melting away in my own stink. Talking to myself was not unusual these days, blabbering nonsense about crap I didn't care about.

On the recommendation of Brother Daniel I took part in the knitting sessions, it was a lot more enjoyable than I had imagined. I made Ted a scarf; it was blue and black, striped. I sat in the arts and crafts room for days knitting away on my piece. I surprised myself that I didn't miss being off my head. I just kept on knitting. faster and faster. The scarf was long and I was good at it.

The first few days I was there I sweated buckets of water. After a week I started to feel better, much better. I called Ted on my first allowed phone call and told him that I was away learning how to knit and that we would go to Camber sands soon. Hang with the uncles, I told him. I missed him and told him I loved him a few too many times. I started to talk to other people in there and made some new friends. I realised that I was just another alcoholic. I was pleased to be free of the burden; I knew I had to watch myself. Strangely I felt genuinely that I'd had enough.

Week two was not as easy. It was painfully boring, I wanted to escape but I wasn't locked in so I could actually walk out. There was a sweet-looking pub down the road, I'd spotted it on the drive here. I tried to talk one of the other guys into it. He then reported it to Brother Daniel and I was taken in for a one-to-one chat with him. We talked it through. I asked for a guitar and I was brought one; it was an old nylon-stringed Spanish guitar with a hole in the back of the body. I suspected the strings had never been changed. I fell in love with it: it was shit, just like me. I played for a couple of hours, took a break, then played for another four.

The guitar had taken me somewhere, somewhere I hadn't been in a long time, perhaps back to Fairhurst Gardens. I was entranced by the sound it was making. My little cell room suddenly felt like the Ritz and being alone was a bonus. I started to think about Sue, my mum. I cried. I played. I took a walk in the pretty gardens. I felt calm, my body relaxed and my mind still. The boredom awoke my creativity. I felt vaguely alive. Pictures of the past started to pop up in my brain. I remembered life before the band, when I had dreams, my mother's dead body on the sofa, my father's watch, my father, my brothers….me. Aunt Linda, the smell of her and her impish attempts to help. I understood why she couldn't, she wasn't strong enough, she was like I was now… broken. She had already passed, we heard she died the same day that we got our recording contract. It wasn't unexpected. To have all these thoughts in my brain felt good. I felt a little like Ed again. I was Ed and I was real. My life, my family's life, wasn't a made-up story about a bunch of sad kids that made some good out of their circumstances, some rags-to-riches fairy tale. It was our life and we had made it work even though we were written off as losers, we had stuck together.

I decided that I was going to give this place a go, a real go. Chant the loudest I could and give in. I went to sleep feeling calm and woke up with a fresh brain. I spent twenty minutes meditating. I had a spring in my step as I entered the breakfast room. It obviously showed.

'You look happy today,' some guy remarked.

'Thanks. I feel good.'

To think that I had been in that place for two weeks before I finally got it. When I started to know myself again, the years on the booze and drugs seemed like a hazy dream. Some crazy memories and many embarrassing incidents kept on playing in my mind. The brotherhood was pleased with me and informed me that I was now allowed to use the phone whenever I liked. I sat down, mobile in hand. Didn't really feel like speaking to anyone, so I put the phone down and went out into the gardens again and helped out with the weeding.

I didn't want to rush this; for the first time in years, I was writing songs that mattered to me. That evening I was chosen to speak, 'big myself up' as my new friends called it.

I had written a note of things I was proud of. First I had listed all the achievements of the band. Countless number ones and record sales and then I rubbed it all out and wrote:

1. Ted.
2. Looking after my little brothers.
3. Learning how to play the guitar well.
4. Coming here.

That was it. I spoke clearly at the meeting, then I rushed back to my room to use my phone. I wasn't scared, first weirdly, I called Gavin, not because he was important to me but I asked him to sort my house out for me. Paint it white and get rid of all the booze and shit furniture, especially the bed. I told him about my various drug stashes so that he could chuck them out.

I called Steve and thanked him for sorting me out and that I was grateful to be there. He asked if I wanted to go to a meeting with him. I replied I wasn't sure. I said I felt good, which I did. I told him about the songs I'd written they were good, and they were not about Alice. Progress, he said, which it was. I told him I'd thought about Aunt Linda, how we missed her funeral. How shit

I thought that was. He agreed, because it was true. I said I wanted to make another record. He said he wanted to, as well. I said I hated chickens and would never live in the country. He didn't agree about the chickens but respected the fact that I did. Then we laughed. I put down the phone and called Ben.

I asked him if he would come and get me in a few days, as I was getting ready to go home. I wanted to get on with my life. Ben tried to sound cool but I could tell that he was happy to have me back to my old self. Fred was there too and we spoke for a while.

Ben had been spending time at his beach house and suggested we go there for a while. He wanted to show me what he had done to it and said that Ted had his own room there and absolutely loved it.

Fred and Steve could come too and we could have some time together. I asked him about Veronica, how she was. Was she angry with me? I could understand if she was, I've been despondent for a long time. He assured me she was OK and that she wanted to be friends. It was nice to be reassured by Ben. All was going to be fine. We would survive another hurdle, stick together and carry on. That was the only way we knew how.

Veronica had looked after the younger two brothers for me, and they still lived together in Hampstead. Fred had started to talk about buying a house, so perhaps he was going to move out soon. Ben had bought the Camber house and I had a feeling he would move there permanently. It suited him, the quiet life. It was near enough to Steve's place. .

It was my turn to help out in the kitchen; peeling onions and garlics was therapeutic. I asked if I could hoover. I enjoyed the gentle humming. I've had cleaners for years and doing housework felt good. Cleaning up my own shit, that's what I was here to do.

At the next meeting in the hall we all sang together. I played the guitar with the nutters and enjoyed their kooky out-of-time percussion ensemble.

I announced that I wanted to leave in five days, at the weekend, and got a cheer and hugs from my fellows. I chanted, 'I am Ed, I am real,' enthusiastically. They all responded, 'He is Ed, he is real.' Then I cried, like a frigging girl, because I felt happy.

I definitely had a light bulb moment, I felt free again and a little stupid that I'd fallen for the seduction of the celebrity life but I had forgiven myself. There was no place for me amongst all the glitzy parties. I was content again. Finally.

Chapter 24:
The Truth hurts

The prospect of leaving scared me a bit. It had to be done, though. I had things to do, a life to lead. I was wrapped in a cocoon here. If I was sad, there were safe people to speak to. If I was tired, I could sleep, surprisingly well on my hard single bed.

Two days before I was going there was a knock on my door. Fred was standing there in the door of my cell-like room. I was speechless. My youngest brother looked like a man. He was still scrawny but his face was older. A proper person. I stood up and hugged him hard.

'I like what you done to the place,' he said and put up with the hugging. I took him to the breakfast room. We chatted about the band. He'd been writing songs and he had a CD with him. We listened to the songs in Mike's car. They sounded so good. I introduced him to all my friends, the fake monks. It felt as if I hadn't seen him in years. Obviously I had but I hadn't been there properly. I apologised to him. It felt good to be present again.

I told him I had been mourning mum; he said that was good. I was so pleased to see him I didn't notice first that there was an air of seriousness surrounding him. I brushed it off, thinking he felt uncomfortable in this strange place that I had taken to.

We took a walk in the gardens.

'I'm moving out of Hampstead.' Fred lit a fag

'About time. You're twenty-three.'

'Yeah, just haven't had time. Touring and stuff always got in the way.'

'True, that.'

'I found a place in Hampstead. It's expensive. I can afford it, though, so I'm going to buy it. Because I can.'

'Can't you come to Primrose Hill? I would like you to be closer to me.'

'It's close Ed, real close, you'll see me. A lot. Promise.'

'I really want to make up for my shitty behaviour,' I said.

'You haven't been shitty, just busy, that's all.'

'I should have been around more.'

'Perhaps you should have. Actually, that's why I'm here. I need to talk to you about something. Something that is hard to talk about.'

I could tell he was really nervous about what he was about to say. His eyes were flickering and he was biting his nails. He didn't want to say what he was about to.

'It's Ben.'

'What about Ben? Is he gay?' I laughed nervously.

'No, he is not. Wish he was though.'

'What do you mean.'

'I have to tell you; I can't be part of their lie. That's why I came. Ben and Veronica, they are together. It's wrong.'

Adrenaline started to pump through my veins. What did he just say? I must have heard wrong.

'What do you mean, together?'

'I mean, they are a couple, sleeping together, playing happy families with Ted.'

That's what I thought he meant. Not now, not when I was just getting well, coming for my family. Not Veronica but Ted and the brothers. I wanted happy times; this was going to get in my way.

'How long for?'

'I think it's been going on for a long time.'

'Why hasn't he told me?'

'He doesn't want to hurt you, I guess. Veronica cares less about that.'

I needed to make sense of this.

Ted kept on coming up in my head, calling Ben Dad, not me. He was my boy. Mine. I felt angry, emotions bubbling up, my fists clenched. Betrayal didn't feel good. All the serenity was gone and all I could think about was how I'd been lied to. What woman sleeps with their ex's brother? How could Ben do this to me? Not Ben. Not the sensible one.

Fred could see I was struggling, trying to figure it out.

I had gone quiet.

'For what it's worth, I don't think they planned it. It just happened and you know, you haven't been there…'

I needed time to think about this, so I asked Fred if he could leave me to it. He was worried, I could tell by the expression in his eyes. He didn't mean it but he looked as if he was patronising me. I wanted to hit someone. Not Fred.

'I think I need to have some time alone,' I finally said.

'You gonna be OK with this?'

'Thanks for telling me, Fred. That was brave. I mean it. Thanks.'

He reluctantly started to walk towards the car. As the car sped off I vented.

'FUUUUUUUCK!'

The timing was bad, but it's never a good time when you hear that your brother is shagging the mother of your child, your first love. I needed to know how serious their relationship was. I wanted to know when it had started. How could I have missed it?

There I was, thinking Veronica was like a mum to him. Some mum.

The thing was, I had been too wrapped up in my own shit to notice. It was wrong but was it really that bad? Yes it was, it was fucking terrible. Ted is *my* son.

How was I going to cope with it? What should I do? Should I hit Ben in the face? Not my style. Should I cut off all contact? Not possible, there was Ted to consider. Ben loved Ted. That was good. In my selfish head I had never considered that Veronica was going to meet someone else. I guess I had thought she was forever in love with me.

What an idiot. I didn't want to be with her, but I didn't want Ben to have her either. I wanted a drink, I wanted a line, I wanted to be numb. Secretly I'd been sure V would always have me back if I so wished.

I was sitting on a bench with my head in my hand when I felt a large hand on my back. It was brother Daniel.

'You must tell me what the matter is. You seem upset.'

I slowly looked up at him.

'My brother is sleeping with my ex.'

'The brother that just left?'

'No, another one, Ben. Seems I'm the last to know. Story of my life.'

'Less off the self-pity, young man. Let's go to my office.'

We sat and talked for a long time. I was starting to calm down a little; the urges to hit someone and to drink faded and I was starting to reason that perhaps it wasn't the worst thing that could have happened. For my ego, it was, but for Ted, it was good. He was safe. At least Ben was a good man. It wasn't easy to keep the demons away and this didn't help. The thought keeps on popping up in my head. I wanted to call Ben; I wanted to tell him what a lying wanker he was. At the same time, having a conversation like that with Ben felt wrong. We never had that sort of relationship. It's like I didn't want it to be true. But it was. It was clear, all the signs I had missed kept on playing on my mind. I am such a self-obsessed idiot; they could have shagged in front of me and I would have missed it. That's what a trusting fool I am.

Brother Daniel kept on reminding me that self-pity was not a good road to go down and he was right. I took his advice but it was difficult.

It was time for bed.

I was hungry but I couldn't eat.

I felt low and broken.

All the work I had done felt undone. I wasn't drinking, though, I was clean. It didn't feel good, not one bit, but at least I could feel it.

I sat for an hour with my mobile in hand, staring at his number. All I needed to do was to press the call button. I was scared–scared it was going to send me back to that angry place.

At 23.05 I did, I called him.

Ben: Ed, hi.

Me: Hi.

I went quiet;

Did he know that I knew?

Ben: I'm asleep. When shall I get you?

Me: Fred came to see me today.

Ben: He did?

Me: Yep. Got something to tell me?

The phone line went quiet, dead quiet.

Me: He told me Ben. I-I-I don't understand. How could you? Our family—our trust—it's the only thing I care about.

Ben: It's not like that.

Me: What is it like, then?

Ben: We never planned it, it just happened.

Me: That's exactly what Fred said, It's really bad for me to find this out right now. I was just getting better.

Ben: I'm coming to see you. Wait there. I'm coming.

Me: Don't fucking bother.

I put the phone down, I heard him say it. Confirmed the truth. Inside I knew I could deal with this one but I was too angry right now. I wasn't ready.

I sat alone with my thoughts; I had an urge to hit someone. I decided to go and make another cup of PG Tips and grabbed the guitar. I wrote a song, it was venomous. I was spitting out insults, it felt good. Music was my venting tool, not my fists. The phone rang. It was Veronica. I didn't answer. Hearing her apologise would only piss me off even more. I needed some time so figure this out. How should I handle this? What would be the right thing to do? Too early to know. Right now, swear words were the only comfort. The wall in my cell looked tempting. Perhaps I should just thump it. Hit it hard, make a dent. I stood up, filled my chest with lungs and thumped the wall like an idiot. It made my fist bleed and the wall had a tiny little dent. I stared at it. Pathetic. I can't even make a fist mark in a wall

An hour passed and the phone kept on ringing. I looked at it and it had eight missed calls from V. Then Fred started to call. I couldn't be arsed to speak to any of them. Ben would be on his way; he would be here soon.

Perhaps I would try and swing my pathetic weak fist at him. Make him bleed a little. Another hour passes. The phone kept on ringing. Wish they would leave me alone. I needed Ben to sort this out. Veronica would make it worse. Fred wouldn't know what to say. Speaking to them would come to no good.

After a little while there was a knock on my door. It was Daniel. He looked serious.

'Come, we need to talk.'

'It's four in the morning. Let's speak tomorrow. I'm waiting for Ben; he is on his way here.

'You need to come with me. Get some clothes on.'

As we walked through the corridors an unpleasant, serious atmosphere surrounded me. I felt sick. What was going on? Something bad was about to happen.

In the living room stood a couple of policemen. They had their hats off.

'Ed Henderson.'

'What's going on?' I said.

'There's been an accident.'

'A what?'

'A car accident.' Slow motion. Stop. Don't say anything more. Be quiet. I wanted to shout, 'Shut the fuck up!'

'It's your brother, Ben. He's been in a car crash. He's alive. He's at the Watford hospital.'

'Is he OK?'

No reply.

'Is he going to be alright?' I shouted.

'It's not looking great, I'm afraid but, the doctors will tell you more.'

'He's gonna be fine though, right?'

'I don't know, Ed. As I said, you have to speak to the doctors. Come with us.'

The faceless policemen started to walk towards the exit; Daniel asked if I wanted him to come. I didn't want him to. I wanted to get to Ben, make it ok. Everything was going to be fine once he got better. He was a Henderson, he was strong. He would make it, he had to. The phone kept on buzzing in my pocket. I picked it up and said, 'I'm on my way.' Then I put the phone down again, I was in shock. The policemen drove smoothly through the narrow country roads. The trees were swallowing the sky with their overhanging branches. It was hard to see round the corners.

'Where did it happen?' I asked.

'On the motorway, on the M1. We don't know how but there is another vehicle involved. The driver made it but his wife didn't.'

'What do you mean, she died in the crash?'

'Yes, Mr Henderson, she did.'

'So, it was a bad crash?'

'I don't want to upset you any more right now. We are going to take you to your family. They will give you the details.'

'How bad was the crash?' I wanted to know.

'It was a serious collision. Your brother was cut out of his vehicle. His car saved his life; it's new, so the airbag was a help. There are other problems.'

'What problems?'

'Mr Henderson, I'd much rather the doctors explain what's going on. I don't want to say the wrong thing. His condition can change; I've seen it before. Do you smoke?'

'Yes.'

'You can smoke, open the window.'

I lit a Benson, sucked on it so hard the filter had a hole in it.

It felt as if I'd been in the car for hours when we finally reached the hospital. It had only been twenty-five minutes. Steve was standing outside, waiting for me. My heart was racing; I nearly opened the car door before we reached the entrance. My senses were on full alert. I wanted to get to Ben, needed to hear he was OK. I could see on Steve's face that this was not the case. Ben was not fine.

I got to Steve, he looked devastated, his face distorted by tears and pain.

'How is he? Is he alive?' I spoke a bit too loud.

'It's bad, really bad.' His voice was shaking.

'He is alive right? He is still here? There has to be hope, tell me there's hope.'

'He is in theatre right now. They are trying to operate. There is a ten per cent chance of survival. His brain is bleeding. He's lost an arm. Every bone is broken, but that is not the biggest problem. It's the brain.'

The rest of them were in the waiting room, all sitting quietly. Veronica looked up, straight at me. She looked like a little scared, injured bird. She walked over to me with her arms tightly around her body.

'It's terrible Ed, we can't fix this.' I felt protective and took charge.

'I want to see a doctor; can I speak to someone?'

'They are all in theatre. We will know in fifteen minutes what the outcome is.'

I started to pace up and down, thoughts marathoning through me.

I shouldn't have reacted. It was my fault he got together with V. How could I have been so stupid? It's my fault, it's my doing. Look what I've gone and done. Hurting everyone. Please make it, Ben. I will never fight with you again. I'm an asshole. I'm a fucking idiot.

I felt an arm around me. I recognised the smell. It was V.

'Ed, it was an accident. It's not your fault. Let's wait and see what's going to happen. Here's some water. Drink it. You look as if you're about to pass out.'

'Let's hope for a miracle. We are due one. I will not give up hope. Ben is strong. The doctors don't know that. They don't know how strong he is.'

We hugged. I buried my head in her hair, closed my eyes. Take this away, please, take away this pain. Wake me up. This is ending, now but it was reality. The walls at the hospital were there cold and grey, I felt them. The broken coffee machine, the shitty plastic chairs, the no smoking sign, the flickering lights, all this was reality. This is where this family had ended up now. Again. The curse of the Hendersons: after every rise, a fall. Ben was too proper, too sorted, too good. He didn't fit in with the rest of us; he was going for better things.

I heard footsteps resonating through the corridor. The automatic doors swung open and two doctors walked into the room with serious faces on. We all stood up. No one spoke. We all looked at them, holding our breaths.

'My name is Doctor Walker. I have just operated on Ben.' He paused.

'I'm afraid I don't have great news. Ben is breathing but his brain… well, I couldn't save him. I tried to relive some pressure on the brain so that the body could do its job but the bleeding was too severe. Even if I could have saved him he would have been a different person. The impact from the crash was too much for any human to handle. I am so very sorry. This is not the news I wanted to give you. It really isn't.' He looked genuinely upset.

I couldn't take it in. Veronica was screaming, Fred fainted and Steve and I stood there, tears rolling down.

'I am sorry I couldn't do more. He is still breathing. He is in a coma so the machines will keep him alive for as long as you wish.'

I was still unable to speak.

'Do you want me to get the priest to come in?'

'No.'

'We have bereavement counsellors,' the other doctor offered.

'We need some time,' I finally said,

'To work things out, how and what to do.'

'All you can do is accept this I'm afraid, Again, I am so sorry.' The doctor left.

I sat down, head in hands. The medical team was attending to Fred, who was still unconscious.

In the middle of this chaos Gavin and Mike walked in.

'What the fuck is going on?'

'Ben's brain dead,' Steve managed to say.

Someone had contacted the press, and outside it was starting to look like a premiere, except it wasn't it was just vultures waiting to get their story about a famous bass player dying in a car crash. They were going to get their story; there was nothing I could do to change that.

'Can you get rid of them?' I shouted. 'Tell them to fuck off.'

Gavin went into management mode, calling in security.

'I want to see him,' I said.

We were told that Ben had been cleaned up and that we could see him, Veronica went in first. She cried so hard; noises came out of her that cut through the doors. She was in physical pain. She was rocking back and forth and we tried our hardest to console her. There was no use, she was heartbroken and the pain was excruciating.

Fred and Steve saw Ben together. I wanted to be on my own. I needed to understand what had happened. Part of me wanted to run out the door.

I walked into the room, machines everywhere. Ben was hooked up to all of them, his head covered in bandages to cover the scar from the accident and the operation. What I could see of his face was bruised but he still looked like Ben. I sat down next to him. I held his hand; it was warm, he always had warm hands.

'Ben, little brother, I love you. And I'm sorry. I will see you eventually. Just look out for us, we need it. We need you. I told you Hendersons are not supposed to drive cars. You are so fucking stubborn, never listen.'

I sat there for a while but I was in physical pain, it was too much to take. I didn't know how to deal with it. I cried properly. Water streaming down my face.

It wasn't going to bring him back. Nothing was, just like the other times I had seen death. It wasn't new to me.

In the end they turned the machines off and Ben managed to stay alive for another three whole days. The final breaths were spent with all of us huddled around him. We were quiet; the sounds of the busy hospital, our faint breaths and the flickering of a faulty fluorescent light were the only noises. Ben was still, like only death can be.

Chapter 25:
The End

Ben was dead and there was nothing we could do about it; he was never coming back. It was definite. I never considered that that could happen. Life is like that. You think you work it all out, relax and then it slaps you in the face.

Sitting by my brother's bedside for these last three days had made me understand that whatever the outcome might be my world would never be the same. The reality was final, no negotiations. Death was here again.

I'd failed him. I had failed Ben, my flesh, my blood. The sensible one in our family, the one who gave us hope. He was never like the rest of us. He was proper.

It was so cold in here, I was freezing. My heart was broken. Was I supposed to just recover from this too? Bounce back. Find my place in this world like nothing had happened? I had to carry on. I stood up. Then I fell to the floor; there was no more strength left. I had to give up for a while, throw in the towel and admit defeat. This was the worst thing life had thrown at me … so far.

Camber Sands, late August 1999

'Faster Ted, faster!'

The kite didn't lift properly. We ran like a couple of lunatics. Ted was tall for his age, a real Henderson. Being just eight, he wasn't quite tall enough to get the kite flying but he tried really hard. I caught up with him and helped him to get the kite to go. We managed to get it up there with the seagulls until it crashed on the sand dunes. The sun was setting and the tide was out as far as the eye could see. We sat really close together, staring at the horizon, silent and content. I reached for his little hand. Ben's beach house was where I felt the most at ease. My son and I, barefoot in our own world. We understood each other, even in silence.

There had been a lot of pain. I had always hoped that Ted was protected from most of it. I didn't want him to feel the way I do and have done all my life, my young shoulders weighed down by responsibility and sadness. There had been a lot of success with the band: it made me proud to think about what we'd achieved.

We, who had nothing and had been written off by everybody, orphaned and chanceless, made it and became rock stars. It had torn us apart. Ben's death had affected me more than any of the other loses. He was young and good. He was different from the rest of us.

The light from the sun reflecting on the softly swaying waves, starting and stopping, going bigger and then smaller. There was a rhythm there, a little like life. Mother Nature taking control. I stared out upon the never-ending horizon and forgot about the pain for a second. The guilt kept creeping back. There was so much I could have done better. I could have looked up and changed everything.

'Go grab my guitar.' Ted shot up and ran to the house, struggling with the pebbles as they rolled under his feet, but he was determined and back in a flash, my Martin guitar in his hand.

'Here, Dad.' So happy and innocent. My only child: I never want to have another. Responsibility had eaten me up, spat me out. Love felt like a threat, a threat of deep uncertainty. A risk I wasn't prepared to take again. My heart had been broken too many times.

This is how I can survive, I thought, as I strummed gently. I just wished had I found out how to do it better, so that no one got hurt.